For Sharo

Friends
THAT'S FOR SURE

AT 8

Brendan McCann

Published by New Generation Publishing in 2020

Copyright © Brendan McCann 2020

First Edition

The author asserts the moral right under the Copyright, Designs and Patents Act 1988 to be identified as the author of this work.

All Rights reserved. No part of this publication may be reproduced, stored in a retrieval system or transmitted, in any form or by any means without the prior consent of the author, nor be otherwise circulated in any form of binding or cover other than that in which it is published and without a similar condition being imposed on the subsequent purchaser.

Paperback ISBN: 978-1-80031-869-4
Hardback ISBN: 978-1-80031-868-7

www.newgeneration-publishing.com

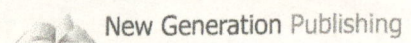

New Generation Publishing

*Dedicated to my daughter and son in law
Megan and Jacko.*

*Sincere gratitude to my wife Ann
who is never far away.*

PROLOGUE

IT'S FRIDAY, 14TH FEBRUARY 2020: another Valentine's Day, another birthday for Liz, aged thirty-five. But this birthday is definitely one she will never forget. Nor will her five children, because Mum is up to her neck in deep shit and not for the first time. This time, her kids are involved. This time, it isn't her casual disregard for the establishment or general morality. This time, it looks as if her goose is well and truly cooked! It all went wrong on the previous, late, wet, windy afternoon and things got worse by the minute. Well into the wee small hours when she finds herself sitting alone in a small, dingy, cold, interview room, with only a small table and two chairs for company, one of which she is sitting on. This time, there is no way out. No excuse, no matter how well played, will suffice on this occasion. This time, it is the last stop saloon and is definitely the straw that broke the camel's back. Is this the end? But where did it all begin?

CHAPTER 1

14 FEBRUARY 1980: Robert McKenna (Robbie) and Cecelia Sloane (Cissy) married in Omagh, Co Tyrone, Northern Ireland, both aged twenty-one. With the help of Robbie's father, who was a local councillor, the happy couple moved into a two-bedroom terraced council house. It was fitted with a small but adequate bathroom, a small and equally adequate kitchen and sitting room, a small back garden, in a small remote area not far from Omagh, known as Drumlyn. Robbie was a general labourer, mostly in the building trade, and Cissy was employed as a dinner lady at Drumlyn Primary School. Robbie was picked up about a mile from home each morning, in an old battered rust-covered red van and Cissy was within easy walking distance from the school. Happy days... For now!

Their first child Leonard (Lenny), named after his paternal grandfather, was born on 21 March 1983 and Elizabeth (Lizzy) named after her maternal grandmother arrived on 14 February 1985, a great way for Robbie and Cissy to celebrate their fifth wedding anniversary! Due to the remoteness of their humble abode, Cissy sometimes found it difficult to find a local childminder. On few but far between occasions the two grandmothers helped out, but it was far from satisfactory, especially when there had been a difference of opinion between the grandmothers and Cissy regarding the way the children were being brought up! Families... Who would have them? Eventually Cissy had to give up the part-time job she loved and settled for being a full-time housewife and mother. She couldn't help but feel that not only was the income to the household depleted slightly, but she had also lost that little bit of independence. Robbie's opportunities for work began to fade away, which was not helped at all by the ongoing troubles in Northern Ireland, thus adding to the financial strain on the household.

As time passed, the nice little house that the happy couple had first moved into was becoming cramped, to say the least, what with the two children getting bigger all the time there was hardly enough room to hang the family washing, especially when it rained, which was more often than not! Play areas for Lenny and Lizzy were limited. Although the main road immediately outside the home was not very busy, it would be tempting fate to allow them to be left unsupervised, so it was either the small backyard or indoors, which led to household utensils and toys, to be found in every and any orifice or crevice throughout the house! Poor Robbie couldn't sit down after a hard day's work without a squeaky toy or a fork stuck up his arse!

Due to a family bereavement in June 1987, of a great uncle on Robbie's side of the family, his only other sibling and elder brother Benny returned home from London to attend the funeral. Because of the short time allowed in N. Ireland between death and burial, which was and still is only three days, Benny could only come on his own leaving his wife Julie and three children behind. After all good funerals in Omagh, Co Tyrone, there was drinking and singing and story-telling to be done, and done with un-bounding enthusiasm! During a lull in the battle Robbie told Benny of his ongoing unfortunate circumstances. Benny immediately suggested that Robbie, Cissy and the two children move to London, where work of any sort was in abundance with great pay and accommodation was not difficult to obtain.

The plan would be for them all to move into Benny's flat in the Kings Cross area of London on a temporary basis. Start work within only a few days, register with the local council explaining that the main reason for the family move was quite simply the lack of work in N. Ireland but also, more importantly, the grave concern for the children's safety, due to the troubles that were being reported not only in Great Britain but around the world! Benny and his wife had no trouble at all when they first moved to London two years previously with their three children. But Robbie was of the opinion that Cissy would find it difficult to move all the way to London even though she was almost at the end of her tether. He also found it hard to believe that Benny's wife Julie would be happy with another four people moving into her nice London flat! But sure, the drink got the better of them both, until they ended up sleeping side by side on the small but comfy sofa in Robbie's small living room.

The next morning the brothers woke up with the hangovers from hell! Although there were two years of age difference, they could easily have been mistaken for twins, especially first thing in the morning, still wearing most of their funeral attire. Cissy was busy making nice, greasy, fried egg sarnies to be washed down with very large mugs of very strong and very sweet tea! Cissy looked at the drunken gobs on the two pitiful men and decided that they were not a pretty sight and both deserved an `X` rating. Robbie had no idea how he should approach the delicate subject that he and his brother had not only discussed but had decided upon the previous night. Robbie could hear his big brother's comments: 'Are you a man or a mouse? Just you tell her that it's for her own good and for the good of the kids and if she doesn't like it... You'll go to London on yer fuckin' own!'

Both men tried very hard but to no avail to disguise their discomfort and need to go to the toilet. After making a gallant attempt to enjoy the egg sarnies and the sweet tea that were now not even lukewarm, Benny was the first to surrender to mother nature's call. Top or bottom... He wasn't at all sure! In his absence Cissy asked Robbie if he remembered anything about the conversation they had had when he and Benny returned home the previous night.

'Och Cissy. Did I make a fool out of me-self again... By... By telling ye that I really, really loved ye? Please don't tell me I was slobbering all over ye in front of me big brother!'

Cissy replied in a very nonchalant manner, 'No you didn't. Benny fell asleep almost straight away, but, I'm ready whenever you are.'

'Ready for what?' asked Robbie.

'Ready to move to London,' she said.

When Benny returned and Cissy was back in the kitchen

making more tea, Benny asked Robbie if he had dared mention the move to London, to which Robbie replied, in a very nonchalant manner, 'Och Aye ... Sure I just told her we were goin' and she could lump it or leave it... And she said okay.'

It was difficult throughout the following few weeks for Robbie and Cissy to explain to family and friends of their decision to move to London. Both sets of grandparents were up in arms and things were quite often said in the heat of the moment, but the promise of a better life and a bit of adventure was too compelling for the young couple to be persuaded to change their minds. Due to the fact that both children were too young to start primary school and pre-school facilities were practically non-existent, there was nothing as far as they were concerned to delay the inevitable. So, on a Saturday afternoon in August 1987, with the money they raised from selling anything of value from their modest little home and a meagre amount of savings, plus a little financial help from family and friends, the young McKenna family made their way to London via Aldergrove Airport.

The journey was a great adventure for all four of them but it has to be said the parents were more than just a bit overwhelmed with their first sight of the metropolis, particularly the London Underground! Benny met them at Heathrow Airport and acted as the duty guide. Robbie was rabbiting continuously throughout the journey about the great times that lay ahead. When they arrived in their new temporary home in Kings Cross, they were greeted with cheers, hugs and welcomes from Julie and her three children. It wasn't long before they all settled down to a feed of beef stew with fresh bread and butter, followed by jelly and ice cream. The following morning was a slow start for everyone, due to the late-night celebrations for the adults and excitement for the children.

Benny and Julie's three children were all girls. Louise aged eight, known as Lou, and twins Samantha and Pamela aged six, known as Sam and Pam. With Lizzy aged two and poor Lenny aged four, well that was five children with Lenny being the only boy. Lizzy was too young to offer an opinion, but Lenny was secretly hoping that he wouldn't have to live with all these screaming girls for too long. His mother had told him and his sister that they would be living in a big, big city from now on. His Aunt Julie was a great organiser and put into operation a temporary plan as follows:

She and Benny would remain in the master bedroom, Robbie and Cissy on the sofa-bed in the living room, Lou would share with her twin sisters who would double up so Lou being the eldest, still got a bed to herself, and Lenny and Lizzy would double up in Lou's room. Job done. The open plan kitchen wasn't massive but there would still be room for everyone to enjoy their meals, even if some of the adults took their food on their knees in the living room.

The flat was in a four-storey block with six dwellings on each floor. Each floor was given a letter of the alphabet. A. B. C. D. The ground floor was A. and the top floor was D. Entry was by a stairwell with two flights to each floor. Each flat was given a number one through to six. There was no lift as was standard for blocks of this type in London in the mid-eighties. Most were built in the mid-sixties. Benny's family lived in the fourth flat on the second floor, number 4B. There was a long walk-way along the front of each flat with a safety wall running the same length giving protection from accidental falls to the ground some distance below and also from inclement weather. There was also enough room for the children to play and run about and to interact with other playmates who lived on the same floor.

Robbie couldn't believe that an interview had been arranged with Benny's boss the very next day on a new development just a few minutes away by tube train. Julie got her three kids off to their nearby school and she, Cissy with Lenny and Lizzy in tow, made their way to the local council office to register for a council flat. Things were moving that fast it was making Cissy's head turn. For Lenny and Lizzy, it was another day's adventure. Although on the job front for Robby things were better than anyone could have hoped for, the accommodation was not as forthcoming. The two wives soldiered on to make things as amicable as possible for the two families. Poor little Lenny was not backward at being forward in offering his opinion on the saga of the four screaming girls who would take it in turns to tease him or cuddle him depending on their mischievous moods. But as they say... blood is thicker than water and this lot, if the truth be told, were all as thick as thieves. No one ever went to sleep on a bad note.

Benny had a reputation as a very hard and dependable worker over the previous two years with his employers and the admiration for Robbie soon followed. The two brothers were also renowned for any job anywhere, anytime, big or small, dirty or slimy, all comers welcome. In truth they were earning a lot of big pay cheques. In the early days of his new job Robbie at times had to pinch himself to make sure that the pay clerk in head office hadn't made a mistake. To see so much money going into his bank account at the end of the first month almost brought tears to his eyes however, as time passed the amount grew more and more each month until after six months, he had paid Benny all the money he owed him and he had now been able to open a savings account for Cissy and the two kids. Robby thought to himself, 'Just think. We have a bloody savings account!'

Because Julie's children were in full-time education, she worked the school hours for a local cleaning company. Cissy was quick to follow suit, albeit only part-time in the early evenings when Julie returned home and could look after all five whipper-snappers. The men were never home before six o'clock due to the amount of work they were being offered. The wives would sometimes tell them to slow down but to no avail. The men were definitely on a mission. A regular baby sitter ensured that Saturday nights at the local working men's club went with more than just a bit of a bang. Most Sundays they all had lunch at one of the many hostelries in the local area. The women and children would return home and the men would adjourn to one of their favourite haunts for an afternoon session of alcohol and banter. The bread winners would return home at about seven o'clock full of the joys of spring, with slightly glazed eyes and big cheeky grins. Each always had a bunch of flowers and a large bag of assorted sweets and chocolates. The usual cheers from the children and the usual smiles from the wives ensured that another great weekend was had by all and another fruit-full week was to follow.

Accommodation for Robbie's half of the family was still outstanding due to the fact that they applied for a three bedroom flat in the same block as his brother. Others became available some distance away but Cissy in particular stuck to her guns. The bond between both families had become so strong, especially with the wives, that they felt the need to remain living in close proximity. The children had become great friends and even poor little Lenny quite enjoyed the antics he and the girls got up to on a daily basis.

Almost a year after their arrival in London another letter arrived from the local council. It arrived on a Monday morning in the usual brown envelope with the official council stamp across the front but Cissy was frightened to death to open it, in case it contained bad news. They had turned down two previous offers of accommodation so this one could be put up or shut up! Cissy waited patiently until Robbie came home from work that night. The five children were playing in and out of the bedrooms causing the usual commotion when the four adults crept into the sitting room for the grand opening of the brown envelope. Without any fuss at all Robbie ripped the brown paper, read the letter within and informed those present that they had indeed been offered another flat at the following address: 2B Broderick House, Broderick Street, Kings Cross, London, NW1.

Robbie quickly asked, "Where the fuck is that?"

Cissy burst out laughing and shouted, 'It's two doors along the way from here!'

Robbie began to look around the sitting room and shouted, "Along the way from here? You mean this flat here? This fuckin' flat here? What's that number again?"

All three shouted, 'Two B!' To which Robbie orated, 'Two B or not two B... That is the fucking question!'

Everyone burst into a cheer with back slapping and laughter which in turn, brought the herd of children bounding into the room to find out why the adults were making more noise than they were. Although it was a work night the brothers insisted that a few half-ins would be in order. The girls agreed and even the offspring got a treat of fizzy orange and crisps. Benny's three were on school summer holidays so it didn't really matter how late they went to bed.

At the beginning of August 1988, Robbie and his family accepted the keys for number 2B. Over the next three weekends Robbie and Benny with the help of their work mates, turned a not so pretty flat into a beautifully redecorated home. Cissy and Julie added the women's touch even though the children continually got in the way. The summer holiday for both families on the Isle of White was postponed as the preparation of number 2B took priority. By the time Julie's children returned to school in September and Lenny starting primary school in P1, number 2B was fully occupied. Both families were in and out of each other's flat so often, it was if there was one big home within two flats. All four of the children attended St Mark's Primary School situated on the Kentish Town Road which was about a ten-minute walk from their homes. It was agreed that Cissy would drop off and pick up all four of them each school day. A kind-hearted neighbour agreed to look after Lizzy while the school runs were ongoing. This enabled Julie to work full-time during the week and Cissy to work part-time in the evenings. Saturday nights at the local club remained the same. Both families usually ate out for Sunday lunch but on special occasions one of the wives would prepare a Sunday roast at home on an alternative basis. The dads did not mind as long as it didn't affect their usual Sunday afternoon of drink and banter with their mates in the pub. The mums insisted that the usual routine of flowers and sweets on their return from the pub also remained in situ.

Over the coming years, time seemed to fly by and both families flourished, much more than anyone could have ever imagined. Each summer they all holidayed together. Various locations up and down the country saw them travel far and wide but the old favourite, Butlins at Bognor Regis was always top of the pops. Both families also enjoyed separate holidays in Omagh, but sometimes the troubles that remained ongoing would result in their relatives travelling from N. Ireland to London, which was always a most enjoyable experience for all concerned.

Along the way Benny and Robbie formed their own painting and decorating service. Being self-employed gave them a great deal of satisfaction and a great deal of financial gain. Julie and Cissy formed their own cleaning service. It was a lot slower to get off the ground but eventually the driving force of these two very determined ladies, had it overtaking its competitors in all aspects. It wasn't long before both services had a number of employees and was in need of a qualified accountant, which resulted in two limited companies being formed. Julie and Cissy wanted something with their initials in the title of their company and Benny and Robbie wanted something catchy in the title of their company. After a great deal of discussion and deliberation, falling out and falling in, drunk and sober, the two names of the companies would be as follows:

J. C. Miracles. Cleaning Services.
Slicker & Flicker. Painters & Decorators.

Throughout the coming years Benny and Robbie increased their business interests so much that they were able to employ four teams of three employees, with a team leader in each. They leased four work vans, one for each team, and two smaller vans, to be used by each of the brothers. When the occasion arose they also used other contractors for electrics, plumbing and any other specialised jobs. As well as growing the painting and decorating business, they also branched out into the property auction scene. Houses, flats, former business premises, everything and anything that they could turn into a reasonable profit. On one particular occasion they bought a very large reprocessed property and over a period of about two years created two large detached four-bedroom bungalows. Each had a spacious back garden with a gravel driveway at the front and a large garage at the side of each house. The two, brand-spanking new, all-singing, all-dancing houses were situated in West Croydon, which was a town in its own right but also a large suburb of South London. The two families had to agree that their new homes certainly had the wow factor.

It was now 1998. Slicker & Flicker. Painters & Decorators were flying high. The brothers had a small office and vehicle yard with a small store area in Station Road, not far from where they lived. Benny's eldest, Lou, was now nineteen years of age and after a long summer break backpacking in Europe, was now employed as the office manager. Although she had no experience at all as a manager her father and uncle agreed that it wouldn't be a problem. She had a good head on her shoulders and she would be the only one in the office. Her mum and auntie agreed to spare some time to help with 'training on the job.' Lou took to the new challenge like a duck to water.

The twins, Sam and Pam, were now seventeen and were attending sixth-form college. Both mums agreed with the idea that when the twins left school the following year, they would be employed by J. C. Miracles Cleaning Services. They would start on the bottom rung of the cleaning ladder. The cleaning company had also grown to the extent that they had increased their employees to eight. They leased four small vans with two cleaners in each van which were taken home by the said staff at the end of each shift. J. C. Miracles had not yet progressed to opening a small office and yard. They were still depending on mobile phones as the only form of communication but both sets of parents agreed that by the following year, both companies would move into joint premises with all the mod cons. By that stage both mums and Lou would staff their joint head office and eventually Sam and Pam would be team leaders on the road.

Robbie's two children, Lenny and Lizzy, were aged fifteen and thirteen respectively. Lenny sometimes helped with his dad if he had to work on a Saturday, or better still, during the school holidays. Lizzy was mad about being a hair dresser when she eventually left school, so a part-time job as a tea/coffee maker, cum sweeper-upper was arranged at a local salon. Once again Saturdays and school holidays were the preferred work routine. The McKennas were as close as ever. That's for sure.

CHAPTER 2

BY 2003, ALL THE GOALS, that the McKenna families had set had in fact been achieved, and achieved in no uncertain terms. The joint head office, vehicle yard, stores area and necessary back-up logistics were all in place. The bumper new set-up was still in Station Road West Croydon but they bought the existing site and the two smaller sites either side and completely redeveloped all three sites to a very upmarket standard. The brothers' property portfolio had increased beyond anything they could have imagined plus, work was still coming in fast and furious through the painting and decorating company. The brothers were now equal directors.

The wives' cleaning company was also in overdrive. By this time Lou was twenty-four years old, Sam and Pam were twenty-two. All three had shown their worth time and time again with Lou now a very experienced and well-paid office manager and the twins not far behind as operations managers. Cissy and Julie had also progressed to equal directors. J. C. and Slick and Flick were definitely on a roll.

Lenny, who was now aged twenty, had chosen not to follow in his father's footsteps. Although he had become very handy in all aspects of the painting and decorating service, he wanted to travel more and experience a different type of adventure. So, at the age of eighteen he joined the Royal Navy. At this stage he had completed his basic training with flying colours, had taken part in a continuation training course and was presently specialising in radio technology. He was stationed in Portsmouth and would be putting to sea soon for a period of six months. His best mate in the Navy was a very presentable young man who was from Newquay in Cornwall. He was the same age as Lenny and his name was Edward Perry-Webster. His father was a freelance architect and his mother was the editor for a local newspaper in Cornwall. He was an only child and, like Lenny, wanted to travel with more adventure than his well-to-do parents would allow. He liked to be called Ed, much to their dismay.

Both mates had visited each other's homes on several occasions, with all visits being a complete success but sometimes they liked to get away together like all good mates do. Although it has to be said that Lizzy, who was now aged eighteen, had a bit of a crush on the soft-spoken Ed and always, always, looked forward to his visits to West Croydon. Lizzy was now working full-time as a trainee hair stylist and had little love for the family cleaning company. She preferred to get soap and dye on her hands rather than smelly water and disinfectant. A few weeks before Lenny and Ed were due to begin their first adventure at sea they were awarded some well-deserved leave, part of which would find them both in West Croydon for a farewell party. Both McKenna families agreed that it should be the party of a lifetime for the two intrepid sailors. Lizzy was hoping that, just maybe, she could steal a first kiss from Ed. Well... A girl could dream... Couldn't she?

It was now the last Saturday in April 2003. With Easter behind everyone this was to be the night for the eagerly awaited farewell party for Lenny and Ed. It was held in the small but well-decorated and well-furnished function room of the Eagles Nest on Station Road near the local railway station. It had become the favourite pub for Benny and Robbie, who quite often used it on Sunday afternoons for their impromptu sing songs with their fellow cronies. A local four-piece band had been booked, who were known as Blueberry Buckle, and a buffet supplied by the pub's owner, the one and only Big Frankie McCracken, would be excellent value for money. Big Frankie was a tall sturdy Dubliner, with black wavy hair and a hint of grey on the temples who had been in the pub game in London for more years than he cared to admit. There were about seventy guests invited with two local hard cases on the door, to ensure that any gate crashers would be crashing outside rather than inside.

At eight o'clock on the night the doors opened and

within a very short period of time the party of the millennium kicked off. There were no set tables or chairs for anyone. It was a case of sitting or standing, dancing or singing, with whoever was closest at any given time and stomp your stuff, everywhere and anywhere. YAHOO! As the night grew older Lizzy could hardly contain herself and eventually gave into temptation and asked Ed for a dance, to a set of slow love songs that the band was playing. Ed, being the gentleman he was, gladly accommodated the impressionable, love-struck teenager and held her close and personal. The lights of the function room were turned down low and the small dance floor was packed so, no one noticed the odd peck on the cheek that Ed conveyed to Lizzy, who in return held Ed that much closer. Occasionally, their eyes met, their noses touched and their hearts missed a beat. Lizzy was in love-heaven. When the band changed tempo to a slightly faster set of dance songs, the young couple continued to gyrate and then broke into an old-fashioned jive routine to the delight of all the other dancers. The crowd began to move back a little bit at a time, until they formed a human circle with Lizzy and Ed strutting their stuff in the middle. The culminating point, of the final song in that particular set was a solo by the lead guitarist and finished with a crescendo of noise from all four of the band. Lizzy and Ed fell into each other's arms to yelps and whistles from everyone there, including Big Frankie and the two hard cases at the door.

When the noisy commotion settled down, the two guests of honour were coerced into making a joint farewell and thank you speech. Lenny and Ed, to everyone's surprise gave a very creditable account of themselves. And the party rolled on and on and on. At one stage Lenny mentioned to Ed that he never knew he could dance as well as he had done earlier with his little sister. The only reply Ed could muster was: 'She's not that little, mate!' Lenny gave a slight frown and said, 'Lizzy might be eighteen but she's still my little sister, mate!'

But, undeterred, the two mates soldiered on, or should I

say, sailored on and continued the motion, sometimes in slow motion, as they partied the night away until the taxi service arrived at about two o'clock in the morning. Both families ended up in Robbie's house for a few night-caps. What with Benny's three girls and their boyfriends, the two married couples, Lizzy, Lenny and Ed, the small cocktail bar next to the patio door became slightly crowded so Robbie and Benny took the opportunity to slink away into the garden, to light up a well-earned King Edward cigar. None of their wives allowed smoking in either of the houses much less a great big cigar. They were even restricted to smoking in certain areas in head office. They both agreed that only God could help them if the much-talked-about smoking ban ever came in.

Meanwhile, back at the cocktail bar a sing-song ensued. It has to be said, that it would have given the local moggie brigade a good run for its money. But the wisecracks in-between verses made up for the lack of vocal talent. The family bathroom was in continuous use so the ladies decided that the en suite in the master bedroom would be exclusively for them. On one occasion, Lizzy, who was more than just a little bit tiddly, was making her way back through the house to rejoin the others when she literally bumped into Ed, who had taken a wrong turn from the family bathroom and they immediately kissed. Not just kissed, but passionately kissed... And continued to kiss and caress each other for what seemed like a life time. Ed realised that someone could come along and see them and reluctantly pulled away. Lizzy was disappointed at his hasty withdrawal and asked, 'What's wrong Ed? It's only a natural reaction between a boy and a girl. No one will mind. We are both adults.'

Ed stood back a little and replied, 'Listen, Lizzy. I fancy the pants off you but you are my best mate's little sister. I don't think Lenny would be too pleased.'

Lizzy enthused, 'But Mum and Dad think the world of you. In fact, everyone does.'

Once again Ed took another pace back and said, 'Let's

talk about this when we wake up tomorrow.'

Lizzy smiled and quipped, 'It's already tomorrow.'

Although the drink had definitely taken its toll, Ed decided to take the initiative, 'Look, Lizzy. I'll go back into the sing-song and you follow in a few minutes and then I will make my excuses and go to bed in the usual spare room. When you think it sounds okay then you say the usual goodnights and off you go to your room. Give it a few more minutes and if you think the coast is clear, creep into my room. Okay?' Lizzy nodded in agreement and the said plan began to formulate. No one really noticed who was going where or when. Those not in bed were beginning to drop off on the soft comfy chairs around the cocktail bar and some of the boys, including Lenny, were falling asleep on the large comfy sofas in the sitting room. Both sets of parents were weaving their way along the hallway to the front door so that Benny and Julie could go next door to their own house and Cissy could shove Robbie into their own bed.

'Every man for himself,' the two brothers shouted and then burst out laughing and apart from the music from the CD player, which had by this stage been turned down to a reasonable level, there wasn't another sound to be heard, bar the odd fart or snore. When Lizzy closed the door of her room she quickly undressed and put on her usual night shirt. She didn't wait long before tip-toeing along to Ed's room. As quick as a flash she was inside, which initially gave Ed a bit of a fright.

'Did anyone see you?' he whispered.

'What do you think?' was the brisk reply.

There was a small bedside light in the bedroom that Ed had left switched on. Lizzy motioned to turn it off but Ed shook his head and whispered, *'No.'* He pulled back the duvet cover just a little, to reveal his muscular torso and then he pulled it back completely to reveal his manhood, which, it had to be said, was more than just a pleasant surprise for the trembling eighteen-year-old. Without prompting, Lizzy quickly removed her night shirt over her head and stood there completely naked. The shadows created by the small bed side light gave an almost erotic flavour to this very special occasion. Without saying a word, they both realised that this was to be the ultimate deflowering of this beautiful young virgin. She quietly slipped into the bed.

Initially they caressed slowly and carefully, exploring each other's contours. Licking, kissing and devouring each other's tongues. Lizzy began to tremble almost uncontrollably but then the same uncontrollable tremble began to creep over Ed. She had experimented a little with boys before but never to this extent, thus she was finding it difficult not to become over excited, but why was Ed shaking? Could it be that he was also a virgin? Surely not! This was a tall, good-looking, sexy young man who had the most magnificent penis, which took all the strength of her two small hands to manipulate. The two trembling lovers positioned themselves in the centre of the bed, Lizzy laid back with her legs open, while Ed balanced on his elbows each side of her sweat-covered face and slipped his huge, stiff sex organ a fraction at a time inside her tight wet channel.

As he gently manoeuvred himself deeper into his virginal accomplice, gasp after gasp was released from her throat but she managed to stem the passionate cry which was imminent, by placing the corner of the duvet a little way into her mouth. She began to caress and pinch as much of his tense buttocks as she could, coaxing him deeper and deeper until he was fully engaged to the hilt, and then she climaxed into an unknown world of passion and ecstasy. Within only a few seconds she felt Ed's bulbous expand and explode inside her sweat-soaked body, with a flurry of spraying and bucking that seemed to last forever. They clung to each other, not wanting to let go. He remained deep, still hard, still fully engaged and she could still feel him throbbing, like a quickened pulse beat inside her. Eventually, he slipped from the wanton grasp of her juice-covered pouch and relaxed on his back beside her. They gazed at each other and with a mutual nod she crept out of the bed, replaced her night shirt, gave him a peck on the cheek and whispered, 'See you later?'

He smiled and said, 'You're right, you'll see me later!'

It was a bright sunny Sunday afternoon, before all the sleeping beauties finally arrived in the kitchen, each suffering a severe hangover, all apart from Ed and Lizzy. Coffee or tea and toast with strong pain-killing tablets were the preferred menu. The two mates insisted on carrying on with the party at the Eagles Nest, as there was always live entertainment provided on Sunday afternoons. Everyone apart from Lenny and Ed refused as they were all up for work on Monday morning. Robbie and Benny would have a hair of the dog sometime that day but would not entertain another heavy drinking session. The two sailors were not due for duty until their first parade at eight o'clock on Tuesday morning, so a few drinks that afternoon and then to bed would still give them time to recover on Monday before heading back to Portsmouth on Monday night. Lizzy hinted that she may be tempted to go with them to the pub but with a disapproving grimace from Ed, she said that since it was such a nice day, she would spend the afternoon sunbathing in the back garden.

'Not topless,' joked Ed.

And with a cheeky little grin she teased, 'Not likely. Not with two sailors knocking about!'

Well now, the two mates once again began another over-the-top drinking session in the Eagles Nest. The music and the banter were great and every man and his dog wanted Lenny and Ed to have a good luck drink before their first long trip at sea. Lizzy's sun bathing didn't last long because, once again, the rain arrived. Initially it was just a drizzle and then it began to bucket down for most of the afternoon. She played with the idea of joining the boys in the pub but decided that staying put would give people less to talk about.

At about nine o'clock both households were quiet, with those not already sleeping, preparing for an early night. Lizzy's dad was snoring and her mum was trying to read a book in bed but had trouble keeping her eyes open.

Suddenly, in the quiet and still Sunday night in that leafy suburb, the sound of a car pulling up outside in the street could be heard, followed by the opening and closing of the car door, followed by whispered goodnights and almost silenced tittering. The boys were back.

Lizzy looked through a small gap in her curtains to see that Lenny was practically legless and Ed was doing his best to keep her brother upright. Her mum stirred a little, but Lizzy popped her head round her parents' bedroom door and assured her that the two party animals had returned home safe and sound and would probably go straight to their beds. Robbie was still snoring so Cissy turned over to her side once more and quickly fell into a deep sleep.

Lizzy opened the front door to Ed's delight, as he could not persuade Lenny to part with the front door key. Together they guided Lenny to his bedroom and after taking off his shoes and shirt, they loosened the belt and the top button of his jeans and laid him down on his side. They left the bedroom, hand in hand and once again gazed into each other's eyes and with a mutual nod Lizzy went to her room and Ed to his. The coded silence did not need any words. In less than ten minutes Lizzy and Ed were together again, in a warm lovers' embrace, both naked, both under his duvet. There was no uncontrollable trembling on this occasion. Just a chemistry of tension and a war of wills as to who would be first to release their energy or would the orgasm be in unison. Bingo! It all happened at once and there was no need to suppress their gasps and cries of passion this time. No one was awake to hear them, not that they seemed to care.

They lay closer than skin itself but there was to be only a short lull in the battle. This time it was Ed who lay on his back and allowed Lizzy to take control. She gazed at his manhood as it resurrected itself in only a short period of time. She cupped and squeezed that impressive stallion's organ between her gentle hands and teased the tip of his erection with both of her thumbs. His back arched so much he thought it would snap. Lizzy straddled him and guided his large, stiff, pulsating muscle inside her. Once again she teased it, putting only a little bit in at a time and then removing it before he had time to thrust. When she knew that he was almost at the stage of no return, she enveloped him in one swift motion and felt his back arch once again. They writhed and twitched and dug their fingernails into each other's flesh until an electric flash overcame them both as they clutched and grabbed and gasped for air. When she finally rested her forehead on his, it was as if there was no oxygen left in the room. They remained like that for some time, dozing on and off but they remained coupled until she climbed off him, with an effort of an exhausted rodeo cowboy. A few minutes later she slipped out of the bed, which was damp with sweat, and replaced her night shirt once again. She sallied to the bedroom door, paused briefly, turned her head over her right shoulder and blew a goodnight kiss to her lover, who had once more drifted back into a comfortable slumber. Within seconds she was in her own bed with a smile like the cat that got the cream.

Monday morning saw everyone, bar the two mates, up and away to work. The boozing buddies never heard a thing. At about eleven-thirty, Lizzy was having a coffee with Sharon Jackson, her fellow trainee in the hair salon, as was their usual tryst on Monday mornings. They were in a small cafe not far from Lizzy's home and the topic of conversation was usually about their encounters, or lack thereof, since they last saw each other on the previous Saturday night, at the end of the working week. Lizzy gave Sharon the shock of her life with the detailed history of her sexual encounter with Ed, but kept a little in reserve.

'Bloody hell, Lizzy! Are you sure he didn't split you?'

'Oh, Sharon. It's as if we were meant for each other. Imagine having it off for the first time and with a bloke with a double-barrelled surname like, Perry-Webster.'

Sharon quipped, 'Double-barrelled cock, more like!'

Lizzy gushed, 'Imagine being married to a sailor. Cor Blimey. Mister and Missus Perry-Webster.'

Sharon moved closer to her friend and whispered into

her ear, 'Fucking hell, girl! He's off today for six bleeding months. What do you think he'll be doing with his spare time in all those strange places, with all those strange women? He won't be playing bleeding tiddly-winks will he?'

'You're just jealous, Sharon, that's all that's wrong with you. Bleeding fucking jealous!'

'You're bleeding fucking right, Lizzy. I'm bleeding fucking jealous!'

They both burst out laughing and nearly knocked the empty coffee mugs off the table. Ernie, who was about sixty years of age and the owner of the cafe shouted, 'Oye, you two. Take your filthy talk outside. What are you trying to do? Give an old man a bleeding heart attack or somefink?'

All three began to giggle in unison. The girls made for the door to leave Ernie to get on with his work and as always, he gave them a farewell little wink as they closed the door behind them. Outside the girls gave each other a peck on the cheek and a little hug before going their separate ways, as was always the form on Monday mornings. No work today, for either of them, as like a majority of hair salons in that area, Mondays were always a day off. Their working week was Tuesday through to Saturday. So, Lizzy decided to walk home, knowing of course that her brother and Ed would probably still be in bed. She would sneak in and surprise them with a great big plate of bacon sarnies and a pot of tea, although sometimes Ed preferred coffee. She just could not help smiling as she pictured her handsome lover sitting across the kitchen table from her, with Lenny talking away as usual, totally unaware what she had in mind. A quickie with Ed. Somehow. Somewhere. She didn't care!

Lizzy unlocked the front door and gently kicked her trainers off in the hall. She was about to make her way to the kitchen when she heard voices coming from Ed's room.

'Ah shit,' she thought. 'They are already awake. Never mind. I'll just creep up to the door and scare the living daylights out of them.'

As she got closer to Ed's room, the door was slightly

ajar. She thought she heard Ed say, 'Everyone else is at work.'

She tried in vain to listen to the conversation but the voices were a little more than a whisper. She ever so gently eased the door open, just a fraction of an inch. The large mirror on the dressing table showed part of a reflection on the bed. Not enough to see fully just yet. She ventured another fraction and the full view of the reflection became apparent. She could see Ed lying on his back on the bed. She could see Lenny squatting over him with his back to the mirror. Yes, it was definitely Lenny. They were both completely naked. Then before her very eyes, she watched in horror, as her brother mounted his mate's large, erect, specimen of manhood. She watched as it was inserted deep inside her brother and they both gyrated and grunted their approvals, oblivious to the unbelieving and shocked spectator just a few feet away.

Lizzy squinted in disbelief. Then her eyes were open so wide she thought her eyeballs would pop out of their sockets. She slowly began to back track along the hall with one hand over her mouth and the other keeping her balanced as she almost staggered in a circle. She quickly made her way through the kitchen and out of the sliding patio door trying not to spew up. She continued not knowing what foot to put in front of the other until she came to her favourite spot that she normally used for day dreaming about Ed. It was underneath the small apple tree next to the small hedgerow at the end of the garden. Just out of sight from the house. She slid down the bark of the tree into a crouched position on the grass with her chin resting on her knees. The tears were streaming down her face as the noon day sun-rays crept over the hedgerow as it had on so many wonderful day dreaming excursions before. She managed to muffle her sobs but not her temper. With gritted teeth she muttered: 'The dirty fucking pair of bastards. How could they do this to me? He's screwed the both of us. Under the same fucking roof! In the same fucking bed. Bleeding, fucking, Ed!'

Meanwhile in Ed's room, the two lovers, who had satisfied their hunger for each other, lay in their naked embrace, forehead on forehead. Ed couldn't help but indulge in a little smirk of satisfaction and thought to himself, 'Like sister, like brother.'

Lizzy felt disgusted and let down. She didn't want anyone to know what she had seen and how hurt and degraded she felt. She sneaked into her bedroom and crept under the duvet. Out of sight. Out of mind. She must have dozed off, for the next thing she heard were the voices of her mum and dad. They had knocked off early to ensure the boys had a good meal and a bon voyage, before their return journey to Portsmouth. Lizzy was nowhere in sight. Cissy called her name several times before Lizzy found the courage to answer.

'I'm in bed, Mum.'

'What the hell are you doing in bed? It's the middle of the afternoon.'

Lizzy had to do some fast thinking. 'I've got the dreaded hay fever again, Mum.'

'Have you taken your antihistamine?'

'Yes, Mum. I've taken a double dose.'

Cissy hurried herself to Lizzy's room to find her still well under cover.

As Cissy began to edge the duvet away from Lizzy she said, 'Come on, love. Let me see your smiley face.'

Well, when she saw the state of the poor unfortunate teenager's blotched face and bloodshot eyes, her heart sank. 'Oh, love. You've got it bad this time, haven't you?'

'Yes, Mum. I've got it bad,' was the brief reply.

'Well now, will you be up to seeing the boys off? On second thoughts I'll send them in here before they go. Alright?'

There were only three words that Lizzy could think of. 'Fuck! Fuck! Fuck!'

Then her mum added, 'Ah, here they come now. Look, boys, Lizzy is bad with the hay fever. She's a wee bit embarrassed, so say a quick bye-bye and let her suffer in peace.'

The two mates entered the room with great big smiles offering sympathy and a cold drink. They both simultaneously kissed her gently on the back of each hand. Lizzy gave a hidden cringe disguised with a false smile and almost burst into tears once again, but she held her own and showed no sign of weakness, just the want of revenge. And then she saw it, the cheeky little wink from Ed. She found it difficult once again to curtail her anger but thought better of it and as her mum and the two mates left the room, she slid down under the duvet for another bout of nearly silent sobbing. She finally dozed off with one last thought in her mind, 'Fuck the both of them!'

CHAPTER 3

IN THE WEEKS AND MONTHS THAT FOLLOWED, Lizzy never mentioned to anyone what she had witnessed that Monday morning. Any time that she found herself alone, the picture of Ed enjoying her brother as much as he had enjoyed her brought on another tearful tantrum. With clinched fists she promised herself that she would try to forget, but she would never forgive. The family doctor prescribed a stronger medication for her worsening hay fever. Her best friend Sharon would often tease her about the lack of communication from Ed but Lizzy assured her that she and Ed had agreed to put their love-making down to experience, and if he felt like hooking up on his return, Lizzy agreed that she would give it careful consideration. With that said, the two girls burst out laughing and Sharon quipped, 'I hope you didn't break his heart or, should I say, his hard!'

At the end of their six months at sea the two intrepid sailors returned to good old Blighty. However, their relationship was not what it was before their departure. When they were away they found themselves mixing more often than naught in different circles and also working in different shift patterns, throughout their Navy manoeuvres. Shore leave at various locations was also in different groups. Although it was unintended on both parts, Ed thought it would be for the best.

The mates were given four weeks' leave and spent time off with their respective families but agreed to meet up somewhere special and private, as Ed had something he wanted to tell Lenny before it became common knowledge. Although Lenny would be returning to Portsmouth at the end of his leave period, Ed had in fact been given a posting to a submarine base in Scotland known as Faslane. His secret ambition was always to experience life as a submariner and this was a once in a lifetime opportunity. Lenny was a little disappointed at first but agreed that Ed should follow his dream. They shared a five-day break at a secluded four-star country hotel and spoilt themselves with the spa facilities and other personal attributes. Life on the ocean wave. You couldn't beat it with a big stick.

By the time Christmas came that year, Lizzy had, against her better judgement, secretly forgiven Lenny for a betrayal that he knew nothing about.

'After all,' she mused, 'he was as betrayed as much as I was but he must never, ever, find out. Ed would eventually get his comeuppance. Of that, I am absolutely sure! Fuck Ed!'

Christmas was celebrated in the usual McKenna fashion. It was an unwritten law that both families would party together in and out of the two homes, for the full forty-eight hours. There was an array of visitors coming and going throughout the continual bedlam. It came and went with a bang, as usual. New Year however, was down to where the offspring wanted it to be. Benny's three would be out celebrating with their boyfriends and Lizzy would be out and about with Sharon. Lenny loved to party in Portsmouth any time so New Year was always going to be a blast. Benny, Julie, Robbie and Cissy would always be among the first to arrive at the Irish Club in Croydon and almost always be the last to get a taxi home. The McKennas were as close as ever. That's for sure.

By late January 2004, with all the festivities firmly behind them, it was time once again, for the two families to knuckle down and begin what was forecast to be another busy year. It was agreed that more staff would need to be taken on and as usual, each set of directors was responsible for hiring and firing in their own domains. If the businesses continued to grow at the rate that was predicted, then a full-time personnel manager would be on the cards that would facilitate both parties. All family members were more than happy with their lot, so to speak, and it was a discipline that was not favoured by any of them so an outsider would need to be considered. Who would they be able to trust? Not a stranger surely? Lenny was never going to leave the Navy any time soon and Lizzy was happy at the hair salon and anyway, she was far too young for such a prestigious position. As one of the locals would say, 'It was all a bit of a palaver!' It was decided to put the dilemma on the back burner but not for too long.

During the years leading up to this point in the McKenna family's success story, Benny and Robbie's love for darts had grown considerably. Although they were both handy players and represented the Eagles Nest at a local level, they both thoroughly enjoyed watching some of the top players at local and national competitions. This resulted in a few weekends a year, when the brothers would travel up and down the country as regular supporters at first-class venues. Of course, they were accommodated in first-class hotels. Their excursions would typically last from Friday to Monday with the exception of the World Championship, held annually at the Lakeside Country Club in Surrey. This was always a seven-day hooley of darts, beer and song. Their twin room was booked for the full seven days, in the adjoining Lakeside Hotel, each year well in advance, as were the tickets for the competition venue, all of which were guaranteed by a mate on the inside. Nudge-nudge wink-wink.

Julie and Cissy also had several trysts away each year. In their case they looked forward to a nice long weekend break, in the peace and quiet of a country hotel without the hustle and bustle of London and absolutely no children. Of course, they would spoil themselves with pampering sessions including pedicures, manicures, massages and absolutely top service for all meals and drinks. They would never have an early night and always had room service deliver breakfast each morning, sometimes in bed. But as some folk would say, 'It's a hard life.' It was during their first weekend away in 2004 that Julie came up with an idea, concerning the ongoing problem of hiring a personnel manager for the family businesses. It was the first week in March and time was marching on if they wanted to solve the problem before the start of the new financial year in April.

On their frequent visits with Benny and Robbie to the Irish Club on Saturday nights they often shared a table with a lady called Ann Wishbone. She had been a widow for some years but was always accompanied by her gentleman friend Ernie Ferris. He was always known by his nick name: Wheelie, as was his father before him: Wheelie Ferris. They were of a similar age group as the McKennas (middle-aged, although no one was prepared to admit it), which was probably the main reason that they all got on so well. Wheelie was a local man born and bred and a self-employed window cleaner. Ann was originally from Skibbereen in Cork in Ireland and had been a nurse for many years in the Croydon General Hospital. Wheelie's great cry to fame was that he had never been married and never had his heart broken. Ann had qualified to a certain degree as a nurse in Cork but decided to move to England the summer of 1974 when she was twenty-two years of age, after spotting an advert in her local newspaper for qualified nurses to relocate to a spanking, brand-new, modern hospital in Croydon.

Soon afterwards she met her late husband William who was seven years her senior and a very handsome 6' 2''. After what most people would call a whirlwind romance, they married in 1975. William had emigrated from Jamaica five years earlier and had a good job in the London Underground based at Waterloo station. After ten years of trying, Ann gave birth to their only child, a boy named Michael, named after Ann's father. Unfortunately, William died of a heart attack when Michael was ten years old. He was now nineteen years old and studying music at Royal Tunbridge Wells University. Ann took great delight in casually letting people know this fact.

After twenty-five years of job satisfaction, working on the hospital wards and attaining the position of ward sister, (the position of matron was gradually phased out over the years), Ann was asked to consider moving into management, in the personnel department in the same hospital. The hours were better, Monday to Friday, no night shifts and the biggest carrot of all was the pay rise she would receive on completing her training courses and probationary period, as she would be promoted to the position of personnel manager. She would share an office with another personnel manager with more experience but with equal seniority. The powers that be insisted that with her experience and dedication, she would be ideal for the job. There would be the usual formalities prior to her acceptance but the personnel director assured her that this position was to be kept in house. Her predecessor had retired after many years and although there would be a big pair of shoes to fill, Ann was the first name on everyone's lips.

It took Ann a full year of courses, probation and on-the-job experience to feel competent enough to hold her own with her counterpart. Years two and three were challenging to say the least and then the rot set in. Ann always maintained her loyalties to the nurses on the wards and could not and would not accept some of the money saving and sometimes rash decision-making regarding these unsung heroes. She had head-to-head arguments, not just with her fellow personnel manager but on many occasions with her boss, the personnel director. This did not hold well among the Board of Directors at all. The following were a few of their comments, although not recorded, which were passed on to Ann, via the secretary responsible for typing up the notes from their meetings.

'Who the hell does she think she is?'

'Who gave the nod for her to get the job in the first place?'

'She will have to bloody go!'

Ann knew she was on a sticky wicket but would not desert her basic beliefs on the correct staffing of the wards, and the welfare of not just the patients but also the nurses was absolutely paramount.

Due to reorganisation within the NHS and just shy of thirty years' service, Ann was made redundant early in the New Year 2004. She was given an excellent package and pension and was given three months gardening leave which was coming to an end and as far as anyone knew, she had not been actively seeking further employment.

Julie and Cissy thought that she was just what they were looking for: an experienced hard-nosed character, who calls a spade a spade. On their return home they quickly contacted Ann. She agreed to meet all four of the McKenna directors. 'Just for a cup of tea and a chat,' Julie had said. Ann started her new job at the beginning of April on a six-month trial. The trial period was Ann's idea.

The summer months were always hectic for both companies so the holidays abroad were always in September and possibly, if the price was right, a bargain early in the New Year. The husbands still had their weekends away, as did the wives. On one such weekend the boys were in Liverpool for a North versus South charity fundraiser. All the top names would be there and the chance to play a world class name was too good to miss. It was being held in the Adelphi Hotel in the city centre, less than five minutes from the railway station. No driving involved so it would be a piss up from getting on the train in London on Friday afternoon, until their return on Monday, at whatever time they decided to roll home. Ah well, boys will be boys.

The girls as usual, were keeping an eye on things for both companies with the help of a duty manager designated by the boys. Most weekends came and went with very few problems but it was always prudent to keep the mobile phones handy. As it happened, Saturday was always busiest for Lizzy and Sharon in the hair salon. They would sometimes not finish work until after seven o'clock so it was always a mad rush to get home, get changed, get dolled up and get out, and see what was on offer at the local pubs and clubs. But on this particular Saturday, Lizzy was suffering really badly with the dreaded hay fever and it was for real this time. She was popping pills like Smarties but to no avail. Her boss, Jethro, felt really sorry for her but it didn't sit well with his customers when she sneezed and spluttered around the salon and almost spilt the coffees onto the customers' laps. The blue rinse brigade was not happy. So, at about two o'clock she sniffed through her goodbyes and apologies and headed for home. The fresh air seemed to do her some good so the short walk was a temporary relief. When she arrived at the house she noticed that her mum's car was not in its usual place but Aunt Julie's was parked up next door. She thought that there must have been a problem at work and her mum had gone to sort it out. 'Ah well,' she thought. 'I'll have the house to myself this afternoon and hopefully make it out tonight to meet Sharon.'

After about an hour and another dose of antihistamines, the sneezing and sniffles began to fade away as she slipped into a gentle slumber. When she awoke sometime later she felt much better but had a bit of a headache, which was unfortunately an after effect of over-medicating her prescribed drugs. If she was going out on the pull that night she would need some of her mum's extra strong headache tablets. She glanced out of her bedroom window but her mum's car was still missing. 'Fuck it,' she said. 'Aunt Julie will probably have some.'

So, without further ado she made her way through the house to the patio door and into the back garden. There was a small gate in the garden fence dividing the two properties, which was always used at weekend for access between the two houses. On entering the kitchen via the patio door, she called out for her aunt but there was no answer. She knew that Julie would sometimes have a lie down as she occasionally suffered from migraine headaches, thus the reason for the extra strong tablets available. Lizzy could hear some sort of soft music coming from the other end of the house. 'Probably Aunt Julie's bedroom,' she reckoned. 'I'll tip-toe down and see if she's alright and tap two tablets off her. She'll understand.'

When she got close to the bedroom door, which was slightly open, she could still hear the soft music. She also heard the duvet cover being moved on the bed and what sounded like a stretch. 'Oh good,' she thought. 'I won't have to waken her. Sounds like she's getting up.' But then silence. Lizzy grimaced, scratched her head and decided to peek through the hinge crack in the door.

She could see Julie's head just above the duvet and what appeared to be a large bulge in the middle of the bed. Lizzy could not make head nor tail of what was going on. Then she heard Julie gasp. Then she heard whispers but couldn't work out where they were coming from or who was making them. Then, oh then, Lizzy spied another pair of feet at the bottom end of the bed as if someone was crouching, yes crouching between Julie's legs. Julie gasped once again, only this time it was almost like a cry for help. The unknown assailant was definitely in their stride as they both writhed throughout the turmoil of their sexual chemistry and wanton lust for each other. All hell broke loose as Julie's legs wrapped themselves tightly around the torso, or was it the head, of her benefactor until they came to rest, two lovers together. The duvet was covering Julie's waist, exposing her heaving breasts but hiding the identity of her partner in crime. Then, oh then, Lizzy spied a head slowly appearing from beneath the duvet, that began to kiss and lick the crevice between Julie's breasts, as if to sooth her ongoing palpitations. Julie put her hands down to assist her love tease, to stretch up and kiss her on the lips. It was then, and only then, that Lizzy could make out the identity of her aunt's illicit lover. Lizzy heard her own voice inside her sub-conscious mind and without making a sound, she cried out to her inner self:

'It's not. No, it's not. It can't be. It can't fucking be! It can't fucking well be! It can't be her! It can't be my fucking mum! Aghhh!'

Lizzy, almost frozen to the spot, felt her chin fall forward, until it rested on her breast bone. She slowly turned to make her way back, the way she came. Quickly and silently she exited the house to her safe place under the apple tree in her own back garden. Still standing and resting her hand against the tree, she puked up from the depths of her soul bringing phlegm and remnants of her medication to the fore, with a little catching the back of her throat. Some of the liquid came out like a spray while some seemed to remain slowly dripping from her mouth, resting and then dripping from her chin. At the same time a similar concoction was making its way down through her nostrils. Tears were also in abundance but she never made a sound. She began to shake her head in disbelief, trying to make some sense out of the situation but the nausea took over once again. Such was the ferocity of her convulsions she was beginning to experience severe cramps in her stomach and had to sit down on the grass with her legs fully stretched, with a hand at each side to steady her. She sat in silence for a few moments, until the urge to empty her insides in disgust subsided. She was emotionally drained and felt completely numb.

Meanwhile, in the bedroom the two wives remained in their embrace, totally oblivious to what Lizzy had witnessed and her subsequent condition. Cissy knew that she needed to be making a move soon as her car was being returned between half four and five and time was getting on. The local garage was replacing the front two tyres and Cissy had told the rep to take his time as she had housework to do that afternoon.

As Cissy was getting dressed, Julie said, 'You know something? We've got it all. Great jobs. Great houses. Great kids. Great husbands. And we have ourselves to thank for our exciting and unusual sexual appetites.'

Cissy smiled and replied, 'Yeah. You're absolutely right. But do you remember the first time we decided to experiment with each other?'

'Not half. We were at secondary school and at the fourth-year barbeque. We had fumbled and toyed with each other a few times before but none of us would make the final move, for a proper kiss or an intimate grope. That day we smuggled six cans of cider into the school grounds. We hid them in a plastic bag down by the stream near the woods.'

'Yeah,' agreed Cissy. 'We said we were going home as soon as we had something to eat but took a little detour, to have our dessert in private. Our just desserts, so to speak.

We drank the cider and did all the things we shouldn't have done. We were there for ages. How we didn't get caught, I don't know.'

Julie smiled and said, 'Then we left school and although we stayed in touch, on and off, eventually we went our separate ways and did what all girls did in our day. We looked for a half decent fella to marry, have kids, have no ambition and wonder why we all missed the boat of opportunity. Who would have thought we would rekindle our relationship in the circumstances we now find ourselves?'

'You know something Julie? There really is a God.'

They both laughed and Cissy asked, 'Do you think the boys get up to any mischief when they are away?'

Julie almost shouted her answer, 'Don't be ridiculous! They're so predictable. The only thing they want is a boys' weekend on the bloody piss. A leg over on Sunday mornings suits them just fine. I know they are great guys and our kids idolise them, but we are doing no one any harm by enjoying each other, especially on our weekends away and the odd afternoon perk like today. Anyway, they get their fair share of us, when we are all on holiday.'

When Cissy returned to her own house via the garden, she did not notice Lizzy, who remained out of sight between the apple tree and the hedgerow. Lizzy heard her mum but took no notice. She forced another potential puke back from whence it came, adding further discomfort to the dryness of her throat and the taste in her mouth, which was like a rugby player's jock-strap. The headache she suffered earlier was now well and truly gone. Lizzy made up her mind to meet up with Sharon that Saturday night, the sooner the better. She was definitely going for it, like she had never done before. Anything in bloody trousers.

By ten o'clock that night, Lizzy was completely pie-eyed. Sharon was raging as two potential good-looking bunk ups had plied them with alcohol and flashing the cash in no uncertain terms. They were at a disco bar in Bromley, which wasn't too far from home but far enough away from knowing eyes that might be only too willing to relay the unladylike behaviour to their parents. The two fit guys in question had invited the girls to a very upmarket night club in the West End of London. They were both in their mid-twenties and had booked a taxi for their journey, which was due to arrive at any minute but Lizzy, although willing in spirit, (spirit being the optimum word) was not totally in control of her bodily functions. At this stage it was either a rift or a fart, the fart was silent but deadly, if you know what I mean. Sharon was being loyal to her friend. There was no way she could leave her in that state and no way would she get home on her own so, reluctantly she said farewell to the two studs and blew them a sexy kiss as the taxi pulled off for what would have been a night with a bang.

When the girls arrived at Sharon's house, her parents were amazed at the early return home on a Saturday night. Sharon quickly pushed and dragged Lizzy upstairs and onto the spare bed in her room. She phoned Lizzy's house knowing that her parents would be out at the Irish Club and left a brief message on the voice mail. Poor old Sharon had to make do with a cup of tea and a slice of toast to finish off her Saturday night out. Her parents were tee-total.

The next morning Sharon quizzed Lizzy as to why she got so drunk, so quickly, the previous night. Lizzy could not think of a logical explanation so, just fobbed her off with, 'What's wrong with getting pissed now and again? We are always too bleeding careful in case someone gets the wrong bleeding impression. It's time for Lizzy's lib. Fuck everyone else. Who cares, who thinks, fucking, what. That's what I fucking say!'

Sharon was amazed at her mate's outburst. They both liked a good time, they both liked a good drink and they both definitely liked a bit of hanky-panky but within reason. 'But,' thought Sharon. 'Maybe Lizzy's right. Maybe we do worry too much. Maybe we should let our hair down more often, just, not so early on a night out and definitely, out of sight of prying eyes and ears!'

In the end, over a cup of coffee that morning, Lizzy

sincerely apologised to her best mate for mucking up what could have been their best night out in ages. Their devious plan of phoning their respective parents when they were up to no good, to say that they were staying overnight in each other's house, had in fact worked a treat on that occasion. Later that Sunday, they ended up in the Eagles Nest with Benny and Robbie and after a great afternoon's partying and semi-misbehaving, they headed their separate ways home, leaving the brothers McKenna holding court as usual.

When Lizzy arrived home, she made her excuses to Cissy and slipped into bed. The last person she wanted to speak to at that particular period in time was her mum. She then made herself a solemn promise that early evening. She would never use the word mum again. Mum was too kind a word. It would always be mother and she would never again use the word aunt or auntie regarding Julie. It would always be Julie, plain and simple. They deserved nothing less, nothing more. Fuck them both.

'And another thing,' she thought. 'From now on I will not answer to the name of Lizzy. Lizzy is a name for a slip of a girl. I am a full-grown woman. From now on my name is Liz. Yes, Liz McKenna sounds much better!'

CHAPTER 4

OVER THE NEXT FEW WEEKS, Liz and Sharon played the field like two old pros. They ensured that gullible, well-oiled young men, and some not so young, paid for drinks, taxis and sometimes a late supper or, after a late-night workout, a well-earned breakfast in a secluded hotel. On some occasions, after a stand-up fumble with their benefactors for a particular night, they would spend the night together in one or other's home, to validate their cover story for the nights when they scored a jackpot.

During the third weekend of May that year (2004), the two strumpets made their way a little further afield for possible new conquests. A few of their regulars or irregulars were becoming a little too possessive and same old, same old. They had heard great reports from like-minded, young ladies that the Lewisham Irish Centre was the 'in' place for great music and there was plenty of fresh totty, just dying to be taken advantage of. On their first visit, which was a Saturday night, they arrived just before ten-thirty and were damned lucky to get in. It was packed to the gills. Other venues didn't get remotely warmed up until much later and women arriving before eleven o' clock gained free entry. Not so in Lewisham.

It was first come first served, and if the guy on the door said that no one else was allowed in due to overcrowding, then a tip of a tenner would be the least anyone would be expected to cough up, to get to the ticket office in the foyer. The small ticket office was like a little hut which was protected by a metal grill, with barely enough room to pay and get a stamp on the back of your hand in pink ink, which stated the current date. The girls paid the normal entry fee of £10 and after what seemed like an eternity, squeezed into a small space at the bar created by a young man of about twenty, who staggered off into the ensuing madness, with a pint of Guinness, taking a slurp and then spilling a slurp. The disco sounds from the resident DJ were almost deafening but the crowd loved every shake, rattle and roll as they gyrated in a mass orgy of foot-stomping, arse-wiggling, tit-bouncing, ear-licking, touching-up promiscuity.

Eventually they each managed to procure a cocktail, when they noticed a dark-haired hunk of about thirty years of age, who would not be out of place in somewhere like Hollywood. He was sitting at a table with four other guys who appeared to be slightly younger than him, a short distance from the bar but on its own and away from all the other tables in that area. There was a sign on top of the table which spelled RESERVED in bold black letters. Both girls glanced at each other and then slowly made their way in the general direction of the table. When they were pretty close, Liz pretended to slip in her six-inch-high heels and grab hold of the dark-haired hunk's shoulder and as quick as a flash he was on his feet, with a steadying hand around her waist. Liz's hand remained on his shoulder, almost, as if they were about to dance. Sharon moved in for the kill, apologising for intruding and adding that if they didn't rest their weary feet they would have to head off somewhere else. Next thing you know, all five men made space for the girls to join their company. Everyone's drink was replenished and Liz made sure she was next to Mr Hollywood. Sharon had eyes for all of the other four, who were equally infatuated with both of these seemingly, fancy-free young vixens. The night was still but young.

In the conversation that followed, it transpired that these five fit blokes were in fact, the live entertainment for the night. 'All bleeding night,' thought both girls. They were all from in and around Dublin who had travelled by ferry in a converted sixteen seat minibus. It was big enough for the five guys, their instruments and their kit to travel far and wide. Quite simply, wherever the money was.

The gig in Lewisham was only one of twelve that they were contracted for, over a seventeen-day period. They were a band known as *Steve Walker and The Walkmen*. And guess which one was Steve? Only Mr Hollywood himself and Liz, was already giving him butterfly kisses with her well-groomed eyelashes. Just before eleven-thirty, Steve and the boys made their apologies as they were required on stage for their ninety-minute performance. Steve arranged for the club entertainment manager to keep the girls company at the table, with drinks aplenty until the band completed their showbiz routine. Liz and Sharon couldn't believe their luck. A reserved table, free booze, a bunch of well-groomed shags and all on their first night there. 'Oh bliss. We're on the piss. We can't miss. Thanks a lot, for the fucking jackpot.' They couldn't help themselves, as they sniggered in unison.

The DJ gave the band a really big intro, enhanced by a loud, slow, teasing backing track, from his spot at the left-hand side of the stage. The large heavy stage curtains were drawn back as if by magic, the overhead lights came on, just a few at a time until all five members became clearly visible. The crowd began to edge closer to the stage, waiting with bated breath. The drummer was on a raised platform so that he and his array of percussion could be clearly seen. The guitar ensemble consisted of a bass, a lead and a rhythm, in front of the drummer, all in a line with Steve playing acoustic and standing slightly in front of the others to take up his place as the lead singer and what proved to be the star of the show. They all wore open-necked white shirts, dark trousers and sparkled jackets, each jacket a different colour. Steve's was jet black, matching his hair and his equally dark eyes.

The live music was fantastic and the packed house of punters from all age groups showed their appreciation with their energetic dance routines, chorus join-ins and thunderous applause followed by cheers and whistles. Every up-tempo number the band performed was a floor puller of wannabe show-offs, while the few love songs or heart breakers signalled the formation of numerous groups with interlocking arms, legs and torsos and anything else that was on the loose side. The ninety-minute routine was over in what seemed like no time at all. The band left the stage but only for a few moments as the baying crowd demanded an encore. Steve and the boys did not need much persuading and banged out another popular song and then once again vacated the stage.

This time the resident DJ immediately took over the reins to keep the party going, adding his own patter to once again take control of the venue and dictate in which direction the music was going. He was definitely a master at work.

When the boys returned to their RESERVED table, the entertainments manager dutifully handed over Liz and Sharon with no harm done and then headed off into the oblivion, shouting over his shoulder, that drinks would be on the way. Although each member of the band had a quick dry off and changed their shirts, the sweat was still visible on the sides of their faces, all except Gino the drummer. His favourite saying was that it took more than a few songs to make him sweat. This brought a wry smile from Sharon.

As the night wore on it was obvious that Liz and Steve were an item. They didn't dance. They just sat, drank and tried to talk over the noise of the packed revellers until, in desperation, Steve suggested they move to somewhere a little quieter. Liz nodded her agreement and they both headed for the exit. Gino grabbed hold of Sharon's hand and they both quickly followed suit. Out of the main door, all four shared a London taxi to the band's digs. It was only a ten-minute journey but both couples took advantage of the closeness of the taxi to swap some spit.

Steve paid the fare as they were dropped off outside what appeared to be a run of the mill bed and breakfast. The girls were a little disappointed, for they were expecting some sort of a hotel, to say the least. Anyway, Steve unlocked the front door and all four made their way upstairs to the first floor, where Steve once again unlocked another door, this time to his humble abode. He switched on the bedside light to reveal a spacious, well-decorated room with an equally spacious double bed.

From the small fridge near the window Steve and Gino

produced bottles of beer for themselves and in turn, white wine for the girls. They apologised for not having any spirits for the two well-oiled mates, but by this stage, neither Liz nor Sharon seemed bothered about what they drank. Their only concern was: who was having the big double bed? Not all four surely? At this stage Gino asked Sharon if she would like to see his room, which was just next door. The two girls gave their usual signal, a wink and a nod and in only a few seconds Liz and Steve were alone. It wasn't long before they were both stark naked.

The following Sunday morning Liz awoke to find Steve standing at the end of the bed in his boxers, holding a tray. She was pleasantly surprised to see that it held two mugs of what proved to be strong sweet tea and two slices of burnt toast. Just the way she liked it. Sharon popped her head round the door wearing a t-shirt and shorts, to check on Liz, as was their usual plan, when they found themselves in separate rooms after a heavy night of booze and debauchery. One would always seek out the other, depending on who was up and about first.

Gino soon joined them with his offering of the same mini breakfast fare, dressed only in a pink bath towel. He couldn't find his underwear. Little did he know Sharon was wearing his boxers, as she couldn't find her thong. Over the next hour or so the boys explained that the boss of the bed and breakfast was a man of about sixty years of age and didn't mind turning a blind eye regarding late-night visitors, as long as there were no noisy parties. 'Don't take the piss!' was his main house rule. Steve also explained that he always got the double room, while the other four shared two twin rooms, quite simply because he was not only the lead singer but also the booking and road manager. Plus, he was in his early thirties while the others were just pups in their very, very, early twenties. Liz was more than just, very impressed with her newfound heartthrob. The emphasis being on the word, throb. The other golden rule was that if one of the other four copped off with a bird then his roommate would bed-down, on the floor in the alternative twin room. No probs. Everyone's a fucking winner.

Their present gigs were booked around three weekends. Friday, Saturday and Sunday nights by three, in Irish-orientated dance venues. Two Wednesday nights in top class pubs of renown and one Thursday night for a wedding reception in a hotel, giving a grand total of twelve gigs. The only exception on this trip was that the last Sunday was an afternoon show, in a monstrously large pub in Croydon that was holding a music fest, over the second bank holiday that May.

Liz and Sharon quickly worked out, that this particular Sunday in the bed and breakfast was part of the middle weekend, so they suggested that they all meet up again the following Saturday night, which was once again to be the Lewisham Irish Centre. Steve and Gino did not need much coaxing but both suggested, in the nicest possible way, that a little more action between the sheets would be definitely on the cards, providing the girls were not in any hurry to get home. Smiles all round but the girls insisted that they all have a shower before the next round of events. Steve and Gino looked at the girls and whispered, 'All together? In the all together?' Liz and Sharon whispered, 'Not this time... Boys.'

About four o'clock that afternoon found Steve and Gino fast asleep, in an attempt to regain some energy prior to the band's performance that night, while the girls swapped notes on their mobile phones from the privacy of each other's bedroom. They were both home and safe and hatching a plan for the following weekend and if they had their way, the boys would think Christmas had come early. The emphasis being on the word come: or would it be cum. It was going to be a plan with a big fucking bang.

Throughout the following week, the two girls were continuously whispering what can only be described as unbelievable infidelities to each other, which on a few occasions infuriated their boss Jethro who, if the truth be known, would have given more than his right arm to familiarise himself with their final, dastardly, evil, mind-blowing plan. Whoopee do!

Steve had taken the whole experience the previous weekend in his stride while Gino was a complete nervous wreck of fantasy and delusion. He could hardly leave himself alone. Saturday seemed like years away. The other three band members actually felt sorry for him.

That Saturday night finally arrived at the Lewisham Irish Centre and the girls arrived just before ten o'clock. They paid their entrance fee and made their way to the band's reserved table once more. They slowly manoeuvred between the other dancers, sallying forth and side to side like two professional cat-walk experts, as if moving in slow motion. As they came into view the five band members looked up and each of them, including the incomparable Steve, could just about hold on to the roots of their tongues as they were all hanging out like dogs in heat. The makeovers the girls had invested in earlier that night were undoubtedly a very wise decision, to say the least. Gino nearly filled his boxers.

Drinks appeared as if by magic and the girls settled down for a prick-teasing routine that had passers-by, male and female, rubbernecking the two dolly birds flashing their wares. Both hairstyles had that 'just been shagged' look. Their make-up was extremely subtle which, in turn, effectively enhanced their eyes and the contours of their faces. Both wore bright yellow shirts unbuttoned, almost to the waist and tied in a knot to reveal their trim mid-drifts. Each set of nipples could be clearly seen through the fabric as if trying to escape captivity. Both had a small shiny silver stud in their navel. The black tight mini-skirts could only be described as: bras with pelmets. When they crossed their legs every so often, a brief glance of their white underwear was absolutely eye popping. The six-inch, black, sling back, patent stilettos, were the icing on their well-prepared honey traps. They were definitely on a roll, and definitely well ahead of the game. All five of the band spilled their drinks or missed their mouths on several occasions but the alcohol just kept coming. The two vixens smiled and Liz whispered to Sharon, 'The only way is up.'

The remainder of the night in the Irish Centre went like a tidal wave of horny innuendoes and complete abandonment of morals and scruples, with more than just a hint of, 'I'm gagging for it!'

Men and women both, who passed the RESERVED table found it extremely difficult not to bump into each other as they shuffled, google-eyed in disbelief at the French kissing, (boy on girl and girl on girl) and the touching up (boy on girl and girl on girl). Sinning was in no one's dictionary that Saturday night. Steve was beginning to tremble, Gino had to cross his legs continually and the other three were about to have a nervous breakdown. Wet dreams, while they were still awake!

When the band took to the stage at eleven-thirty, they performed as if they were on fire. Liz and Sharon continued to sip their cocktails and enjoy the show from their RESERVED table with the entertainment manager standing guard. The atmosphere around the entire dance hall was absolutely electric. It was like a free-for-all. There was no encore that night. The boys couldn't get off the stage quick enough. Steve, Gino and the girls headed for the main door and into a taxi for a fast getaway to the bed and breakfast. The other three band members were practically mauled as they came off the stage. One of them shouted:

'Every man for himself and fly the flagpole, high and dry!'

Sunday morning found Liz and Steve completely naked on top of his double bed. Their garb and bed clothes were scattered all over the room. Some on the floor, some on the armchair and some on top of the small dressing table, even on the top of the wardrobe. They were both completely fucked. Liz stirred and gazed around the room, a little unsure where she was and then Steve began to rouse. He also was not sure what had actually happened. If he had the ride of his life or was it a mixture of a dream come true and a nightmare?

Liz slipped off the bed and wrapped herself in a large

black bath towel, making sure it covered her vital parts. She went next door to check on Sharon and didn't want the boss of the bed and breakfast to suffer a stroke. The door of the bedroom was slightly ajar and it made a soft creaking sound as she slowly opened it. Sharon was alone and shot upright in the bed, covering her breasts with what little bedclothes she could find. She smiled with relief when she realised it was Liz. Her best friend sat on the end of the bed and both swapped points, good and bad of their sexual adventures throughout the night. Liz was full of it as she explained in every detail the various positions and the number of times she had enjoyed multiple orgasms with Super Steve.

Sharon's tale was not as wonderful as she had anticipated. Gino was nowhere to be seen. Liz thought he might be making some tea and toast.

'No such luck,' said Sharon. 'He's not even in the fucking building.'

'What are you on about, Sharon? Where is he?'

'He's in A and fucking E. And the last time I saw him he was bleeding, fucking bleeding!'

'You're having a fucking laugh, girl. Now where the fuck is he?'

'I fucking told you, Liz. He's in A and fucking E.'

'How the fuck did he end up there?'

'We got back here, same as you and old fucking supercock next door. We got into the room, right? He says he wants me to do a striptease, right? To a song on his CD player, right? Well then, off I goes, giving him the treat of his fucking life.'

At this stage Liz, was finding it difficult to keep a straight face but she didn't want to upset her best friend so she managed to cough her way out of the impending laugh.

Liz almost shouted, 'Get to the fucking point, will you!'

'Alright, Liz. I'm getting there. Now, after the slinky striptease, I'm on the bed as naked as the day I was born, wearing just my strap back stilettos and pushing my fingers in and out of my pussy, begging him to come and stick it in me! Well, he yanked his zip down so hard onto his hard-on, so fast that it caught him on the fucking hard-on. Good and fucking proper like. Well, he started screaming and the next thing I know he's bleeding, fucking bleeding. All over the fucking place.

'Old horny bollocks from downstairs, you know the boss of the fucking place, comes running up the stairs, his thick grey hair standing on end, wearing his trackie bottoms and string vest, with his hairy man boobs flapping all over the fucking place, screaming blue bleeding fucking murder. No matter how hard we pulled at his hard-on: well, it was just fucking stuck to his bleeding zip. In the end we had to phone for a taxi to take him to the hospital. Poor old Gino had tears in his eyes.'

(At this stage so did Liz but it wasn't because she was in pain.)

'We put a damp towel over his bits to save his blushes and to soak up the blood but he was ever so brave. He rang me a little while ago to tell me he was waiting for a taxi to bring him back here. He said that no serious harm done and no stitches but he might be a little tender down there for a while, so to speak. He said that the nurse put a little dressing on it. I asked him what he was going to do with me when he got back here. He said that his tongue was still up for plenty of licking exercise and the engine room would be fully functional once the pain killers kicked in.'

Both girls burst out laughing so loud it woke Steve next door. He looked out of the window to see a taxi pull up outside. Gino stepped gingerly onto the pavement and the boss of the place let him in through the front door and asked, 'Where's my fucking towel?' Gino just rolled his eyes and made his way upstairs, to be welcomed by both girls offering lots of sympathy and lots of little cuddles. He was really beginning to milk it. Poor Gino.

Steve popped his head round his bedroom door and asked, 'What the fuck is going on?'

Gino replied, 'You always said that I was just a flash in the pan, and last night was no exception mate, but don't worry, today is another day and tonight... Well now that's another fucking story.'

The remainder of that Sunday morning was spent lazing around the bed and breakfast. The other three members of the band shared a battered old minicab and returned just before midday, full of tales of debauchery and other Sunday morning antidotes. There was just enough time for everyone to down a hot greasy bacon sandwich and a mug of tea, duly supplied by the sex symbol from downstairs. Two taxis were booked asap, to take everyone back to the Lewisham Irish Centre, pick up all the band's gear, pack it into the minibus and make their way to the pub in Croydon known as The Tumble Down Dick.

They arrived in plenty of time to set up all the gear, carry out a thorough sound check, and locate the minute changing room that they were allocated. The main bar was huge, possibly the biggest any of them had ever seen. The gig hall and stage were equally impressive, as were the door men at the entrance and the two fire exits. No one would get in or out without the say so of the well-dressed henchmen. They were charging £20 per head and there were at least two hundred in the main pub, with a queue beginning to form outside on the pavement.

Steve thought to himself that a crowd this big and already in the party mood, on a Sunday afternoon, in a pub rather than an organised dance hall, could be the makings of something really big, or it could easily backfire and turn into a free-for-all. In contrast, Irish dance halls had regular clientele that were out for a bloody good knees-up, as well as a good drink, but tended to remain reasonably civilised in order to get a shag at the end of the night. There's no point in spending money on possible rides to frighten them off with a punch up. But this crowd was growing bigger by the minute and was topping up from the night before. If they didn't get a jump last night they would not be in the best of humour, and if they did, then they wouldn't give a flying fuck anyway.

Steve squeezed the band and the girls into their dressing room and laid out the plan for the rest of the afternoon. It was now 3 pm and as the main band they were expected to open the show at 4 pm. After their first set of about an hour and a half they would have a short break. They would then return to the stage and be the back-up music for several solo artists lasting about an hour. Another short break followed by their second set, once again for about an hour and a half. It was going to be a long afternoon but Steve reminded them that the money was not just good: it was exceptional, especially for a pub. The icing on the cake was that all drinks for the band and the two girls were on the house. Steve warned the band not to go over the top with the drink until they had finished performing.

Immediately after the briefing, Steve organised a large table and chairs to the left-hand side of the stage, only a few feet away from the hallway leading to the dressing room. The crowds were now beginning to fill the main gig hall. The long bar on the opposite side to where they were sitting had no less than six beer stations, each consisting of four standard beers, a fully-stocked spirit selection and fridges consisting of every type of alcopop known to man. There were three bar staff, male and female in attendance at each station and each with its own till. Everything and everyone looked so well organised. Steve had never seen anything quite like it but didn't want to be over-awed as were the youngsters at his table, just in case it all went tits up. If the shit hit the fan it would be up to him to get them all out in one piece. He assured himself that this was the reason he was the highest paid member of the band. The buck stops with him. He placed his head in his hands and thought to himself: 'Maybe I should consider a solo career.'

Just before 4 pm the resident compere cum comedian known as Big Bill, with a mass of blonde curly hair, dressed in a flamboyant, multicoloured, carnival style suit, hit the stage with a magnificent bellowing voice which caught everyone's attention. To say the least, he could have performed without a microphone. He had a most compelling voice and a personality that hit you right between the eyes. His one-liners and jokes were absolutely hilarious. Steve and the boys were waiting patiently out of sight at the side of the stage when they all burst out laughing, almost out of control. Eventually Big Bill announced: 'Steve Walker and the Walkmen!'

Although they had never played this venue before, the applause, cheers and the whistles were deafening. The band just could not believe the reception they received, which was a continual melee of noise until they hit the first note of their first song. Even Steve with all his experience was so impressed, a silly little smirk developed on his face when he looked round the rest of the boys. He gave them a wink of approval and nodding his head as a sign of satisfaction. They all knew that this was going to be a fucking cracker of a gig, maybe their best ever.

From start to finish the band worked their socks off. The solo artists could give them nothing but praise. Big Bill was more than pleased with their performance and of course he kept the party going with his fantastic comedy routine during the short breaks between sets. Liz and Sharon were both itching to get at them because even during the breaks the boys were unable to spend much time with them apart from making sure that they had enough drinks. Big Bill looked after that department in no uncertain terms. He was not only the organiser of the show but was also the owner of the joint.

At about 8 pm the live show came to an end and the disco took over with Big Bill once again on the mic. He made sure the party atmosphere was maintained and then handed over to the resident DJ. Steve and the boys were completely knackered. They had never worked so hard nor enjoyed themselves so much before. It was obvious that the four younger men of the band came of age in the world of entertainment that day. Smiles all round and the two girls were gagging for it. When the dust settled a little, all the band's gear was packed away into the dressing room to be collected the next day. An hour or so later saw Steve and Liz slip away with two bottles of chilled wine supplied by Big Bill. Gino and Sharon partied for a little while longer and then followed suit. The other three thought they had died and gone to heaven.

The following morning, which was a bank holiday Monday, arrived with sunshine and little birds singing on the trees front and back of the digs. However, no one in the building was remotely interested, including the hairy ape of a manager. At about eight o'clock Liz began to stir. Her head was absolutely fucking bouncing! The wine that they had brought back with them went pretty quickly but the re-supply from the manager of the digs was what caused the most damage. He had a substantial amount of poteen, which he procured on a regular basis for a rock bottom price from his maiden aunt in Reading. According to him, Aunt Mary Ellen who was originally from Mayo in Ireland, ran a bed and breakfast for the building fraternity. She had over many years built a do-it-yourself poteen still in the cellar of her town house and had subsidised her income by selling it first come first served. Her best customers were the Thames Valley Police, many of whom came from Irish parentage and their headquarters were only a stone's throw from Mary Ellen's house.

Liz glanced round the room, which was in such disarray that it was difficult for her to orientate her glazed eyes in any direction without feeling intense pain. She thought, 'Where's Sharon?'

She put one foot on the floor, then the other, careful not to wake Steve, who was lying face down on top of the duvet with his bare arse stuck up in the air, then that fucking bass drum in her head began to get louder and louder! She covered her own nakedness with Steve's shirt, which more than covered her vital parts and gingerly made her way to the bedroom door, side-stepping various articles of clothing, wine bottles and coffee mugs.

'Coffee mugs? Oh yes. We were drinking that fucking poteen out of coffee mugs last night. That hairy arse, slobber chops of a manager, I think he said his name was Clifford but everyone called him Cliff because in his younger days, he looked like... Cliff Richard. Fuck. Fuck. Fuck.'

She made her way along the short landing to check on Sharon and gently knocked on the door. There was no response from inside so Liz turned the door handle and peaked round into the bedroom. Sharon was sitting in the armchair beside the window. She looked over her shoulder and smiled, which slowly turned into a great big grin, and beckoned Liz to come in. Liz began to whisper her inquisitiveness but Sharon told her not to worry about noise because Gino was completely and utterly bolloxed and was forming a foetal position under the duvet. Sharon was also wearing her lover's shirt. They both giggled, as the wearing of the lover's shirt the morning after the night before was their secret sign that they had the fuck of a lifetime. Sharon supplied the extra strong and well received headache tablets to her grateful friend, who quickly consumed them with the aid of the not-so-cold water from the adjacent not-so-clean sink.

After a few moments of sharing secrets of their sexual escapades, Sharon said, 'Listen, Liz, I always tell you to do what I do. After a heavy night take the tablets before you get into bed. That way, nine times out of ten you won't suffer in the bleeding morning. But you never listen.'

'But I did exactly that last night. But that bleeding poteen fucked me up completely. You and Gino only had one and then fucked off to bed for a marathon riding session. You jammy bastards. Once me and Steve got the taste of it there was no going back.'

Sharon purred her reply, 'Gino was like an ever-ready battery. He went on and on and on... And on.'

'Well,' said Liz. 'Steve was so bleeding rampant. Well... When he stripped off with his back to me and then turned round, in a flash... Like... Holding his fucking totem pole. I couldn't help myself. I pinned him to the bed and I rode him, as if I was trying to break it in half. I don't know how long we were at it, but fuck me... I'm still dripping.'

Suddenly, the sound of car brakes outside brought their attention back to the window. The girls just knew it had to be a minicab bringing the other three boys back to the digs.

Sure enough, they all piled out of the vehicle, almost all at once, still swigging beer out of the one lonely can between them. All had shirt tails hanging out and unbuttoned to the waist. Either they were trying to show off their macho chests or they had the shirts ripped off the previous night. But they were in fine spirits, slapping each other on the back like winning jockeys after a hard ride.

Cliff, the boss of the bed and breakfast, was woken by the commotion and eventually opened the front door, standing or possibly even swaying, to welcome them back to his humble abode. He was not a pretty sight, that's for sure. Knowing that there was going be a race for a bed, the girls gathered their belongings from both rooms and made their way to the bathroom for a quick shower.

At about nine-thirty they found themselves in the small sitting room of Cliff's ground floor flat, which also contained the kitchen from which the so-called breakfast was to be created, but he certainly wasn't up to the task. Liz and Sharon to the rescue: sandwiches for everyone. Toast with grilled sausages and bacon, all on plates in the centre of the dining room table. First come first served and plenty of hot tea to wash them down. It was now about eleven o'clock and Steve and Gino did not need much persuading to stagger down the stairs for the hot food. The smell of the sausages and bacon was like a red flag to a bull and the other three amigos soon followed. Within twenty minutes there wasn't a crumb or a drop of tea left. All present were more than replenished and the girls were subjected to numerous compliments from all directions. Even the Cliff Richard look-a-like offered a thank you kiss but the grease on his lips and chin was a real put off. They each accepted a little hug instead, at half an arm's length.

By midday the five boys took turns to shower and pack their belongings for the trip home to Dublin. They would first have to return to The Tumble Down Dick pub to pick up their gear, but that wouldn't take long. Two taxis and an hour later all was packed and ready to go. Big Bill was more than impressed by the band's performance and although he paid them the previous night, he slipped Steve a £50 note for a drink on the ferry on their journey home. He also said that they were one of the best bands ever to perform in his huge pub, plus the takings had in fact been through the roof. Steve thought to himself, 'Another satisfied customer.'

But alas, it came the time for the goodbyes. The three amigos were in the minibus trying not to giggle and pretending to have a hush-hush conversation, while the two lover boys canoodled the two love-struck girls in the side ally of the pub. Privacy and seriousness were a priority for the parting couples. Mobile phone numbers were exchanged and also promises to keep in touch were in abundance. In a flash, Steve jumped into the driver's seat and Gino into the front passenger's seat. Almost like two cowboys jumping onto a stage coach. The three amigos were pissing themselves. A wave from Liz and Sharon and the minibus was gone.

Sharon asked Liz, 'Any regrets?'

Liz replied, 'Not a one. Let's go across to the Eagles Nest and join the bank holiday fun with my dad and Uncle Benny. There's always a great band on there and the craic will be ninety!'

CHAPTER 5

THE ONCOMING DAYS PASSED INTO WEEKS. Although Gino was in contact with Sharon there was nothing from Steve. To be honest, Liz had not expected to begin a long-distance relationship, but a quick call now and again would have been nice. Sharon and Gino seemed to be taking their relationship a lot further as they spoke on a daily basis, sometimes three or four times a day. Also, as time wore on, Sharon didn't mind going out with Liz on the town but was very reluctant to go on the pull. If the truth be told neither did Liz.

Then, out of the blue, Sharon told Liz that Gino was coming back to London at the end of August for a job interview. Well, the interview was in Southampton but he wanted to stay for a week or so to spend some time with Sharon.

Liz thought, *Fucking young and gullible... True fucking love. Ah well... Good luck to her... And him. The jammy bastards!*

When the dust settled, Sharon told Liz that Gino had an initial interview and audition in Dublin. He was now on a shortlist for a position with a cruise ship company as a resident drummer. His prospects looked really good and he also said that he had an idea that might suit Sharon. He would explain later when he arrived in London. Lo and behold, Gino arrived in Croydon and based himself at Cliff's bed and breakfast. The British Maritime Cruisers had paid for his travel expenses and two days' bed and breakfast, so his out lay for the seven days was not going to break the bank, especially with a discount from Cliff. He arrived on Monday and was to report to the BMC office in Southampton the following morning. Although he and Sharon met up it was only for a few quiet drinks and then under the duvet for some indoor PT. Of course she had told her parents she would be staying at Liz's house. Their old cover story was still going well.

Oh yes! Gino's idea that might suit Sharon? Well now, Gino had taken the liberty of passing on Sharon's contact details and a brief resume of her qualifications and experience in the hair dressing business. Well, Sharon nearly shit herself.

'What do you mean you passed on my personal details to a complete stranger? I ain't going to work in bleeding Southampton!'

'No! No! No! Will you listen to me, Sharon? I looked at other vacancies that are available with BMC, and you could easily get a job on the same ship as me. We could travel all over the place and be a proper couple. I thought that's what we were both hinting at, during all our phone calls over the last three months.'

Sharon was completely astonished at Gino's proposal, but quite liked the idea. She said she would sleep on it, to which Gino declared, 'Listen, my little darlin'. You won't be getting much sleep tonight.'

The following morning the pair of love birds said their farewells and, to Gino's relief, Sharon agreed that she could be contacted online and by phone, with a view of a job prospect. According to Gino there was a big recruiting drive throughout the cruise business for qualified and certificated hair dressers. One final kiss and he was on his way. She knew he would be back as soon as his little legs would carry him, but regarding the potential job... Sharon wasn't holding her breath.

Gino's interview and what he hoped would be his final audition went much better than he could have ever imagined. It took place on board the *Belle Morrow*. He was invited to stay on board overnight and mix with some of the crew so as to gain a brief insight to life on board a cruise ship. He jumped at the chance and phoned Sharon accordingly. He could just about contain his excitement. What he didn't tell Sharon was that he passed on as much of her professional capabilities as possible to human resources, and also to the personnel manager of Ladies' Hair Salon Services. They guaranteed him that someone would be in contact with her within the next few days.

The week that followed in Croydon was slightly hectic for the two young lovers. Sharon had booked a few days' holiday and told her parents that she was going down to Brighton on a girlie holiday break. So long as she and Gino stayed well out of sight then her parents would be none the wiser. They asked if Liz was also going but were reliably informed that she had been under the weather recently, which was closer to the truth than anyone could have realised. She had been a bit of a wet blanket in and out of work but Sharon put it down to lovesick blues. Gino's seven-day visit came and went as fast as lightning. He and Sharon found it difficult to say another au revoir but hey ho. He had to go. It would all work out fine in the end. No sooner had Gino gone when Sharon's mum appeared with a large white envelope.

'This arrived while you were in Brighton,' she said.

Sharon looked at it curiously. It had a Southampton postmark and when she turned it over the sender on the back was 'British Maritime Cruisers, East Dock Street, Southampton.'

'Holy fuck,' she thought. 'How the hell do I explain this?'

'Well then, what is it?' asked her dad.

Sharon had to think fast. 'How should I know?'

'Well, open it then!' shouted her mum.

Sharon opened up the envelope very slowly hoping that Gino's name would not be mentioned in the documentation. To her relief it was an application form that had been sent on the recommendation of a third party. Her mum was reading it over Sharon's shoulder.

'What third party would that be, Sharon?'

'Oh, I don't know, Mum. Probably one of the old girls that come into the salon. You know, the ones with a few bob. The ones that always leave a good tip.'

Her mum frowned and said, 'I hope you don't think that we are going to allow you to move to Southampton. You're only a slip of a girl. You would never cope on your own.

Now give it to me and I'll get rid of it.'

Sharon clutched the paperwork and shouted, 'I'll hang on to it. Liz might be interested!'

Both parents raised a suspicious eyebrow then her father said, 'Okay then. You give it to your mate, but I can't see her surviving on her own either. Her parents would be of the same frame of mind as us. She's far too young to go off on her own. The two of you have good homes and very little expenses. The both of you should be grateful.' With that said the conversation ended.

'Thank fuck,' thought Sharon.

The following morning during their tea break, Sharon could hardly wait to show Liz the application form and to tell her how she had nearly been caught out by her parents. The two mates had a bit of a chuckle and Liz asked, 'Are you serious about filling in the form?'

'To be honest Liz, it's getting a bit claustrophobic at home. Those few days away with Gino were just fucking fantastic. I could come and go, and was answerable to no fucking one. My mum and dad still think I'm a schoolgirl who should hang on to my virginity until I get bleeding fucking married.'

Liz empathised, 'I know how you feel, mate. I'm fed up doing the same old routine day in and day fucking out, but we can't afford to leave home yet.'

Sharon piped up, 'We could... If we were both successful enough to get a job with this cruising company. Why don't we both apply? I'll phone them for another form to be sent to your address. At least your mum and dad don't nosey when you get mail.'

'There's no point, Sharon. No fucking point.'

'But why, Liz? Why the fuck not?'

'Because, Sharon, I'm bleeding fucking pregnant. That's why the fuck not!'

Sharon's eyes and mouth shot wide open and she froze as if in suspended animation.

A fortnight later Sharon was in Southampton for an early morning interview followed by a salon assessment module on the same day, with just a few minutes in-between to grab a quick bite and a cuppa. There were twelve candidates in total competing for six immediate vacancies in BMC, and there was hardly time to go for a piss never mind anything else. Sharon was taken completely by surprise but had taken good heart in the advice and support Gino had given her over the phone on countless occasions. There were ten women and two men who were all in a competitive frame of mind, with no room whatsoever for fair play. They were squeezed into a local hair salon on a hot August Monday morning, two teams of six at a time (A team and B team). There was a never-ending supply of guinea pigs from the local senior citizens bridge and bingo club. Mostly old biddies with the occasional old, touchy, feely, randy old codger who would probably get his rocks off for some time in the future, fantasising about all the young bits of stuff fussing over them. And all on the house.

'A team out. B team in. A team out. B team in. Make sure your client has got a hot drink! Come on keep going. Keep smiling. Talk about the weather. Talk about *Coronation Street*. Talk about *EastEnders*. Talk about football. Keep smiling. Keep your chin up. Talk about fashion. Talk about *Emmerdale*.' At one stage Sharon almost screamed out, 'I'm sick fucking talking. Any chance of a fucking break?'

All of a sudden there was complete silence. There were no more clients. There was hair, soap, shampoo, brushes, combs, sweat and tears all over the salon. It looked like a bomb had exploded, but everyone was still in one piece. Not one of the candidates said a word. Then the well-spoken, smartly-dressed middle-aged boss woman, who had introduced herself earlier as the salon training executive smiled and, almost in a whisper, said, 'That will do for today. Don't worry about cleaning up as we have a team on standby. Please, can all of you move into the room at the back, pick up your personal belongings and wait for your name to be called out. We won't keep you much longer.'

Two of the female candidates left the salon immediately.

Suffice to say, in tears. The remaining ten waited nervously. Hardly even looking at each other for they all knew at least four would not make the grade for immediate employment. And if the truth be known, a majority of them had not enjoyed the day's traumatic experience. Then, the little head of the spotty faced, flat-chested assistant of the boss woman appeared around the door and called out six names. Two were male and four were female, which included Sharon. All six were herded onto a minibus toot sweet and within minutes they were on board the *Belle Morrow* for a guided tour and would you believe it, a fancy buffet with an assortment of wines, soft drinks and tea and coffee.

Sharon thought to herself, 'I hope they don't think I can go now. I have to go home and tell my bleeding mum and dad first.'

Sharon arrived back in Croydon at about seven o'clock that evening. She was so glad that Liz had agreed to meet her when they spoke on the phone earlier that afternoon. They headed for the Eagles Nest and settled in for a good old chinwag. Sharon explained to Liz that she had been offered a job on the *Belle Morrow* on a three-month probationary period. Her first cruise was a fourteen-day trip around the Mediterranean, departing early September. Just two weeks away. Gino was also on the same ship with the same contract. Sharon's main concern was how her parents would react.

'Listen, Sharon. You're almost twenty years of age. You don't need their permission.'

'I bleeding know that, Liz, but they will both hit the fucking roof!'

'I'll tell you what, mate, I'll come round to your house and we'll tell them together. What do you think?'

'Oh no, Liz. That will only make it worse. They'll think you put me up to it. I'll just have to pluck up the courage and come clean with them. If they throw me out can I come round and stay at yours, just till I get myself down to Southampton. You see, Gino wants us to have a few days together on our own before we board the ship... So, I have just over a week before I pack up and go.'

At this stage Sharon was finding it difficult to hold back the tears, so Liz took her to the ladies to freshen up. While they were there, Sharon suddenly realised that she may have a problem about leaving home but in her emotional state, she had forgotten about Liz being pregnant.

'Oh Liz, there's me going on and on like a bleeding selfish arsehole and you've got the whole world on your shoulders. I'm so sorry, mate.'

'Don't worry, Sharon.'

'Does your mum and dad know about the baby?'

'Not yet but I'm working on it. I'll have to tell them soon. I can sort of feel the little bump. Can you notice it?'

As she asked the question, she pulled the top of her jeans down and her t-shirt up. Sharon stood back, got Liz to turn sideways, left, then right. She squinted her face as she usually did when she wasn't sure what to say, paused, squinted once again and was about to say something when Liz exploded, 'For fuck's sake. Can you notice it or not!'

Tears once again appeared in Sharon's eyes. 'Oh Liz, I feel as if I'm deserting you.'

'Oh dry your fucking eyes and let's have another drink.'

They settled back in their secluded booth in the corner, which was their favourite place in the Eagles Nest when they wanted to connive, slag someone off or just compare notes on their escapades. Sharon received a call from Gino on her mobile. It was in answer to Sharon's request about the whereabouts of Steve Walkman, the father of Liz's baby, although Gino did not know about the forthcoming event. Liz was absolutely positive that it was Steve's, as she had been with no one else since he left London. Gino asked Sharon to put Liz on the phone as it would be easier to tell her direct rather than through a third person.

'No fear,' said Sharon. 'I want to share the news with her. Good or bad.'

'Someone else might hear, you pair of nuggets!'

The girls decided to make their way back into the ladies and carry on the conversation with all three in situ. Gino, at the other end of the phone in Dublin, could only scratch his head in wonderment.

'Right, girls. Now listen carefully. Steve Walkman no longer exists. He never existed. His nickname is PAXO. Nothing to do with stuffing, although he likes stuffing things. If you know what I mean?'

Liz gingerly asked, 'Please explain PAXO.'

'PAXO are his initials. Pascal, Aloysius, Xavier, O'Reilly. PAXO. Get it?'

Both girls were dumbstruck.

Gino continued, 'He's on his way to the States to kick off a solo career. Fuck knows what he'll call himself out there.'

Gino rambled on about what the other boys in the band were doing. Neither of the girls heard another word. Just a mumble in the back ground.

'Hell? Hello? Sharon? Liz? Is anybody there?'

The following day, after a hard day's work at the salon and an even harder day's work convincing her boss Jethro to let her go with only a week's notice, Sharon decided to take the bull by the horns and tell her parents that she was leaving home to work on a cruise ship... In a week's time... No, seven days' time might sound better. Liz had asked her to phone as soon as possible after the potential earthquake to say how it went down... Like a sunken ship?

As soon as Sharon walked into her parents' house her mum greeted her with another large white envelope in her hand. She had obviously read the name and address of the sender on the back, which was the same as the last one... British Maritime Cruisers, East Dock Street, Southampton. On this occasion the envelope had been opened. Her mum began to wave it like a large white feather as if to give some relief from the hot August evening and sarcastically asked, 'What the hell is this then?'

Sharon was furious. She grabbed the envelope and quickly glanced at the contents. It was confirmation of her probation contract and the date of departure from Southampton to the Med. Beneath her breath she said, 'How dare she open up my personal mail.'

Without further ado Sharon went into overdrive and gave her mum such a mouthful that she nearly knocked the both of them off balance and brought her dad running into the hallway from the kitchen. Well, all hell broke loose. Name-calling and ridicule were coming thick and fast from her mum, who was now becoming completely out of control. Her dad chipped in every now and again as if goading his wife to put more oil on the fire.

Her mum screamed, 'Is that bloody Liz McKenna going with you? I bet it was all her idea!'

'No, she's not going!' Sharon screamed back. Then she held her breath to help hold back the tears. 'I've made an important decision for the first time in my life and I'm sticking to it! End of fucking story!'

Her parents were aghast at the language used by their only daughter and began to put their arms around each other's shoulder in consolation. Then both parents were having a go, almost at the same time. Over and over again.

'It's that bloody Liz McKenna's fault. I always said that she was no good. Tell the truth. She's bloody going as well, isn't she? She's bloody going, isn't she?'

Sharon was beginning to feel the pressure but screamed back, 'No! She's not fucking well going!'

Her dad went berserk, 'She fucking well must be! If you're going, you fucking well wouldn't be going on your own. Just who are you trying to kid? She's fucking well going. Isn't she?'

'No, Dad! She's not fucking well going!'

Both parents began to sneer at their daughter. She fought back the tears but she was growing stronger and was beginning to hold her own with these two overbearing and intimidating bullies... Because that's what they were. Her parents were nothing but bullies, always had been. She never realised it before.

'Then tell us why she's not fucking well going. Go on! Go on! Tell us why she's not fucking well going!' By this time her parents were ranting, almost in unison. 'Tell us why? Go on. Tell us why she's not fucking well going?'

Without thinking Sharon screamed at the top of her voice, 'Because she's fucking well pregnant! That's why she's not fucking well going!'

Sharon stormed out of the house making sure she slammed the front door behind her. She realised that she would have to phone Liz straight away. How would she be able to explain how she gave up her friend's secret about her pregnancy? How could she be so fucking stupid? She tried again and again to contact Liz on her mobile but to no avail. It must be switched off. But why? A short time later Liz phoned Sharon.

'Hi Liz. Listen, I've really fucked up. I'm really, really sorry but—'

'No need to apologise, Sharon. Your mum has already done the damage.'

'But Liz. I couldn't have been out the front door more than a few minutes when I calmed myself down and tried to ring you.'

'Well, your mum was definitely on a fucking mission... Blaming me for everything... Late nights... Stop overs. And the pièce de résistance: it was me that convinced you to go on a fucking cruise ship!'

'Oh Liz, I'm so, so sorry.'

'Not to worry, mate. As soon as your mum started slagging me off, my mum went straight for the jugular. By the time they had finished your fucking dad was getting into the act but my mum used some of her Irish charm. Threw more than just a few fucks into both of them before hanging up. And do you know something? As soon as she put the phone down do you know what she said to me? Do you know what she said to me? "FUCKING WELL KNEW IT! NOW TELL ME MORE ABOUT THIS BABY".'

When Liz began to explain about her brief affair... no... it was a brief fling. In the back of her mind, she blamed her brother Lenny and his mate Ed. Rethink... no... It was the devious relationship between her mother and Julie, or was it a configuration of all their misgivings that had sent Liz completely off the rails? She eventually gave Cissy a brief run-down of the disastrous relationship, brief though it was, with an older man, who just happened to be the lead singer of an Irish band, who had the most ridiculous of names and was now somewhere in America! Cissy gave a great big sympathetic sigh and assured her daughter that she would square things with her dad. And true to her word that's exactly what she did. She included everyone else in the family circle, for there was nowhere to hide. Not that there was any reason to hide at all but not all the details were disclosed, especially the father's true name. And Liz's parents didn't push for any further information. This newborn needed to be welcomed into the McKenna family and make no mistake about it. The new arrival was due on or about 1 February 2005.

If the truth be known, Liz's dad Robbie and her Uncle Benny couldn't have been more pleased when the dust settled about the news of the forthcoming baby. Robbie was dying for more information about this guy Steve Walkman. Although that was his stage name, he wondered what name would go onto the birth certificate in relation to the child's father.

The festive season came and went at the end of 2004. Lenny made it home for Christmas but as per usual he headed back to Portsmouth for New Year. The two-day free-for-all between the two McKenna households went once again with a bang, although Liz kept a low profile for obvious reasons. She often wondered what Steve would say if he knew he was going to be a father, but Liz knew in her heart that it was highly unlikely that she was ever going to see PAXO again, well, not any time soon.

The big highlight for Liz in the New Year was that Sharon would be back in London for a well-earned week off, with Gino in tow. They had really hit it off on their probation period of three months and were both on a rolling contract with BMC, renewable every twelve months. The rift between Sharon and her parents was still seething with menace. Sharon had tried to mend the bridges, but her parents were having none of it. They stopped accepting her phone calls, texts and even when she wrote a letter pleading for them to end their vindictiveness, there was no answer. Surprise! Surprise!

When Sharon and Gino arrived in London they decided to stay in a little bed and breakfast near the Lewisham Irish Centre. It was run by a long-lost cousin of one of their shipmates and, of course, mate's rates were part of the deal. When they walked up the driveway of Liz's house it was like the second coming as far as Liz was concerned. All three had a great catch up and Gino had to reluctantly tell Liz that there was no word whatsoever on the whereabouts of PAXO, Ireland or America. They all agreed that none of them were holding their breath.

That night Cissy and Julie joined them for a Chinese takeaway in Cissy's kitchen. Both sisters-in-law were bombarding the cruising couple with countless questions about their work, but specifically about the nightlife, the five-course a la carte menu available each evening and the various styles of cabins. Liz could not help thinking, 'Is this going to be another juice-sum, two-sum?' Conniving bitches!

The first of February came and went and still no new arrival, but Liz was assured by her doctor that the baby would come when he was ready. Liz knew she was having a boy but kept the news to herself so as not to ruin the surprise for her dad. If he knew it was definitely a boy, he would be at his wits end. Would you bloody believe it? The baby arrived on 14 February 2005. Liz's twentieth birthday, and her mum and dad's twenty fifth wedding anniversary! Well, what a knees-up at the Eagles Nest was had that night. The new mum and the seven-pound-two-ounce baby star were none the wiser. Liz and the baby were home three days later. Cissy, Julie, Robbie and Benny were all still hungover from the previous prolonged celebrations. The spare room at Liz's house had been converted into a beautiful nursery. Robbie and Benny had spent almost as much time on that one room as they would on one of their rented properties!

Then, it was like *Mastermind*:

'What are we going to call him? Should we include the grandfathers' names? Maybe just three names would keep all the senior men of the family happy. What do you think, love?'

Liz stood up with her baby in her arms and addressed those present with one simple statement:

'Forget the in-laws and the out-laws. He will only have one name. Steven. End of story! Now, we are going for a lie down.'

With that she turned on her heel and out of the kitchen with her head held high. 'Well,' she thought. 'That's that lot told.'

The two brothers and two sisters-in-law sat gobsmacked. They were almost whispering. Robbie was seething and said, 'Why should that gob-shite have a son named after him, a son he doesn't even know, or want to know?'

'You're fucking well right,' agreed Benny. 'Why don't you try and change her mind. After all it's you and Cissy who will be paying all the bills and helping to bring him up.'

Cissy chirped in. 'It's her son and it's her decision. If she wants to call him Steven, then that's the end of it. They've only just arrived home. The last thing any of us need right now is an unpleasant fall out.'

The following morning everyone was up for the usual early start except Liz and Steven. Apart from a bottle during the wee small hours they were still fast asleep. Cissy looked in on them and thought that they may have a great little sleeper on their hands, unlike the two she had, up all hours and any hours. Never mind. If there were any future problems, there was enough help at hand.

Two weeks later Steven was christened with Benny and Julie as godparents. During the next few months, Cissy, Robbie and Liz were bumping into each other throughout the night. They were all guilty of over-checking to make sure that Steven was not too hot, not too cold, needing a nappy change, breathing okay or if he would like a little song, or two. Many a night all three sat around the kitchen table drinking tea or coffee, just daydreaming about what great times lay ahead with this little bundle of joy.

Liz decided not to return to work for the foreseeable future. Steven would be keeping her busy and she was in no rush to put him into a kindergarten, even part-time. No, her place was with him and besides, she wanted to show everyone that she could cope. Both McKenna households were more than willing to step in and help out. On a few occasions the two brothers almost had fisticuffs, arguing whose turn it was to play with Steven. In the end they sneaked behind each other's backs, but inevitably caught each other out. They always burst out laughing as they entertained their new offspring. Yes, the McKennas were as close as ever. That's for sure.

CHAPTER 6

BUSINESS FOR THE FAMILIES was once again on the up and up. They were increasing their potential in all areas of their companies. The rental market was really taking off and Robbie and Benny were determined not to be left behind. Family holidays were still the norm and even more fun because of Steven. The two couples also enjoyed their time away together and the boys still had their dart tournaments to attend, especially the World Championship at the Lakeside Country Club.

But it has to be said, every time that Cissy or Julie mentioned a short girlie break together, Liz couldn't help but cringe. She had certainly got over her brother being gay, but not that selfish bastard Ed for playing the two of them with the same hand, and certainly not her mother and Julie, for their ongoing, sordid affair. Liz thought she could detect when something illicit had gone on. They would have to be a lot more careful, now that Liz and Steven were more about the house. She just fucking knew when they had been kissing the velvet.

The festive period of 2005 was probably the best one ever. Well, it was Steven's first Christmas and first New Year. Although the poor little mite didn't really know what was going on, he soaked up the atmosphere from as early as November and got to visit Santa no less than five times in December. What a palaver! Still, no name of the child's father on the birth certificate. So what?

So, as they say. Time marches on and march on it did, with Steven getting bigger by the bloody day, or so the two proud grandparents would loudly boast. Although Liz loved her little boy with all her heart, after his first birthday party in February 2006, she realised she had not socialised outside her close family circle for well over a year, which included the usual family holidays, the local park or something indoors. She was in regular contact with Sharon and Gino, who were having the time of their lives. Her brother Lenny, who was now twenty-three, was forging what appeared to be a successful career in the Navy, which also involved world travel.

Benny and Julie's eldest, Lou, who was now twenty-seven, was engaged to an obnoxious, smarmy, bollock of a solicitor and had moved into their first house. The twins, Sam and Pam, who were both twenty-five, shared a nice little upmarket ground floor flat with two bedrooms. Saturday nights for Robbie, Benny and the two wives at the Irish Club was always a goer, especially when Ann Wishbone and Wheelie Ferris joined them at their usual table. Ann's contribution as personnel manager was greatly appreciated by both the McKenna companies and Wheelie was always a laugh a minute.

Liz, still living at home at twenty-one, couldn't help but fancy a night out... But with who? And go where? And do what? Then one day out of the blue Cissy suggested that she and Robbie would keep an eye on Steven and Liz could have a night out. They had spoken to Julie and Benny who thought, that a night out with Sam and Pam would do her the world of good. So, the following Saturday night all three girls got dressed up to the nines and set off for the West End for a tour round the pubs and clubs. If they were going to be late then the twins would let Liz crash out on their sofa, so no need for anyone to worry.

Well, all three of the McKennas turned more than just a few heads, that's for sure. Liz couldn't believe just how much her cousins were definitely up for it. As they said on several occasions that night, 'We always go for it but we make sure we don't get caught out, if you get our drift.' At about midnight all three found themselves in a people carrier with three male hunks. They were heading for none other than the Lewisham Irish Centre. Liz didn't catch on where she was until she was getting out of the taxi. She took one look at the front door of the centre and then placed her head in her hands and almost let out a yelp of frustration, though she was sure the twins didn't know the history that Liz had with that place. Why would they? After a few moments to collect her thoughts she ambled in after her five companions. 'Fucking, fucking, fuck, fuck!' Which were the only words she could think of.

The large dance hall and bar were packed as usual and in a very short period of time Liz was separated from the others. The only upside of the situation was that one of the hunks had bought her a very large cocktail. So, she made her way over to a dimly lit corner, being careful not to spill her drink. And just there, through the haze of sweat and flashing lights she could just about make out a small stool that had her fucking name on it. Down she went to rest her weary arse. It had been such a long time since she had worn high heels! Her feet were fucking killing her! She wiped her brow and thought, 'How the fuck did Sharon and I do this every weekend?'

Sipping her drink, she glanced around the disco filled dance floor, when a soft male voice from the other side of the small alcove asked, 'You alright?'

Liz hadn't noticed him before and could just about make out the long shaggy shoulder-length hair and square jaw. He leaned forward and asked once again, 'You alright?'

She could see him better now. He was fucking fit. Really fit. She spoke just loud enough for him to hear.

'I'm fine. Why are you hiding here? In the corner? In the dark?'

'Waiting for you.'

She leaned forward and said, 'Is that the best you can do? Straight out of fucking Hollywood that is.'

He smiled and whispered into her ear, 'It's the best you're going to get tonight.'

'Says fucking who?'

'Says me. And do you always swear so much?'

'What's it got to do with you then, Shaggy?'

'Well, maybe I've been sent down here to be your guardian angel.'

'Guardian angel, my arse. Come into the light a little bit more, so I can get a better look at you.'

He shuffled the stool he was sitting on a few inches

closer and she was absolutely right. He was, fucking better than fit. 'Mid-twenties,' she thought. Definitely would not be kicking him out of bed. Her head began to do a little spin. Was it the drink, or the heat, or the lust-filled vibes that began to haemorrhage from both their anatomies? He was hard. She was definitely wet.

He suggested that they step outside for a breath of fresh air. There was a side door leading into a patio area that, according to this handsome stranger, had recently been laid by him and his work mates. He explained further that the no smoking ban was due in the next year or so. Many of the big entertainment venues were preparing non-smoking areas in anticipation of the law being enforced sooner rather than later. In the next twelve months, most, if not all, pubs, clubs and dance halls would have to comply.

The coolness of the late February air was a pleasant relief for them both. In mid-flow of the conversation he leaned forward and kissed her full on the lips, without any warning. Not as much as a by your leave. Liz didn't mind at all but there was no way would she consider going much further on this occasion. He suggested they carry on their tryst at his small flat a few minutes' walk from the Irish Centre. Against her better judgement she agreed, and with that he took her hand and led his latest conquest to his working man's lair.

On route they learned each other's name and basic backgrounds. He was from a small market town known as Mount Mellick, in Co. Laois in Ireland and was part of a working-labouring gang organised by his uncle, Ned. Her escort's name was Connor. Connor O'Connor. Everyone called him Con.

She thought, 'Con O'Connor. That's got a good sound to it.'

They soon found themselves at the front door of a three-story town house. There was a two-bedroom flat on each floor each with a small shower/toilet and a galley kitchen. Con's flat was on the ground floor. When he turned the key to his front door he motioned with his forefinger on his lips to keep quite. He later explained he shared with his cousin who, although was a very heavy sleeper, would get a little envious because he couldn't pull a fart out of his arse, much less pull a woman, not even if his life depended on it. Small talk played a very small part of their encounter. The single bed in the small single room left nothing to the imagination. Strip fast and fuck fast, goes better with a buck fast, a bottle of which he had at hand. Never mind the expense.

They slowed down a little in the second of five lengthy sessions of love-making, and the sleeping cousin in the bedroom next door never heard a thing, not that anyone cared. Liz could not believe the sense of relief each time she experienced an orgasm and Con must have had an emergency supply of electric soup, for he never seemed to tire. He may well have published his own version of the Karma Sutra. Conversation throughout the marathon manoeuvres were of an idle nature. Tune up and tune in for the next round. All of a sudden Liz woke up from a short cat nap. She checked her watch. It was six o'clock, still dark. She quickly phoned Sam's mobile and thankfully she answered after only a few rings. Sam and Pam had entertained their own guests throughout the wee small hours but they were having a problem rousing them and most important of all, getting rid of them, for now anyway.

Sam told Liz not to worry, as they had reiterated her cover story to her parents when they spotted her sneaking outside the Irish Centre with that gorgeous guy, within only half an hour of their arrival. Her cousins agreed that Liz was a saucy little vixen. They had to settle for the two mister averages with the big wallets. None of them could say what happened to the third mister average after he paid for the initial drinks. Meanwhile, they knew that Liz was making her way to a mystery shag-palace. At about seven o'clock that morning Sam phoned Liz's parents and told them that a taxi was picking Liz up in a few minutes from her flat to take her home. She also explained that the young mum might be a little tired. Although it hadn't been too late when they got to bed, poor Liz was not used to it any more.

As soon as Liz stepped through her front door, Steven, who was in granny's arms, practically jumped from one to the other. Liz hugged him for what seemed like forever. This had been the first time they had ever been apart. Cissy left them to it. She would ask Liz later how well the night out had gone. She and Robbie should thank their lucky stars that Sam and Pam were such thoughtful girls. It would be a very lucky man that got either of them. After a lazy morning with Steven, Liz checked her phone and lo and behold there was a text from a number she was unfamiliar with. Con's name came up. 'What the ...' Then it dawned on her. 'It's him! It's bloody Con!'

She answered his text like greased lightening and for the next hour or so they communicated as if they had known each other for a lot more than just a few hours. He wanted to see her again, but his heavy work load with his Uncle Ned meant he would not be free until the following Saturday. Liz had to think fast on this touchy subject. Con knew nothing about her baby son. She knew there was no way that she would get another all-nighter so soon, so she suggested they meet on the following Saturday afternoon for a few drinks. She may or may not bring up the subject of her son, she wasn't sure.

The following few days passed very slowly for Liz, but she had Steven to keep her busy. She spent so much time that week playing with him, fussing over him, cuddling him, kissing him, her mum was wondering what all the fuss was about. Cissy thought that Liz may have felt guilty about being apart from her son overnight. 'Well,' she thought. 'Sure, that's not a bad thing.'

Saturday arrived and Liz had told her mum and dad that since the weather had cleared and it looked like spring was on its way, she would take Steven out for the day. Go to the swing-park, then some lunch and then, if the weather stayed fair, a nice walk round the shops topped up with an ice cream for both of them. Cissy and Julie waved bye-bye as Liz pushed the stroller, with Steven waving bye-bye in return and watching glassy eyed at the footpath in front of him. He knew the route alright. Mum was taking him to his favourite place, the swing-park. Half an hour later, after spending the shortest time ever on the swings (much to Steven's annoyance) they were outside Sam and Pam's flat. Pam to the rescue this time as Sam was on duty and was called out to a minor emergency.

Liz had explained to her cousins previously, on the phone, of the dilemma she found herself in. They all agreed that Steven should be dropped off at the flat and Liz could meet up with Con. It was up to her how she went about telling Con about Steven. Both twins said that he would probably run a fucking mile. Typical fucking bloke! Anyway, Liz and Con met up in a small back street pub near his digs called The Harp. There was an old-fashioned snug on the left side of the front hallway so, without actually going inside the small main bar they had their own private table and chairs and via a small hatch they ordered drinks from the old man behind the bar. He shuffled along the back of the bar in slow time producing the Vodka and Coke for Liz and taking forever to pour the pint of Guinness for Con. The young couple didn't seem to mind the slow service for it gave them time to get over their nervousness, you know, the way a couple are after a fierce night of love, only a week ago and then meeting for the first time for a quite drink. None of them knew whether to give each other a gentle kiss on the cheek or a gentle welcoming hug, so both sets of hands met at waist level with a gentle kiss on the lips. Compared to what they got up to a week ago, it looked a little prim and proper, maybe a wee bit embarrassing. Drink-fuelled lust or not, today they were both completely sober... For now.

An hour later, once again they were both buck naked and another writhing session ensued. They were back in Con's small bedroom. His cousin had gone out for the day so they had the flat to themselves. There were various positions, in various places, over various pieces of furniture. After all, variety is the spice of life. And not a word about Steven was spoken.

The child was being spoilt rotten by Pam but she was a little worried about the length of time Liz was taking to break the bad news to Con, when a taxi cab pulled up outside. Liz rushed to the front door of the flat apologising to her cousin as Pam handed over Steven to his slightly breathless mum.

'How did it go?' asked Pam.

'Up and down, you know. I'll bring you up to speed later. Right now, we have to get home. You don't mind if I tell my mum that we met at the shops and you invited us round for a little while. Do you?'

'Not at all, but Liz, you look a bit flustered. Are you alright?'

'Yeah, I'm fine.'

'Liz? Please tell me... You didn't? Did you?'

'Look, Pam. The cab is waiting. I said that I would bring you up to speed later.'

And with that, she was gone in a flash. When she and Steven were safely in the back of the cab, she realised that she had left Con's flat without her knickers!

Over the next few days, contact between the two lovebirds began to wane a little. Although Liz was more than keen, the text messages from Con became shorter and fewer, then nothing. Not a fucking scintilla. After a fortnight of no contact, Liz decided to visit his digs. So, on the very next Saturday afternoon she asked her mum to keep an eye on Steven as she wanted to do a little shopping. Cissy didn't mind at all and encouraged Liz on numerous occasions to spend some more time with her cousins or go out even for a stroll on her own.

When she arrived at her destination, she was beginning to feel very nervous. She thought, 'What if he thinks I'm being too clingy? What if someone told him about Steven? Well, if he doesn't know about Steven already, he'll find out today. Here goes.'

She was about to knock on the front door, as there was no door knocker, when it opened as if by magic and there in the hallway stood a very tall, rotund middle-aged man, with a mop of grey hair.

''Ello, my love. What can I do for you then?' He had the most marvellous smile and she was put at ease almost immediately.

'I'm looking for Con. You know, Con O'Connor. He still lives here, doesn't he?'

The smile on his face turned into a slight grimace and as politely as possible, he tried to answer her questions as truthful as possible. 'I do know him, my love, but he's moved on. They all do, these young'uns.'

'Moved on? Where?'

'Back to Ireland, my love.'

Liz was almost in tears when she asked the next question even though she already knew the answer. 'When is he coming back? I mean, he's got a good job here with his Uncle Ned, hasn't he?'

The big man glanced downwards and then invited Liz to take a seat on a chair that was in the hall and closed the front door so they had some privacy from the street. He began to explain the situation from his point of view.

'Okay, my love. Con works for us or companies like us up and down the country. He works six monffs over 'ere and then six monffs in Ireland. Now, as far as we're concerned, they are all self-employed so it's up to them to pay their own tax and insurance. But, because they move around so much it's just about impossible to catch them out, over 'ere or over there. We don't care 'cause we're covered by casual labour and self-employed bleeding fingy. The boss knows all about those fings. The boss always knows how to cover himself. He's got a bleeding high-powered accountant that keeps everyfing right.'

Liz's head was beginning to spin and then she asked, 'Is the boss his Uncle Ned?'

The big man replied, 'There is no Uncle Ned. Well, not really. You see, my nickname is Uncle Ned, 'cause I organise all the beds for the work gangs in and around Souff London, and beyond sometimes.'

Liz looked completely confused and then he added, 'It's

Cockney rhyming slang, my love. Uncle Ned... Bed. Get up the apple and pears – stairs – and get into your Uncle Ned – bed. Get it? I get all the beds sorted out! That's part of my job.'

Liz tried one more desperate attempt to shed some light on the situation. 'What about his cousin? You know, the one he shares the flat with?'

Another grimace from the large man. ''E's gone as well and I don't think they were related. His flat mate was called Dai Williams and he comes from bloody Wales.'

Liz sat in total silence making sure she did not break into tears. She wondered how many other times Uncle Ned had come across the same situation with so many other daft, stupid, naive, dopey, young fucking birds. Liz stood up to leave and Uncle Ned opened the door like the gentleman he was, for he was surely that and that was the only thing she was sure of that fucking day.

As she walked down the garden path because, lo and behold, she had been led up the garden path, she turned and asked the large man one final question, 'By the way, what's your proper name?'

Quick as a flash he replied, 'Spick, Jimmy Spick, at your service, my love.'

When Liz arrived home later that afternoon her mum was surprised at the lack of shopping bags. She also noticed that her daughter's eyes were quite red.

'Not the dreaded hay-fever again, Liz?'

'Just my bleeding luck but, never mind, just think of the money I didn't spend. Not that I've got that much these days anyway.'

Cissy saw red. 'Now just a bloody minute, young lady. You and Steven are well looked after. You want for nothing. You haven't worked, not even offered to work, not even part-time since you had that child. You sound totally ungrateful!'

'I know! I know I got myself pregnant! I know I got myself bleeding pregnant. And you just won't let me forget it!'

'What's going on, Liz? What's brought all this on?'

'Look, Mother. You don't really know what I've been through. You don't know what it's like to keep a very dark fucking secret. Everyone around me is living a normal life, as if butter wouldn't melt. But I know fucking better.'

'What are you on about, Liz? Tell me right now. What are you on about?'

Liz began to develop a sneer of pure frustration and bitterness. Her head was beginning to spin once again, just as it had done earlier at Con's flat. She began to shake, almost trembling. Her mum grabbed her by the shoulders as an avalanche of tears covered Liz's face. It was a picture with no sound, just silent hysteria. Cissy watched her daughter's red glassy eyes stare into space as if she was looking straight through her. She held Liz as tight as she possibly could and petted her like she did when she was a little girl. She felt the emotion tumble out of the very depths of her daughter's being, and she just didn't know what to do or say. Then, everything seemed to calm down almost as quickly as it had begun. A little gurgle and the words 'mummy,' came from the nursery. Liz came to her senses and rushed to hold her baby son, just as her mum had held her. Cissy left her to it. No point in pushing the subject any more. Maybe, another time. Over the following days Liz seemed to perk up a little. No more tears or tantrums, much to Cissy's relief.

Two months later the doctor confirmed what Liz already knew. Yes, another bun in the oven. Fucking hell-fire. She would have to come straight out with it as soon as she got home. It was a Friday night in April not long after the Easter break. Everyone would be in a good mood as it was the start of another new financial year. Another excellent year of business was had by both companies. Saturday night was going to be a big bash at the Irish Club in Croydon with Liz at home with Steven as was the case on most family occasions in recent times. Liz felt she was being punished time and time again for her mishap of being an unmarried mother. 'Stay at home with your son. It's your own fault.

Look at how well your cousins are doing and Lenny, a career in the Navy. The career seaman. Yeah. Plenty of fucking semen for the seaman and make no mistake.'

When Liz arrived through the front door of the family home, she could hear Steven giggling as he always did when her dad or Benny were tickling him. She thought that the shock and despondency of her news may well be quelled with the presence of her son. When she entered the open plan kitchen area both McKenna families were present including her three cousins. Liz smiled and it came out as bold as you please.

'I have some very important news for everyone. I'm eight weeks pregnant!'

Total silence, except for Steven, who was bum crawling along the floor towards his mother. Liz picked him up and said, 'I'm having a bath with my son. I'll be back to make us both something to eat. I know you lot are going to have a lot of questions so it will give me time to think just what my answers might be.'

Benny, Julie and their three daughters, without saying a word, made their way next door via the patio doors. Robbie and Cissy sat completely dumfounded. They began to ask the obvious questions.

When? Who? Where? How often? Here in the house? No! Too risky! But how, fucking how?

An hour later Liz returned to the kitchen carrying Steven. Her parents each had what looked like a very strong drink in their hands. Robbie's would be whiskey and soda and she knew Cissy's would be Vodka and Coke. They were still sitting at the dining table, one at each end. Liz sat in the middle and let her son play happily on the floor with his favourite jingle toy. There then followed several minutes of complete silence, except for the gentle noise of the toy, then they all spoke at once, and then all stopped at once. Liz nearly burst out laughing. If only they knew what she knew, but that would be for another time. Keep the big guns under wraps for now.

Both parents questioned her from all angles but Liz did

not want to drop her co-conspirators in the proverbial pooh (Sam and Pam). She would only give a brief answer, if one at all, on each occasion. She was determined not to let herself down, on how easily she had become another notch on some man's bed post. She didn't even divulge his name. Why should she? He was long gone, the selfish fucking bastard. All men are bastards. Well, except for her dad and her Uncle Benny. While Robbie and Cissy were topping up their drinks, Liz was making Steven and herself a snack, business as usual. Benny popped his head in through the patio doors and asked Robbie if he fancied a pint. Well, he jumped at the chance. He received a gentle nod of approval from his wife, who was of a mind that she might get more information out of Liz, if her father wasn't there. Benny and Robbie were soon on their way to the pub. Cissy decided to see if Liz would give up just a little bit of information.

'Come on, love. Give us a little consideration. Who's the father?'

'Listen, Mum. He doesn't even know. He's moved on, back to Ireland. He's a travelling casual building worker. He doesn't stay too long in any particular place. The chances of running into him again are pretty remote.'

'How did it happen?

'How do you think, Mother?'

'Don't be flippant with me.'

'Oh, using fancy words now, are we?'

'Oh! For fuck's sake, Liz. Give me a straight bloody answer. Weren't you on the pill?'

'I haven't been on the pill since I fell pregnant with Steven. There was no need to. I didn't go anywhere, didn't do anything, then one time, just by chance I jumped between the sheets.'

'What about the morning after pill?'

'Well, I didn't get a chance to get it until the second day after the event.'

'Oh, we're calling it an event now, are we?'

'For fuck's sake, Mother, give it a rest. Then the second time it happened, I had the same problem getting the pill, the morning after pill I mean.'

'What bloody second time? You're like a fucking rampant rabbit! Have you no shame?'

'You of all people, Mother... Are asking me about shame. Get your own house in order, Mother!'

'What the hell do you mean by that? You're an ungrateful little hussy.'

'Me? A hussy? Why, Mother dear... As if... What do you do, to get your rocks off?'

'What the fuck are you talking about?'

'Kissing the velvet, Mother... With good old Auntie Julie... Mother? Does a yodel up the canyon ring any bells?'

Cissy glared at Liz, not knowing what to say. She was definitely caught on the backfoot. She felt as if her Adam's apple was about to choke off her air supply.

With that said, Liz gave a little smirk of satisfaction. There... She'd got it off her chest in one foul stroke. The other dirty little secret about the prodigal son Lenny would keep for now.

Liz made her way to her room with Steven. They would stretch out for a while on her bed and watch the TV. They both loved to cuddle in and watch a bit of TV together. The smirk was now a full-blooded smile and she nearly burst out laughing with devilment.

A few moments later Julie received a text message from Cissy. It read: 'We need to speak, sooner rather than later.'

CHAPTER 7

JULIE AND CISSY DECIDED THAT, with their husbands in the pub and Julie's three gone on their own merry way, the safest place to plough through their delicate situation would be Julie's kitchen, over a very strong drink, or two, or three. The two wives were at their wits' end until the alcohol kicked in, and then a sort of metamorphosis took place. Their minds began to slip into a scheming overdrive and with each large mouthful of Vodka and Coke, which they administered freely to each other, they agreed to a compromise that would suit all three of them. Cissy and Julie would pave the way for the bad news to be turned into good news. It could be worse, couldn't it? They would convince the two brothers that it was just an unfortunate lapse in judgement by a young mum, who could have and should have been shown more love and care, and a lot less criticism, from all members of the family circle. It would be all hands to the wheel to ensure the safe arrival of the new addition to the McKenna family and a lot more consideration shown to Liz, who had every man and his dog on her case. They knew that when their husbands returned from the pub that they would be in good spirits, to say the least, and the two wives would top up the good spirits by shagging both their brains out. Who cares if they have an unplanned lie-in the following morning? That would be the ideal time to explain to both husbands the way forward regarding Liz, thus implementing their devious plan to avoid an embarrassing confrontation with all concerned.

Robbie and Benny welcomed their night-cap of whiskey and soda like two gullible teenagers. Their wives led them to their respective bedrooms and produced the roughest sex that either man had ever experienced, especially with the girls on top. The breakfast in bed the following morning had the brothers thinking that Christmas had come early. Each wife instructed their puppet husbands exactly how they were going to handle Liz's pregnancy and how things were going to happen for the foreseeable future. Robbie and Benny had little option but to agree wholeheartedly.

Later that morning Cissy and Julie were having a cup of tea in Cissy's kitchen awaiting Liz's arrival. When she popped her head around the kitchen door Liz was taken by surprise and said, 'I know it's Saturday, but you two got no work today?'

Cissy answered the question with a question, 'Has Steven gone down for his usual mid-morning nap?'

Liz nodded not knowing what to expect next.

'Well then,' said Cissy. 'Sit yourself down. Julie will pour you a nice cup of tea and we can have a little chat, okay?

Liz had lost a little bit of the arrogance that she had displayed the previous night but she was still just about holding her own. She had no idea what was coming next but she could tell by her mum's tone of voice and of the body language of the two women sitting at the kitchen table, that whatever was about to be discussed, may well be in her favour.

Cissy explained in fine detail what was going to happen, including all the frills that went with the plan. In return, Liz would keep what she knew or what she thought she knew to herself. Julie further explained the repercussions of any scandal becoming public knowledge. What it would do to the family and the family business of both companies. Liz listened without saying a word until her mum and aunt had finished speaking. All three sat in silence for what seemed like an eternity but was in fact only a few minutes when Liz broke the ice.

'What you're saying is, as long as I keep shtum, I'll have an easy ride and also be on the gravy train?'

Cissy and Julie looked at each other and then nodded in unison.

Liz smiled and said, 'You've got a deal. There is a lot to be said for blackmail. But you know what they say? Keep it in the family!'

Baby number two arrived on 15 December 2006, a boy

that Liz named Connor. It couldn't have happened at a better time. What with Christmas just around the corner everyone was in good, if not great form. The two-day festivity party between the McKenna households was the typical roaring success as in previous years, topped up with the attendance of the prodigal son, Lenny. The only fly in the ointment was Connor's christening, which was on Christmas Eve. Liz's second baby christening, with no father present at the service and also once again no father named on the birth certificate. Benny and Julie were godparents. Who else? New Year as usual came and went with a bang, however Liz and the two children stayed at home on New Year's Eve, which suited her right down to the ground.

January 2007 saw the family circle pull together with both businesses towards the end of another tax year in April. Their good fortunes continued to grow to such an extent that there was talk of branching out even more than had been discussed at the director's meeting with Robbie, Benny, Cissy and Julie. Ann Wishbone was also in attendance as she had been promoted to personnel director and company secretary. Their local business accountant and financial advisor had nothing but good news and suggested further investment. He advised organic growth rather than acquisition. Make the McKenna stamp on all their ventures. There were smiling faces all round.

It was generally agreed that both companies should merge and a brand-new name be liveried. After all, J. C. & Slicker & Flicker sounded a bit outdated. If they wanted to really get into the big league and be taken seriously then a name change was an absolute must. These items would be on the agenda for their AGM at the end of April.

When that meeting took place, it wasn't going to be all plain sailing. The only one to show any concern was Robbie. He agreed wholeheartedly to the name change, whatever it might be, but thought that they should count their blessings for at least another year before committing themselves to further investment. The other four directors were almost in uproar. No one wanted to miss the boat of opportunity and make a lot more money. Robbie's argument was that they had made a lot of money already and with another potentially good year in the offing, why tempt fate when they could weigh the pros and cons for another twelve months. One of his favourite sayings was, 'Let's not get greedy.'

Benny piped up, 'Look, Robbie, all our contemporaries are all branching out. We have a great name in this game. We clean up, paint up, refurbish up, sell on or rent out. We should keep the contracts we already have with the local council but buy up smaller contracts and make a killing. Lots of the one or two-man bands are moving on. They don't seem able to keep up with us.'

Robbie replied, 'Weren't we advised organic growth and not acquisition? Why don't we stand fast with what we've got? Just to see how the land lies.'

At this stage Cissy and Julie were giving their tuppence worth. Ann was staying on the fence. Never get between a man and his family, even if you agree with one side or the other. Then Benny put further comment to his argument.

'Look, everyone. Let's look at the other firms in and around London who are growing as we speak. Right, there's the Watson family, AKA the Beastie Boys. There's Mad Jock Davidson and his crew of ex-squaddies. They've got most of north London sewn up between their two firms but only with little fiddly diddly jobs. They have to do a lot of jobs to make a lot of bob. Get it? So they're buying up lots of other jobs for next to nothing and the dosh must be flowing in!'

The sisters-in-law nodded in agreement. Robbie tried to interrupt but Benny bulldozed him, simply by raising his voice and waving his hands and continued, 'And another thing, Big Mick Keane is keen to sell on some of his jobs in South-East London. He's getting near retirement age and wants to cut back a bit. Sort of offload a few, if you know what I mean? That leaves us. If we sort Big Mick out with a good handful of cash, as well as a few of the other smaller firms, we can start to monopolise the whole of South London. Then, in no time at all we could well move over the river and crack or buy the business on our terms. Just look at the company accounts. The bank will easily advance us the money as they have done in the past. I can't see any problem.'

Robbie looked round the table. Ann was busy catching up writing the minutes and the other three were waiting patiently for Robbie's comments. There was a short uneasy silence. Ann decided that she would not look up from her task in hand, just listen and write. Robbie began to speak in a slow and deliberate manner. He knew he would be outnumbered in a vote but he had an ace up his sleeve.

'I hear everything you say, Benny, and I know the girls agree with you, but everyone is forgetting about the recession that is supposed to be on the horizon.'

Benny piped up once again, 'Ah, for fuck's sake, Robbie. That's all just talk so that the banks can hike up the interest rates again. We've ridden high before when everyone else was tightening their belts. If we're not in… Then we can't win!'

There was another pregnant pause and then Robbie realised he had to use his ace. He smiled at those around the table and although he didn't want to, he delivered his sucker punch. He spoke softly so as the remainder all had to lean forward to catch what he was saying.

'If it comes to a vote, it is my duty to remind you of the following agreement. When we set up our directorships within the companies, there is a clause that will prevent the plan, of which you are all so in favour of. Ann may not be aware of it as the situation we find ourselves in has not been brought upon us before. Our family business agreement all those years ago has been recorded and copies are in the safekeeping of both our solicitors and accountants. It plainly states that in the event of a vote being taken, it cannot be carried unless all directors vote yes. A re-vote on the same proposition may take place after a period of six calendar months when the majority vote will be carried. With that said, I suggest we adjourn our plan of acquisition and investment until October this year.'

Well, fuck me. You could have cut the atmosphere with a fucking knife, and if there had have been any knives handy, they would have all found their way into Robbie's back.

They didn't wait until October for their next meeting. In August of that year, the much-talked-about recession struck without mercy, which in turn manifested itself into the worldwide credit crunch in 2008, the ramifications of which resulted in the complete breakdown of international commerce and banking without prejudice. In the words of the Irish philosopher: the shit hit the fan! But hey, Robbie was smiling like the cat that got the cream.

By April 2008 in North London, the Watsons, AKA the Beastie Boys were almost out of business and Mad Jock Davidson found himself facing criminal charges for tax evasion. Big Mick Keane in South-East London was sitting pretty, having sold off all his contracts to the highest bidder, and was enjoying his retirement. The wily big Irishman made a great ally when he advised Robbie McKenna to play his cards close to his chest. And you never know... Big Mick may wish to invest as a silent partner, with a family-run business when the dust finally settles.

The McKennas were holding their own regarding all their contracts, a majority of which were with the local council. As long as they produced the usual brown envelopes containing the appropriate amount of cash to the usual councillors then all would remain in situ. Any properties already bought and not sold for a decent profit would be placed onto their rental portfolio until the tide turned in their favour. Yearly dividends would remain restrained in order to keep adequate cash in reserve. This exercise would continue for the foreseeable future should the unexpected raise its ugly head again. All company staff would remain in employment but hours may have to be cut occasionally depending on the demand for contracts outside the local council's jurisdiction. All five directors would be able to continue in the same lifestyle but advised not to advertise the fact that they too, were sitting pretty. Robbie was voted in as the Chairman and the new company name launched that year was: McKenna Enterprises Limited (MKE Ltd).

Both couples, Ann Wishbone and of course her gentleman friend Wheelie Ferris, continued to meet up on most Saturday nights in the Irish Club in Croydon. Robbie and Benny still managed to slip away for their much-favoured darts matches, especially at the Lakeside Country Club for the biggie of the year. Cissy and Julie in April of 2008 thought they would try something different. They decided to test the water, so to speak and embark on their first cruise ship experience. It was only for a week however it sailed from Southampton with four shore stops, one in Spain, two in Portugal and one in France.

While they were away they encountered a lady of similar age and tastes, with a husband who was absolutely loaded. Her name was, Daphne Deloris de Courtney. She was as posh as fuck and according to her she was not having any luck in that department. Her equally posh husband, who was at least ten years older than her was called Simion Bertrum de Courtney.

They had been married for just over ten years and it was the first time for both of them. No children by mutual consent, although a secret lovechild by either of them would not be out of the question.

Cissy and Julie sniggered to each other as the conversation was taking place: Daphne and Simion sounded like a firm of solicitors or estate agents. Ho! Ho! Ho!

He didn't mind her having lady friends, but if he even got the hint of a man getting too close had threatened to cut her off without a penny. He had suspected her of infidelity in the past but put it down to his own mid-life crisis. If only the truth be known. Daphne also let it slip due to the amount of alcohol she was consuming, that her old man had been impotent for the past couple of years. This all came about while the three ladies were having large cocktails on the very first night of sailing, while Simion was playing a game of bridge with two other equally boring old bastards.

Well now, the three wives got on like a house on fire. Simion joined their company for dinner and that first night was a laugh a minute and poor old Simion didn't realise that he in most cases was the butt of their jokes. He was actually quite intelligent, and charming to a fault, but was not particularly streetwise. He could probably complete the Times crossword in no time at all but didn't recognise the flirtatious behaviour of the three women, that continued until well after they had eaten their five-course meal and consumed a reasonable amount of alcohol. Simion decided at about ten-thirty to retire for the night with a bloody good book.

'Don't stay up too late, my dear,' he crooned to Daphne.

'I won't, my darling,' was the disingenuous reply. He was gone for only a matter of minutes when the three wanton women made their way back to Cissy and Julie's cabin with a further tray of drinks carried by a very young, handsome, Spanish waiter, who thought that his boat had come in, excuse the pun, but alas not. The three rampant women were in the mood for a pussy-only night, tonight and any other night, so the Spanish waiter got the old, heave ho!

Daphne, who liked to be called DD, confided to the other two women that she could spot from a mile away that they had a special relationship. They might be wearing wedding rings but their body language told the true story, which was probably not the case when they were at home or at work. During the remainder of the cruise, although DD had pleaded guilty to a litany of misdemeanours and much more, she could hardly contain herself when the other two women confessed to their outrageous sexual appetites amid the closeness of their families. Three out of the seven nights resulted in a prolonged ménage-et-trios. The incarnation of ecstasy!

The cruise from start to finish was a complete blast for the girls and Simion was none the wiser...

Or maybe he was. Maybe he didn't mind his wife cavorting with another woman or women. He just didn't like the idea of another man ploughing her. She may or may not have given him explicit details after each event, which may or may not have been the only way he could get his rocks off. Cissy and Julie discussed these possibilities on several occasions but both agreed that neither of them gave a flying fuck. This was another chapter in their illicit sex lives and it was indescribably erotic! On their return to Southampton, all three women swapped phone numbers and promised to stay in touch. This was not going to be goodbye but... au revoir!

May Day bank holiday 2008 arrived with sunshine and laughter. The McKennas decided to have a family barbecue over the Saturday and Sunday, similar to their Christmas festivities, with the two families getting together for a two-day/night hooley. The main reason being that Lenny had been at sea over the previous festive period. Lou and her fiancé George, Sam and Pam with their latest boyfriends in tow were all there, and the unofficial guest of honour, Lenny, was absolutely lording it! Ann Wishbone and Wheelie Ferris would also make an appearance. Robbie even paid for a duo to provide live music to entertain them on both afternoons. Some of the neighbours promised that they would pop in. It was a crazy two days and nights and Liz's two kids had a whale of a time. The McKennas were as close as ever. That's for sure.

By mid-morning on Monday the clean-up began. Steven and Connor were having a well-earned nap so Liz began to clear the area of the two back gardens. Cissy and Julie had begun in Julie's kitchen area but the two brothers were still in their pits, as was that big lazy lump Lenny. Liz couldn't help but wonder why all men seemed to have it all their own way. Those three would make an appearance just in time for the usual toasted bacon sarnies looking for sympathy and the usual, 'There, there now. Have some headache tablets and that nasty old hangover will soon go away. Ah, come and have a hair of the dog, love. Are you alright now?'

Under the small tree at the end of the garden, there were what appeared to be the remnants of puke in several serviettes. Liz nearly puked herself but as she was wearing rubber gloves, she decided to put the foul debris into the black plastic bag she was wisely carrying. Immediately under the serviettes she noticed a mobile phone. After wiping it clean she realised that she didn't recognise who it might belong to. It certainly wasn't a company phone as they were almost all identical and the personal mobile phones were a lot more upmarket than this, almost discarded model. Liz slipped it into the pocket of her jeans for fear it might belong to one of her allies, Sam or Pam. The least said the better for now.

True to form, the three dozy men all appeared as if by magic when it was announced that tea, coffee and toasted bacon sarnies were ready. After the clean-up, Liz didn't fancy anything more than a mug of strong coffee, which she decided to take to her room. That way she wouldn't have to suffer the usual bollocks with the three useless excuses for mankind being waited on, hand and foot. Her two boys were still catching up on the sleep they lost over the hectic weekend. So now it was Liz time, oh yes, and the mystery mobile phone. She removed it from her pocket and it wasn't long before she began to navigate her way through the various menus. It was relatively easy, considering most mobile phones have a series of security gadgets. It was as if it was inadvertently left insecure.

There were a few exchanges of normal chit-chat text messages between what Liz surmised, were two females just having a bit of a laugh. A get-together seemed to be on the cards somewhere in Surrey not too far from Guilford. Then photographs began to appear, and Liz thought these may well unravel the mystery identities. From what she could make out they seemed to have been taken in a small room of some sort. Yes, a small bedroom with two single beds? Then the photos showed two pairs of legs or no, maybe three pairs of legs? Liz couldn't make head or tail of it. It was as if those taking part were taking turns to record the events. In her impatience she began to scroll much quicker until she could make out what might be going on.

'Fuck me,' flashed through her mind. What appeared to be three women completely naked in a dimly lit sort of bedroom. She couldn't make out what was really going on and then, whatever button she pressed on the phone, resulted in a video that began to play. Three middle-aged women spread out over two beds, cavorting like nothing she had ever seen before. Swapping sex toys, spit, fingers and tongues in all angles. It looked as if the events that unfolded had taken place on several different occasions, then, lo and behold the sound became loud enough for Liz to hear the laughs, moans, groans and animal-like grunts. She knew, she just fucking knew, even before the light in the small room increased to a recognisable level. She just fucking knew who they were, well, two of them anyway! She played it over and over, again and again, over and over, again and again. She was so overcome with anger and disgust she nearly screamed there and then, but she realised she had to control her emotions for now, until she could get her head round the whole situation and understand the consequences of making a fuss. She began to shake in the same way as when her infrequent anxiety bouts would kick in. Her bedroom door opened and her dad popped his head in to say, 'Come on, lazy lump. Get those two kids up and we'll have a little play in the garden before we all go out for a well-earned family lunch. Your mum and Aunt Julie deserve something special, after the way they always look after us all.'

Liz replied, 'Okay, Dad, just give me a few minutes.'

All through the pub lunch at the Eagles Nest, Liz could hardly contain herself. Mother and Julie were lapping up all the attention they were getting from the two gullible husbands. Lenny was also joining in and the two wives just soaked up the grandeur of the afternoon. Liz was so pleased to have the kids with her as a buffer zone until one or other of the sisters-in-law picked them up for a great big kiss and a hug. Liz made an excuse to shift them back round the table for she knew what their granny and great aunt had been doing with their mouths in the video. God only knows how long or how short a period of time it had been since the last episode of erotic entertainment. Liz tried very hard not to grimace but if the truth be known she was at, no, she was passed, boiling point!

At one point that afternoon both wives were sitting on their husbands' knees and kissing them lovingly on the cheek and on the lips. If only her dad and uncle knew where those lips had been and where they were going to be in the future. Liz felt that the whole situation was out of her remit. How was she going to accept the responsibility of the circumstances she now found herself in? It just wasn't fair. Who could she confide in? No one, that's fucking who! At this stage she felt completely alone... Except for her two beautiful boys.

When both families returned to their respective homes and the cheery goodbyes were made, Liz and her two sons escaped to the sanctuary of her bedroom. After sharing a bath with them, the two boys were soon fast asleep in the nursery they shared. Steven was now just over three years old and his little brother Connor was almost one and a half years old. 'Where does the time go?' thought Liz. She was still very concerned about what she witnessed on the phone, both the photos and the video. The images were difficult at first but with her usual persistence she managed to improve the quality to a degree of no doubt, that her mother and Julie were rampant, unrepentant, unfaithful, fornicating slags.

And whoever the other slag bitch was, well, she seemed to be the instigator of all of the swap-overs, including sex toys, bondage, and the use of every orifice available, of which each participant had three. She wanted everything with no holds barred, all the way through, everyone and all, of the sordid filthy exposures. All three deserve to be ousted! But Liz felt she was completely trapped. Angry and disgusted as she was, her hands were tied. What would the reaction be, from her dad and Uncle Benny? What about the reaction from the remainder of both families? Why did she have to carry this burden all on her own? She would sleep on it tonight and keep the mobile phone in a safe place for the time being. She would have to think long and hard before deciding what to do.

She took two 5 mg diazepam... Instead of the one that the doctor had prescribed since Connor was born. Then she took two co-codamol 30/500 caplets... Instead of the one that the doctor had prescribed, to ease the dreaded headaches. Doubling up on the medication seemed like a good idea. Her whole life was once again turned upside down, with only orchestrated sleep for comfort. Never mind. Tomorrow would be another day.

CHAPTER 8

THE FOLLOWING FRIDAY MORNING AT, 10.45 am precisely, found Lenny in the main Royal Naval Administration Building in Portsmouth. He was in a reception area on the second floor, to see the officer commanding reference his promotion to petty officer third class with immediate effect, and his imminent posting to Gibraltar the following January, 2009. He was initially offered a seat by a rather rotund lady, who introduced herself as the petty officer first class, chief clerk to the officer commanding. Lenny sat opposite a large oak door with a brass plate that read: 'Lt Commander R.N. Lancaster'.

Lenny had also submitted a written application to see the said officer to discuss a private matter. Although he couldn't help smiling when it suddenly dawned on him, that the commander was named after a WW2 bomber, with initials that matched Royal Navy.

At 11 am the large oak door opened and a junior officer appeared and introduced himself as the administration officer, Lieutenant Mc Hugh-Dick. He briefed Lenny to march into the office, halt in front of the commander's desk, salute and then remain standing to attention until told to do otherwise. 'Got it?' Lenny replied a very weak 'Yes, sir.'

In he went and all the official jargon was over in a flash, which finished in a very hearty well done and handshake from the commander. The commander then sat down and asked Petty Officer McKenna what it was he wanted to discuss regarding his written application. Lenny paused and then the commander asked, 'Would you prefer it if I invited the lieutenant to leave the office, so as to address the subject one-to-one?'

'Thank you for the offer, sir, but I don't think that will be necessary. You see, it's quite simple. I formally request, that it be officially recorded, in my personal documents, that I am gay… Sir.'

The commander and the lieutenant both grimaced in unison, and allowed Lenny to continue.

'And, if possible, sir, with the proviso that my record is not changed until my posting to Gibraltar in January... Sir.'

The commander and lieutenant raised a curled up right hand to their mouths, to smother a little cough, in unison. After a brief pause the commander regained his composure and nodded and said to his subordinate, 'Take a note of this change Lieutenant, but we must make sure we adhere to Petty Officer McKenna's request, that it does not become public knowledge until January 2009... On his posting to Gibraltar. Is that absolutely clear?'

'Absolutely clear, sir. Aye-aye, sir. Absolutely, sir. If there is nothing else, sir... With your permission, sir... We can let the petty officer be on his gay-lee way, I mean, merry way, sir.'

Lenny turned about and marched smartly out of the office and away to the nearest pub, to celebrate his promotion with his mates and with a great sigh of relief that he would be officially coming out in the New Year.

On his departure from the commander's office, the lieutenant could not help but notice the tall, handsome young man with the tight booty heading out through the door. 'Ah,' he thought. 'A possible short-term liaison could be on the cards? Ah, why not?''

The commander snorted to the lieutenant, 'Bloody hell, Bertie! We were lucky with that one. Bloody shirt-lifters. They're sprouting up all over the place. It's only been legal, yes bloody legal in the armed forces for about two years. It's like a bloody infestation for pity's sake. Got to keep a lid on it. You know what I mean, Bertie. Keep a bloody lid on it. Brings a completely new meaning to that old phrase at reveille... Hands off cocks! On socks! You totally agree... Don't you, Bertie?'

'Absolutely sir. Abso-bloody-lutetly, sir!'

At around the same time, on the same Friday morning of Lenny's promotion, Liz arrived at MKE Ltd Head Office. She had phoned ahead to get the thumbs up from Cissy and

Julie, that they would be free to discuss a small domestic situation that just needed to be cleared up. Phrases of exasperation were exchanged between the sisters-in-law, like: 'We wait with baited breath. And all will be revealed.'

As soon as Liz arrived, her two kids were immediately the centre of attention. Members of the office staff were more than willing to entertain them while their mum spoke to Cissy and Julie. At Liz's insistence all three moved into the small but private boardroom to the rear of the main office.

As they sat down at the table, arms folded, Cissy was the first to speak.

'Okay, Liz, what's so important that it couldn't wait until we got home?'

'Found this bad boy in the back garden on Monday morning just gone.'

Liz slowly and temptingly withdrew the mobile phone from her jacket pocket and placed it on the table. The partners in crime sat riveted to their chairs, absolutely gobsmacked. They unfolded their arms slowly, as if to reach out and snatch the item, which they knew contained untold evidence of their debauchery. Liz gave a wry little smile and added, 'Oh, it's okay. You can have it back. I've managed to download all the action onto a memory stick, quite a large memory stick, actually.'

Julie couldn't hold back. 'You are a conniving little bitch!' But Cissy stopped her from going any further by simply placing her fingers over Julie's mouth and asked a simple question, 'Okay, Liz. What do you want?'

'Fuck me, Mother. You've changed your tone since we first sat down. I'll tell you exactly what I want. I want to be relieved of the burden of your sins. I want to not wake up in the middle of the night and not think about what you and your slag sister-in-law are doing to me, our family and most important of all, what it would do to Uncle Benny and Dad if any of this ever gets out. But I know that that is just pie in the sky. You have both gone too far to ever stop and my wants and the wants of our family are the last things on both your selfish fucking minds. I'll tell you that I won't get any of those things. So, bitches united, this is the fucking deal! I want driving lessons starting next week, three double lessons per week until I pass my driving test. I want a nice little run-a-round. Not a fucking banger. Something no more than, say, two years old. I want my independence back and this is going to be the fucking start. Okay, so far?'

Julie piped up, 'Now listen, Liz, where is the money to pay for all this coming from, without causing suspicion? We all feel sorry for you and your predicament. What with the two youngsters and all. The medication you're on, well, we are all of the same frame of mind that you may not be ready for a car. We all help to ferry you around whenever the need arises. Don't we?'

Quick as a flash Liz hit back, 'Fuck you, Julie! Put the car on the company vehicle property list and put me on the nominal roll, as a ghost part-timer. You lot have had ghost employees on the books before, part-time and full-time workers, to cover those under the table expenses. To fill those nice brown envelopes with loads of wonga to ensure the council contracts keep rolling over, year after year. And what about all the unofficial cash-in-hand jobs? Eh? Do you think I don't know what's going on? I've been around you lot for far too fucking long. I could run this company with both hands tied behind my fucking back!'

After a short pause she continued, 'And as for your new play mate, DD. The size of her melons it would be more like... DOUBLE FUCKING DD! Watching you two, sucking and biting, what was it she called you, oh yes, her little piglets. Snort, snort. Grunt, grunt. Come on then, girls, how do you like those fucking apples? Are we ready to fucking rumble? Liz is on a fucking roll... Please say yes. Pretty, pretty please?'

If Cissy and Julie had not heard and seen it for themselves, they would never have believed that it was Liz who was sitting there, totally defiant and totally in charge and moreover holding all the winning cards. They nodded in agreement and promised that Liz's demands would be met. They would ensure that Robbie and Benny would not ask any incriminating questions and convince them that this was the way forward.

Before leaving the intrepid duo to stew in their unfortunate situation, Liz, casually as you please, announced that she would like to avail herself of an invitation on the following next Friday night. Sharon and Gino were in town for a week and she would be delighted to join them in the Eagles Nest for a few drinks and a catch up. Liz would ensure that she would use the usual dependable taxi driver to pick her up from home at about 8 pm and get her home around 1am on the Saturday morning. The voluntary services of Aunt Julie and/or Mother would be gratefully appreciated by babysitting the kids. With that said, she left the board room, and with her two boys and a smile on her face, exited the building, convinced that this fine Friday morning was the start of a new beginning.

Julie closed the board room door and said to Cissy, 'You never mentioned that you had mislaid our little cheap non-traceable mobile phone, did you?'

'Well, don't you bloody start. After the weekend boozing session, I thought you had it. The last time I can remember seeing it was with you on Sunday night, under the tree in the back garden when we were skipping through it, tempting fate.'

They both smiled and shrugged their shoulders.

'Right,' said Julie. 'It needs to go back into its little hidey hole. I will return it to our joint safe deposit box in our secret little bank, with our joint secret little bank account, to ensure that the history of our outrageous sex-ploits and the definitive proof, that we are both habitual electronic peeping toms, is kept out of sight but not out of mind.'

The next Friday night at 8 pm saw Liz dolled up to the eyeballs as she bade a temporary farewell to Steven and Connor, prior to stepping into the waiting taxi outside her home. It took Cissy and Julie all the willpower in the world not to make any wry comments. When Liz arrived at the pub, Gino and Sharon were sitting on stools at the busy bar.

After about fifteen minutes, the trio decided to move upstairs to the function room and grab a table and chairs, to enjoy the live duo that would be supplying the entertainment for that night. The music would typically start about 10 pm but the room was already more than half full. They settled for a table a short distance from the bar. Liz couldn't wait to hear about Gino and Sharon's travels and also how much they enjoyed a life on the ocean wave. She also learned that they were putting quite a bit of money into a joint savings account with a view of investing in a small property on the south coast. Their plan was to buy for rent and continue their relationship on the cruise lines for as long as it suited them both. Liz may have been envious, but she couldn't have been more pleased for her two mates. Oh yes, at that moment in time Gino was still not welcome in Sharon's parents' house, so a visit there was not on the cards.

Just as the live music was about to start, two strapping twenty-something guys strolled up to the bar not far from their table. They ordered a pint of lager each and then searched in vain for a free table, but to no avail. Gino was also at the bar ordering drinks for himself and the girls. He noticed the disappointment on their frowning faces and the unimpressed shrugs of their shoulders, as if they had nowhere to go, and he couldn't help but smile and said, 'Should have got here sooner, boys. It's always bouncing on Friday and Saturday nights. Some of the best pub music in South London play this place.'

The two mates smiled and then one of them said, 'You got any room on your table then?'

Gino looked round at the two girls and answered, 'I'm here with my girlfriend and her mate. There's room enough at our table but I don't see a spare seat anywhere.'

The same guy replied, 'We're here at the behest of the owner, Big Frankie. We're both in the army with his nephew and arranged to stay here over the weekend before flying out to Germany on Monday this coming week. So, I wonder if he could sort us out with a couple of seats or stools, anything really.'

The words had just left his lips when Big Frankie appeared from the door behind the bar with a small stool in each hand. He smiled and nodded to all three and then checked with Gino and then the two girls, if anyone minded if his nephew's two army mates could squeeze in at their table. Everyone was in agreement and Big Frankie even sent over a round of drinks for all five of them a few minutes later. A big thumbs up from everyone concerned.

Over the next half hour or so, they all introduced themselves and impressed each other with stories from far and wide. However, the only stories Liz could tell were about her two boys, but she was assured by the remainder that she had more to talk about than the other four put together. The drinks were going down well as was the standard of music from the very talented duo as they belted out various styles of music. The two army guys had a great sense of humour and said that in their unit, the Royal Artillery, just about everyone had a nickname. Because in their case, you would rarely see one without the other they were known as Mix and Match. Well now, everyone around the table howled with laughter because, according to Mix and Match, sometimes they got so drunk they didn't know which one was Mix and which one was Match.

A short while later Mix insisted that it was his turn to buy a round of drinks, even though there were protests from around the table that he was buying out of turn, but he was having none of it. While he was at the bar, Match explained that their mate Billy, Big Frankie's nephew had organised free accommodation with a bit of grub thrown in over this weekend so they could piss it up in London, before flying out to Germany on their next posting. The least they could do is spend a few extra quid at the bar with the locals. Mix re-joined them with a fresh round of drinks and a shot of Sambuca for each of them for good measure. They all shouted 'cheers' in unison and the shots were gone in an instant. The little party at their table was now really beginning to take off, with lots of friendly banter and the odd innuendo. Liz was really enjoying her night out despite the illicit revelations that had raised their ugly heads in recent weeks. Suddenly she felt a little dizzy. Not dizzy drunk, just dizzy strange. She had not taken any pills that day because she knew she would be drinking with Gino and Sharon that night but to be fair, she had not been out for a while.

Even when there was drink taken at home, she would never have more than three or four as the kids were always there and she wouldn't have anyone criticise her for overindulging.

Mix and Match were really knocking them back and were making plans to go to the Lewisham Irish Centre. Lots of people in the bar had been raving about the place since the two mates had arrived that afternoon. Liz checked her watch and it was only just turned 11 pm. Her eyes began to sting a little. She thought that maybe this partying lark was too much for her these days and that it might be a good idea to call it a night and get a taxi home. Sharon was so disappointed when Liz told her that she wasn't feeling great and wanted to pull the plug.

'Oh, come on, Liz. How often do we get together these days?'

But Gino intervened, 'Listen, Sharon, if Liz is not feeling well then I'll get her a taxi on my mobile and we can always call round and see her sometime tomorrow.'

After a few more minutes Sharon reluctantly agreed, but it didn't really matter as Gino was already on the phone organising the lift home and assured Liz that transport was on its way. Of course, Gino, being the perfect gentleman that he was, insisted that he would walk Liz down the stairs and see her into the taxi. As they stood up Mix and Match were returning from the gents. They were surprised that Liz was going home so early but Gino briefly explained the situation to them.

'I'll tell you what, Liz,' said Mix, 'we have a taxi on the way to take us over to Lewisham. Can we offer you a lift?'

'No thanks,' she answered. 'I live in the opposite

direction.'

'Not to worry,' said Match. 'We'll see you downstairs and save Gino the trouble. You don't want to leave Sharon on her own for too long, otherwise she may not be there when you get back.'

They all had a good old chuckle, even Liz. Gino was happy enough to let the two mates escort Liz downstairs and see her into the taxi. When all three reached the pavement the night air seemed to take Liz's breath away and then a nice, comfortable warm feeling seemed to creep over her. It felt as if it was coming from the back of her head and then over her face. A nice, comfortable warm feeling. A safe, drowsy, feeling. In the background she heard someone say, 'Fancy a spit-roast, love?'

She tried to explain that she wasn't hungry but the only response she heard was, 'A nice spit-roast is just what you need, love.'

She became aware, as if she was awakening from a slumber, that she was in a car of some sort. She tried hard to focus but everything seemed to be jumbled up. She rubbed her eyes with the forefinger of each hand and then she realised that she was in the back of a taxi. She glanced at her watch. She thought, 'It can't be bloody half past one.'

She shouted at the driver. 'Is that you, Gerry?'

He replied. 'Of course it is. Who'd you think it was? Gentleman Gerry at your service as per usual. I've been driving the McKennas around for more years than I care to remember and I always get you home safe and sound.'

'But Gerry, I thought you were to pick me up just after eleven o'clock.'

'That's right, young Liz, but one of Gino's mates phoned back a few minutes later and cancelled both yours and their lifts. Said you lot changed your minds. No probs though. They rebooked your lift for one o'clock but I got a bit held up in traffic like, you know, and got to the pub at about quarter past one but I'll soon have you home safe and sound. If anybody can: Gerry can.'

She just couldn't get her head round the whole crazy

story. Quick as a flash the taxi pulled up outside Liz's house. She offered Gerry the normal fare but he shook his head and said, 'No need, young Liz. The two young lads paid your fare up front and threw in a very handsome tip. Yes, very nice they were. Very nice indeed.'

When Liz opened the front door, her mother was there to greet her.

'Everything okay, love? Did Gerry pick you up as usual?'

'Yes, yes, no probs. Were the kids okay?'

'Of course they were. Aren't they always?'

'Listen, I'm sorry I'm a little later than planned but Gerry got caught up in traffic.'

'Look, Liz, you pop in and see the kids and jump straight into bed. You look knackered but as long as you enjoyed yourself. You can tell me tomorrow all about Gino and Sharon and what they have been getting up to. Off you go. Goodnight.'

Liz found herself shuffling along the hall to say goodnight to her two boys. She felt a little bit tender down below. After giving each of her sons a goodnight kiss and a cuddle she stripped off and crept in under the duvet. The duvet had a nice warm comfortable feeling. Soon she was sound asleep, but not for long.

She jumped up into a sitting position on her bed with the duvet wrapped around her feet. Beads of sweat were running down her face and the bed sheet was damp. She thought that she had partially peed herself, until she realised that she was perspiring from every pore on her entire body and then she began to shake. She crept out of bed and dried herself down with the bath towel that was always laid over the nearby stool. Wrapping herself in the soft towel she slowly sat on the armchair next to the bed. Then a series of flashbacks took place. The smell of alcohol, the smell of tobacco, the smell of aftershave. Hands and then more hands... Being undressed by hands... Hands that appeared to have no owners... Sitting on a bed... On a bed? Whose bed? What bed? Liz felt her whole body shaking almost out of control. She closed her eyes as they began to sting with tears, salty tears.

Then, as if she was re-dreaming a dream, she could picture the two tall figures in a dimly lit room. She could feel the harshness of their faces against hers as they kissed her incessantly. Their rough hands were grabbing and clutching and their hungry mouths bit and sucked hard on her trembling nakedness. Fingers with long nails nipped at her from every angle with no thought whatsoever of her discomfort, investigating and channelling inside her. She was then lowered onto the bed. They took her in turn, then both at once. She heard them laugh and snigger. They spun her around the bed like a rag doll, over and over again as if she were in a recurring nightmare! She felt the spit of their foul breaths as they devoured her like a medieval feast. She had no control of either her physical or mental state... Then there was quietness... A very still quietness... She felt a warm sponge gently caressing her body... She was standing... From top to bottom the sponge made its pleasant journey... Paying particular attention to her most nether region. And then she was in the taxi, the taxi home.

The flashbacks continued until dawn and the only thing Liz could do was pull her knees up to her chin and silently sob. Suddenly she got a hold of herself. She couldn't let her two boys or her parents see her like this. Grabbing a set of sportswear she made her way to the bathroom and proceeded to have the longest shower in history. The nail brush was used to the extreme, to scrub away the stale scent she imagined was still there. Her teeth were scrubbed so hard that Liz threw the toothbrush along with the nail brush into the pedal bin underneath the sink. Talcum powder, a little perfume and clean underwear seemed to defuse the situation... For now.

Saturday afternoon found Mix and Match sitting at a secluded table in the corner of the downstairs bar at the Eagles Nest. They were comparing notes on the previous night's escapade.

Mix asked Match, 'Do you think she'll say anything?'

'Not a chance, mate. She loved it. You didn't hear her complaining, did you?'

'No, I suppose you're right. But what if she comes in this afternoon or even tonight?'

'Listen, Mix, even if she does say anything. It's our word against hers. She's already got two nippers. It's not as if she's a fucking virgin, is it? After all, it was you who slipped her the fucking pill, wasn't it?'

'Only after you told me to. It was your idea to put it in her Sambuca, wasn't it?'

'Ah, will you stop splitting hairs. We both had her in every position known to man. I didn't hear you worrying about it last fucking night. You were too busy poking her and shooting your fucking muck all over the fucking place. You nearly got me in the face once, you horny little bastard!'

'I know, I know, but I always felt a bit guilty after we've done it.'

Match crouched down, leaned across the table, sneered at his mate and whispered, 'Those little blue jobs we swallowed. Always do the trick, don't they? Keep us both up, all fucking night, oh yes.'

Meanwhile at the bar Big Frankie was having a chat with one of his regulars, Wheelie Ferris.

'Nice to see you in last night, Wheelie. Do you still go to the Irish Club in Croydon on a Saturday night?'

'Definitely Frankie. Me and Ann and the McKennas go most Saturdays. I hear it was busy in 'ere last night. Packed house upstairs and down 'ere.'

'That's right. Can't complain though. Sure no one would listen.'

'Who are those two over in the corner, Frankie? Don't think I've seen 'em before.'

'Ah now, they're two army mates, on their way to Germany. They were up in Yorkshire with my nephew Billy. In a little place called... Thirsk. Yes, I think that's where Billy's posted. My sister Jean's boy. Her and her old man have lived up in Birmingham for years, all her three boys of which Billy's the eldest, all born and bred Brummies, for their sins.'

'Where are those two staying, Frankie? Can't be cheap anywhere round 'ere.'

'My nephew Billy asked for a favour, if we could put his two mates up over the weekend. They're staying in our backpackers' room. You know? The one we use for temporary staff when they come through London. They come from all over, Australia, New Zealand, South Africa, anywhere really. If we give them a room, then it saves them a fortune on digs. Throw in a bit of grub and they work for next to nothing just to be in London. Everybody's happy, know what I mean?'

'But Frankie, how do those two get in and out of the pub when they could be out to all hours.'

'Ah now, Wheelie, we give them the key to the side door which takes them up a staircase and onto a small landing, then to a small room which I have to say is en suite. The connecting door to the function room above us, is permanently locked so they can't set off the alarm by walking through and they have a bit of privacy to enjoy themselves, if you know what I mean.'

'Do you know somefink, Frankie?'

'What's that, Wheelie?'

'You fink of every fink!'

Liz and her kids lazed around all day on Saturday. She put off Sharon and Gino until Sunday, using the excuse that she had another bad headache, which wasn't really a lie. Every so often the reality of what had happened the previous night hit her like a hammer, but who could she confide in? No one, that's who. On the one hand her medication seemed to settle her mind and then again on the other hand a flashback ignited the clouds of anguish and resentment and the torment of the nightmare that was her so-called Friday night out!

She daren't go back to the pub and confront those two despicable bastards because they would say that she was ready and willing to take part in the off-the-wall threesome!

She didn't remember screaming or trying to get away, so the gossips would say that she got what she deserved. Going off with two bloody soldiers and complaining they were a bit rough after being bedded by both of them, well, they would say it was a bit rich. Maybe, the least said the better. It may take some time but she decided that she would just have to put it behind her. Get over it. Get fucking over it. Bastards!

CHAPTER 9

MONDAY 15 SEPTEMBER WAS, a nice bright sunny day. Robbie was sitting in the passenger's seat and his clever daughter Liz was driving the gorgeous little sky blue, one-year-old, five-door Nissan Micra that they had picked up only five minutes before. She had passed her driving test a week earlier, had taken this nice little motor for two trial runs and was now driving her dad around South London, without a care in the world. Robbie had a smile like the cat that got the cream. The only spanner in the works was she was four months pregnant!

Liz decided to reveal her unfortunate circumstances the following Sunday afternoon. She had realised that she was beginning to show, although no one else seemed to notice. Her parents would have a late night the previous night, as per usual, and would really appreciate a hot brunch. Liz would prepare one of her famous Ulster fries that would undoubtedly go down an absolute treat. Benny and Julie would also be there to satisfy their fierce, hangover hunger. Just before midday they all sat down to what appeared to be a most wonderful meal. Liz also produced a selection of fruit juices, tea, coffee, a mountain of toast with marmalade and blackcurrant jam. The two married couples were like kids in a sweet shop. The smiles on their faces and the eating spree that was to follow was accompanied with very little verbal input. After the feast the two men made their way to the patio for a well-earned cigar. The two women followed with four glasses and a renewed jug of fruit juice and they all sat down on the loungers around the wooden garden table. Absolute bliss... Then, WHAM!

Well, Liz just about got the word pregnant from her lips when all hell broke loose. Jug, glasses, cigars and the wooden table all went up in the air, amongst the most insulting profanities known to man. It was only then that Liz realised that she began her story with the end rather than the beginning. So, she began her story once again, for she definitely had everyone's attention. As her version of events unfolded, one step at a time, from her arrival at the Eagles Nest until she arrived home, she avoided some of the intricate sexual depravities recovered from her never-ending flashbacks. No matter how she tried to soften the blows, she could just about see the steam coming out of Robbie's and Benny's ears. They both sat wide-eyed, with gritted teeth and simultaneous clinched fists. Cissy and Julie were equally upset and held their heads in their hands. All four found it difficult to take in the information that Liz, found necessary to spoon-feed them. Once she had completed the whole sordid encounter Liz sat down and found herself reliving the whole scenario once again. Her almost silent sobs followed by deep intakes of breath resulted in her mother and aunt taking her inside to the kitchen area and all three settled down on the large sofa. Their arms entwined each other with Liz in the middle and no one said a word, because at that moment in time, there was nothing any of them could say. They just cuddled in silence.

Robbie and Benny made their way to the kitchen next door to have a very large family measure of Irish whiskey. They also found themselves in total silence. As Benny was pouring them both a second glass Robbie could contain himself no longer and began to cry. A little bit at first and then it developed into a weeping wail. His brother held him as tight as possible for he knew that if he didn't, Robbie most certainly would make his way to the pub and have it out with Big Frankie for allowing those two gob-shites to attack Liz, or anyone else for that matter.

Meanwhile Cissy and Julie were doing their absolute best to comfort and console Liz. The whole world seemed to be turned upside down. A little later when everyone had calmed down to a certain extent, they once again met in Robbie's back garden. Cissy and Julie had reassembled the garden furniture and swept up the broken glass. Robbie was the first to speak.

'Right then, what are we going to do about this fucking

situation?'

Almost before he finished his sentence Cissy piped up. 'Nothing... Absolutely fucking nothing.'

Both Robbie and Benny screamed, 'Nothing! What the fuck do you mean?'

Then all four of them began to argue amongst themselves as if Liz wasn't there. The two brothers were shouting over each other, 'Burn down the pub, give Big Frankie a fucking hiding, find out where those two rapist soldiers are. What were Gino and Sharon thinking of?'

The two women were trying to calm the situation when Liz shouted at the top of her voice.

'Stop it! Just fucking stop it! I'm right here you know!'

That seemed to do the trick. Once again Liz had their undivided attention and she continued.

'Look, I know you all mean well but there's very little any of us can do.'

Robbie was still angry but managed to keep his voice under control, 'What do you mean love? What about reporting it to the police?

'Look, Dad, it happened four months ago. They'll say I'm crying wolf.'

'Look, love, I'm your father and I think that something should be done about those two perverted bastards. What about one of those rape centres, love. Surely there's someone there that could do something?'

'Dad! You're not listening to me!'

At this stage Cissy stepped in, 'Look, everyone. There's nobody more than Liz who would like to see those two rapist bastards strung up by the balls, have their cocks cut off and shoved as far down their fucking throats as possible, but Liz has gone through enough without having to go through every detail again and again to complete strangers, who will do nothing else except judge her for all the wrong reasons. Is that what you're trying to say, Liz?'

'Yes... And I don't want you all to fall out with Big Frankie. It wasn't his fault. He was doing his nephew a favour by putting those two fuckers up for the weekend...

And what do you think people will say about me, eh? My track record doesn't stack up well does it? Anyway, that's the main reason I didn't say anything about the attack. Because of what people would say about me! I put it down to a very bad experience. Didn't know I was going to get bleeding pregnant, did I? That was the last thing on my mind. I just wanted to put it all behind me. Get on with my life.'

Robbie found if difficult once again to contain himself but had to make one more point.

'So they just get away with it? Do they just get away with it? Is that what you're fucking saying?'

'Look, Dad, there's not much more I can do. Everyone will say I wandered off with two fucking soldiers and got what I deserved. "She was asking for it." That's what they'll say. I know it doesn't sound nice but it will sound a damn sight worse if we try to make it public. It's over... I'm well and truly up the soapy bubble... End of story.'

Silence once more was the only option for all concerned as the reality of the situation kicked in. Someone put some music on in the background and another round of whiskey for the brothers was quickly produced as Cissy and Julie knew that was the only way to calm their husbands. A conversation of a totally unrelated subject was cleverly induced by the wives that would eventually give way to a more civilised tone. Eventually the group decided that the wellbeing of the new arrival and Liz had to be the priority. The discussion went on for some time, as did the replenishment of drinks. Eventually Liz slipped away to the sanctuary of her boys' room and spent some quality time showering them with kisses and hugs before she had an early night. She was so glad that she had got the bad news off her chest at last and most of all – whatever the future might bring – she still had her two beautiful boys, Steven and Connor.

Christmas 2008 went well with the usual antics of the McKenna family, although Lenny was unable to attend due to being on duty and on call in Southampton, however he did have three weeks' embarkation leave at the beginning of December. He spent his time equally with his family and with a few of his mates in various parts of the country. He would spend New Year as usual in Southampton but assured everyone that he would be home for a few days before his posting to Gibraltar on 15 January 2009. Robbie and Cissy were bent on a lavish farewell party but Lenny had persuaded them that a Sunday lunch at home at the weekend prior to his departure with just close family in attendance would suffice. He didn't want to make a fuss and he also dropped a little hint of some news that was for family members only. Well, Cissy and Julie were like clucking hens as they both hoped it would be some sort of announcement, maybe a steady girlfriend or maybe something with a little more commitment, an engagement even. He usually kept his cards close to his chest and he hadn't said anything about bringing anyone with him but you could never know with Lenny. The other news that everyone was talking about was the date for Liz's latest arrival. The baby was due in early March 2009. Robbie was hoping that she could hold on for a couple more weeks and produce the new offspring on 17 March... St Patrick's Day! Ah well, fingers crossed.

Lenny arrived home for his farewell visit on Thursday 8 January for five days' leave. He had to report back for duty in Southampton the following Tuesday by 2 pm. His flight to Gibraltar was on Wednesday 14 January, which gave him a period of twenty-four hours to settle in before starting his new job on the 15th. He had previously explained, especially to his mother that he would be home on regular leave periods during his three-year posting and to soften the blow suggested that she and his dad could come out to Gibraltar for a holiday. They could all come out. Cissy couldn't help herself and just had to coo, 'My Lenny. He thinks of everything. He never lets us down.'

The first few days of his visit Lenny found himself visiting every man and his dog as well as visiting every man and his pub. By the time Saturday night came the Irish Club was the last place he wanted to go, but his parents and his aunt and uncle would hear none of it. Old school pals, some of which he hadn't seen for ages and some he didn't need to see showed up on the night and a great time was had by all. Robbie and Benny were showing off the seasoned sailor who was going off for Queen and country. They were as proud as punch and made sure to let everyone know of his recent promotion. He would be carrying on the McKenna name with a great career and proud sons of his own one day.

Sunday began in slow time for both households with the exception of Liz and her two sons as they crept around the house almost on tiptoes. It was a game they played most Sunday mornings when the others had a late night. Liz making funny faces to see which one of them would succumb and giggle out loud. Steven was almost four years old and Connor had just turned two. Sometimes it would turn into a complete calamity, but if the grandparents heard them they didn't seem to mind as the two boys would eventually climb into bed beside them. Poor old Lenny was dead to the world.

By about two that afternoon everyone in the close family circle were tucking into a beautiful buffet, spread across the huge dining table in Cissy's kitchen. With Julie's help it was decided that it would be less hassle to make a finger buffet rather than a three-course meal for everyone, and Lenny had been equally enthusiastic about the change of menu. Steven and Connor were the first to the table and attacked the cocktail sausages with the enthusiasm of two stormtroopers. Liz made sure they remained at the top end of the table, furthest from the bar, with her, so as not to spread too much of a mess. Robbie and Benny were behind the bar dishing out drinks, while the remainder were scattered around the open plan area adjacent to Liz, making use of the two comfy armchairs and the large sofa. Lou was there with her fiancé George, as were Pam and Sam, although they were not accompanied by their latest squeezes. Lenny found himself leaning on the bar with a slight hangover. His dad and uncle were still making back slapping comments about this highly thought of member of the Royal Navy. When Lenny had mustered up enough courage he tapped the bar with an empty bottle and said, 'Can I have everyone's attention please?'

The usual wisecracks were made referencing public speaking and what have you until Lenny tapped the empty bottle a second time.

'Right, folks,' he began. 'As you all know I will be flying out to Gib on Wednesday to take up my new posting on Thursday. Thank you all for the last few days. It's been a real blast. I couldn't have asked for more, especially as you've all turned up this afternoon and... And, I would like to thank my mum and Aunt Julie for laying on this wonderful spread.'

Cheers from everyone including screams from Steven and Connor.

Lenny continued, 'Well now, before I have too much more to drink, I would like to make a very important announcement. My headquarters have already been notified and I would just like, to let you lot know as well... that, that, I'm... gay.'

There was total silence, apart from the munching of Steven and Connor.

'I hope you all heard, what I've just said. I am gay! Yes, I am gay!'

Liz stood up and announced, 'By the way, I'm having twins!'

The following Saturday Liz received a phone call from Lenny explaining all about his new job and he also inquired if the dust had settled since the previous Sunday's revelations. When he left for Southampton on the Tuesday morning the atmosphere was far from good, to say the least. He was so thankful to Liz that she had decided to make her equally unexpected announcement at the same time as his. He could hardly believe his ears when she said, 'Sure, that's what sisters are for.'

He thought for some time that they had grown apart but that sentiment changed somewhat in the two days that followed the Sunday afternoon shock waves. His mother assured him that there was plenty of time for everyone to accept his unexpected news and for the present, Liz's twins were the topic on most days.

Sunday 1 February began with complete panic. Liz woke at about six o'clock that morning with blinding pains in her stomach. It was as if she had severe cramps. She tried to crawl out of bed and make her way to the bathroom, but to no avail. She got as far as the bedroom door and then screamed for her mum. She hadn't used the term 'mum' for quite some time but the little girl in her needed her mum right now. Cissy was there in a flash. For some unknown reason she had found it difficult to sleep, even though she had quite a few drinks in the Irish Club the previous night. Maybe it was a premonition that her daughter was going to have a problem with the birth? On hearing the commotion Robbie was soon up and about. Cissy knew after a brief investigation, that an ambulance was the only solution. Robbie raced next door and returned with Julie, who would look after the two kids. Benny arrived a few moments later and had to be talked out of using his car as the ambulance had already been called, plus if the truth had been known, all of them would have been over the drink drive limit. Ten minutes later the ambulance arrived and after a quick assessment of the situation Liz was stretchered into the vehicle accompanied by Robbie and Cissy and they arrived at the hospital only a few minutes later. Steven and Connor slept through it all, and although they were a little perturbed with the absence of their mummy at breakfast a couple of hours later, accepted their Auntie Julie's reason that Mummy had just gone to the doctor for a quick check up on the new babies.

'Remember?' she'd said. 'There are two new babies coming to live here soon so Mummy just has to be careful. She'll be home in no time.'

The brothers didn't seem to mind and as soon as Julie had them dressed Benny was playing silly games and chasing them all around the house.

Meanwhile at the hospital, the twins had decided it was time to come out to play... Four weeks early! They were immediately transferred to the special baby care unit. Liz did manage a very brief cuddle before the nursing staff whisked them away, but they assured her that they were healthy and well and it was standard procedure, for premature newborns to be scrutinised and monitored in a sterile environment. Better to be safe than sorry. As they say, belt and braces. By early evening Liz had been allowed to visit and hold their hands and pet them a little, by means of the small access points in their incubators, but the proud grandparents would have to wait at least until the following day before they could get that close to them. However, they were allowed to see them via the viewing gallery window.

Julie and Benny brought Steven and Connor to see their mummy in the recovery ward and of course all four of them got to see the twins from the same viewing gallery as Cissy and Robbie. Steven and Connor could not hide their delight when they realised that they had two new brothers. They were jumping up and down and screaming with delight and of course all the adults were extremely emotional. Bambi tears in abundance! Liz could hardly contain herself but was very vexed that Steven and Connor were a little bit teary at having to leave Mummy behind when it was time for them to go home, but Granddad and Uncle Benny to the rescue. Promises of fish bites and the one and only knickerbocker-glory. They soon kissed and hugged their mum and were quickly on their way for their treats. They also conned their way into a late-night cartoon DVD of their choice when they got home, and of course a return trip the following day to the hospital. By the end of that week mother and babies were home and of course the house was turned upside down. There was a home visit by a nurse on a daily basis with a very strict regime as part of the care package. It was difficult to put family and friends off visiting without putting their noses out of joint, but those basic precautions had to be implemented for the sake of the twins and for Liz. The two big brothers, Steven and Connor, were running around the house almost demented with joy and excitement. Liz felt that her head was continuously turning around and around but she was completely overcome, with a feeling of sublime happiness. The slight downside was that she had four children all under the age of four!

The names she had chosen for the two new arrivals came in a most unusual way. When she was alone in her hospital bed she had plenty of time to think, not just of their names but of the two callous bastards that helped to create them, which in turn lead to the frequent flashbacks of her terrible ordeal but she could only remember the nicknames of the guilty pair, Mix and Match. She recalled that they were in the Royal Artillery. She thought that maybe her two new sons should have the initials of R and A. After a great deal of personal reflection, she decided to call them Ryan and Anthony. No one else needed to know how she came about this decision but it was the only thing at that time that made any sense to her. Best kept secrets?

In no time at all the twins were christened and the reception afterwards was held in Julie's house. There were smiles all round, however Robbie was more than just a little concerned with what he thought was the overcrowding issue in his own house. At that moment in time Ryan and Anthony were in adjoining cots in Lenny's room. Steven and Connor remained in what used to be the spare/guest room and of course Liz had her own room, all of which was good and dandy, for now.

But Robbie just felt that although he loved them all so very much it might be time to think about setting Liz up with a place of her own. Cissy had gone through the roof at the first mention of the idea but Robbie, with a bit of help from his brother, was beginning to wear her down. They needed to get Julie on side before broaching the subject with Liz. The plan conjured by the two brothers was as follows:

With the help from their friends in the local council, who would fund the operation, which would also include extra benefits that may not be as easily available if Liz and the four kids continued to live in the family home, a four-bedroom house about ten or fifteen minutes' drive from their present address would be ideal. Now, according to the council reps Liz and her family, due to budget constraints, may well only qualify for a three-bedroom property, Robbie and Benny to the rescue. They agreed to rent Liz one of the upmarket semi-detached four-bedroom houses in their portfolio, at a reduced rate to appease the council and everyone's a winner. All they had to do was decide how they would approach Liz without causing a great deal of controversy.

It was decided to wait until after Paddy's Day in March. Robbie and Cissy asked Benny and Julie to keep an eye on the kids while they took Liz out for a well-deserved treat. Lunch at a posh bistro with all the trimmings including an expensive bottle of wine... Or two? Robbie tried in vain to mention the delicate subject in a very diplomatic way but diplomacy was never his strong point and he began to jumble and almost stutter his well-rehearsed lines, when Cissy interrupted and fired straight from the hip. She was brief and to the point, making sure to highlight all the pros and avoid any of the cons, although she could not identify any negatives of substance. There was a short period of silence as Liz sipped her very expensive wine. She glanced to her mum, then her dad and then she produced one of her ear-to-ear smiles which in turn signified her approval. They all raised their glasses and Liz proposed a toast 'to the future.' The Mc Kenna's were as close as ever.

That's for sure.

Over the Easter weekend of 2009, Liz and her four boys moved into what could only be described as a dream home. It had been fully furnished by her parents and a little help from the council, and had a small off-road parking area at the front with a modest back garden. As far as Liz was concerned all she had to do was make the situation work. She would still need her family for support but she would be, for the first time in her life, almost totally independent. Summer was followed by autumn and then the festive season and all went as smooth as silk for everyone. It was great popping round to her parents' house and into Benny and Julie's place. Cissy and Julie loved to get away for a few hours and spend time with the kids. Occasionally Liz had a night out but would normally be in the presence of her parents or aunt and uncle. Sometimes it was just the three women who had an afternoon out with Robbie or Benny or sometimes both responsible for babysitting.

The subject of the sister-in-laws' sordid private life never came up at the all-girl trysts, but Liz knew that it was most probable that it would raise its ugly head sometime in the not-too-distant future. At least one Sunday each month was earmarked for a family lunch in either Julie's or Cissy's house. Steven, who was almost five years old, had started full-time primary school in September of that year and he absolutely loved it although Connor couldn't understand why he couldn't go as well. He had the same reaction when Steven started nursery. Ryan and Anthony were coming along really well and apart from the odd infant sickness routine, life in general was great. The family business was doing equally well and the big news for the New Year was that at long last, Lou and her fiancé had set a date. They would marry on Saturday 28 August 2010.

Lou was thirty-one years old and George was ancient at about thirty-five, so it was about bloody time. Liz didn't think they would have kids any time soon as their careers came first and they also loved their very busy social life. Liz knew that if she was to attend the wedding that Lou would be undoubtedly embarrassed. A cousin with four young kids and no man in sight well, tongues would wag, wouldn't they? What would she tell George's family and friends? Most of them would be stuck-up gits, even on a good day. So Liz decided when the invitation came, she would hang on to it without reply until the very last minute, just to make the bride and groom sweat, just a bit. Cruel, but that's life.

True to form, Lou and George's wedding in August 2010 was like a high society affair. Liz made them wait right up to the last few days before politely declining their invitation and both bride and groom feigned their disappointment in typical snobby fashion. Liz didn't mind as she had enjoyed putting them both through the ringer for as long as possible.

Lenny of course attended the wedding, coinciding with one of his leave periods, however he did not bring a guest. Ann Wishbone, Wheelie Ferris and Ann's son Michael were also in attendance. Michael was having some time at home after completing his seven-year stint at Royal Tunbridge Wells University. He had achieved a bachelor of arts in music, followed by a master's degree. It had been a long hard haul but he was highly qualified in classical music, majoring in the Cello and the French horn. He was also a dab hand at various percussion instruments! He had recently returned from America from a very successful audition at the Massachusetts College of Music, whereby he qualified for a three-year scholarship. Now these particular scholarships were very few and far between, however it was deemed well-deserved and would undoubtedly be a stepping stone to greater things. Michael had his eyes on the Boston Philharmonic Orchestra and he planned not on a stepping stone but a spring board to a very successful musical career.

The McKenna family had not seen much of him over the years, mostly photographs that his mother proudly presented on certain occasions that she had acquired at the university when she sometimes dragged Wheelie along. Although he didn't show it, Michael resented his mother's relationship with Wheelie, for he had many fond memories of his late father and there were lots of family photographs around the house. He thought that his mother had a right to a social life but found it strange that it had to be with a window cleaner that everyone called Wheelie but anything for an easy life. Ann had supported him financially throughout those seven long years at university but now he was on his way to the good old USA with a scholarship under his belt but he knew that she would still see him right for money, no matter how long it took for him to be a success. He would be heading to the States in September, only a week or so away and to Ann's dismay he hadn't planned to return home for a visit until August the following year.

He was also assured at his audition that there would be plenty of opportunities to earn a lot of spending money in his spare time performing with other students in various venues the length and breadth of not just the state of Massachusetts but in other parts of the country. He was now twenty-five years of age and at 6' 2" tall, the same height as his father, with his jet black hair, dark piercing eyes, mixed race complexion, he was a handsome devil of a man who made many a woman, young and old, stop in her tracks just to catch their breath. He could well prove to be Hollywood material!

Ann brought him to the McKenna households to show him off one more time before his departure and it has to be said that Cissy and Julie were staining their knickers, crossing their legs and trying very hard to leave themselves alone during and after the event. Each of them thought: 'Local boy does good. He could do me good, any time!'

They both swapped notes in private a little later, over a large glass of wine, and then let their fingers linger. If only Michael knew that he was the subject of their mutual masturbation.

The next twelve months flashed by and Liz took everything in her stride. To the surprise of her parents and the remainder of the family, there was nothing she couldn't cope with. Early in August 2011 her mum and dad took Liz and the four kids to the old family favourite holiday location: Butlins at Bognor Regis. They had various trips away in the past but usually for a week or less due to the stress that the four kids could easily muster. This time it was for a fortnight. Cissy wasn't too bad, but Robbie was always a nervous wreck. Benny and Julie went once in the distant past, only for Benny to say, 'Never say never but not again... Not anytime soon.'

Usually on the last Saturday of each month, Liz and the four kids were invited for a sleepover at Granny and Granddad's house. This was always a great treat for the four boys: Steven now aged six and a half, Connor four and a half and Ryan and Anthony two and a half. They were allowed to stay up late and Liz just loved to step in when it all got too much for her dad. She developed a talent for smiling wryly when no one else could see her, but if the truth be known sure they all relished the whole experience. Even Benny and Julie made an appearance but had the easy option to withdraw to their own house next door, when everything seemed to go bananas! The main perk for Liz was that she could have a well-earned drink on those nights without worrying about the kids. If any of them had a problem through the night her parents would rise to the occasion.

It was on the last Saturday of that August, when their close friends Ann and Wheelie, arranged for Ann's son to join them for a special dinner at a very posh restaurant in Croydon town centre. Michael was home from the States for two weeks but unfortunately for his mum, not the four weeks he had promised, so this particular little get-together had to be brought forward with little explanation. Ann had reserved the table for eight o'clock and a taxi for half past seven but kept herself scarce throughout that afternoon so as not to let the cat out of the bag. Michael assumed that it was her way of getting over her disappointment of his brief visit which was now reduced to ten days. He knew that Wheelie would be there but better the devil you know.

On arrival at the restaurant Michael knew instantly that it was very upmarket, and Wheelie gave a little whistle of approval as they stepped out of the taxi. They were welcomed at the door by a very impressive maître d' who showed them to a candlelit table beside the window. The whole evening went better than Ann could have imagined. Wheelie making his funny wisecracks and Michael actually laughing out loud, which made a pleasant change as Ann knew that her son had reservations concerning Wheelie in the past. She was more than pleased that they were having such a lovely dinner night. Three courses with wine and several Irish coffees later the two men were leaning back in their plush, upholstered carver chairs, putting the world to rights when Ann decided that she should share her good news. Politely as possible she asked for their attention and to move a little closer to her at the table. The two slightly pie-eyed, newfound friends leaned closer as instructed and gazed intently at Ann.

'Right' she said. 'I have good news for you both and when you hear it, I'm sure it won't come as too much of a surprise.'

Both men looked at each other and then back at Ann, finding it difficult to suppress the laughs that were just, dying to get out.

Ann glanced over both shoulders and said, in little more than a whisper, almost a mime:

'I'm getting married.' Both men answered in a similar mime:

'What?'

And then she announced in a much louder voice, 'I'm getting married!'

Both men asked at the same time, 'Married?'

'Yes!' she shouted.

'To who?' asked Wheelie.

'To you... You dope!' she cried.

'To who?' shouted Michael.

'To Wheelie! If he'll have me?'

Well, talk about complete shock. Wheelie jumped up with tears in his eyes and shouted, 'Of course I'll bleeding have you!

Michael jumped up with tears in his eyes, tears of a different nature. 'Mum? How could you?'

At this stage the surrounding diners could not but realise what had just taken place and those closest to Ann's table gave a little round of applause and smiled, not fully understanding why the youngest of the three looked a little upset. Ann and Wheelie held hands across the table and both held on really tight. No one was going to take this moment away from them, not even Michael. A few moments later Ann asked for the bill, paid by credit card and left a £20 note as a tip. All three left the restaurant with the same maître d' offering his best wishes to the newly betrothed couple.

Michael hailed a taxi and they made their back to Ann's house. 'Can't go to Wheelie's flat,' thought Michael. 'It's probably a fucking dump.'

Silence prevailed on the short journey. When they pulled up outside the house Michael jumped out and almost ran to the front door and let himself in with his key. Wheelie almost had to put his foot in the door way as it looked as if it would be shut in their faces as an act of defiance, by what Wheelie had realised was a very spoilt upstart. Meanwhile Ann paid the taxi fare and gave her eyes a little wipe and then she and Wheelie entered the house with both heads held high. Michael had stomped upstairs to his bedroom and slammed the door.

Ann put the kettle on for a well-earned cup of tea and gave Michael a shout, not once but on three occasions before he answered and came downstairs. He stomped his way into the sitting room where he found his mum and man friend sitting side by side on the sofa, once again holding hands. He could manage nothing more than a grimace. Three mugs of steaming hot tea sat on the small table in front of them, with milk and sugar close by. Ann gestured for her son to sit down in the armchair, opposite her and Wheelie. As he did so he picked up one of the hot mugs of tea and made a sweeping movement, as if to accidently spill it over Wheelie but Ann, sensing straight away what her son was doing, jumped up to protect her intended and the whole mug of hot tea splashed over her face!

Twenty minutes later the ambulance arrived to find Ann's face covered in a damp hand towel. Wheelie was sporting a bloody nose and a small cut to his left cheek. Michael was in a complete panic and shouting at the top of his voice that it was just an accident. He pointed to Wheelie and shouted, 'If it wasn't for him, none of this would have happened!'

In the immediate aftermath of the 'accident' Ann insisted that Wheelie call their good friends the McKennas but this led to a complete meltdown by Michael. All that he was worried about was what people might think of him, but Wheelie insisted, which lead to a brief scuffle between him and Michael that resulted in Wheelie's facial injuries. Ann then asked for an ambulance and Wheelie stepped into the hall and made two quick phone calls: the ambulance service and to Robbie McKenna.

Robbie, Cissy and Liz were topping up their drinks and listening to some Irish country music on Robbie's new all-singing, all-dancing top of the range music system that he had bought that very day. Talk about boys and their toys. All four kids were fast asleep. When Robbie answered the phone and heard about the 'accident' he and Cissy called for a taxi and rushed over to Ann's house but the ambulance had already been and gone. Michael explained that the ambulance crew had assessed the situation and would only allow one person to accompany the patient. Ann had insisted it was Wheelie. The McKennas realised that Michael was on the verge of some sort of breakdown and was in no fit state to go to the hospital. They suggested that he accompany them in the same taxi and drop him off for a cooling down period at their house. They would then make their way to the hospital to check on his mother. Surely Liz could sort him out with a cup of sweet tea or even something stronger if required.

Liz was more than willing to help out and her parents were soon on their way to the hospital. As soon as Liz mentioned a hot mug of tea Michael went into one, yet again, so she poured him a large brandy to help calm the situation. When he sat down on the stool at the bar Liz noticed that his hands were still shaking a little and his shirt was absolutely soaked in sweat and it also had small blood stains down the front. Well, he downed the large brandy and was soon sipping another when Liz suggested that he could go to the bathroom and use one of the bath towels to dry off and she would provide one of her brother's spare shirts to make a quick change. He nodded his approval and made his way there. When he was inside he couldn't help but notice that his lower lip was slightly swollen and he had a small bruise under his right eye. Wheelie must have given a better account of himself than Michael had given him credit for. 'Little fucker!'

He took off his sweat-soaked shirt, turned on the taps of the sink and proceeded to throw the water over his head, around his torso and under his arms but was not achieving a great deal apart from soaking the floor. He decided to strip off completely and jumped into the shower for a well-deserved lukewarm drench. Meanwhile Liz was returning with the spare shirt and noticed the bathroom door was slightly ajar, gave a quick knock and walked in. To say that she was shocked was an understatement. She didn't expect him to be completely naked! She made a humble apology and retraced her steps back into the hall still holding the shirt. Michael wasn't even slightly perturbed and just produced a silly little grin, the one that had always worked wonders in the past.

Liz couldn't help herself and just had to have another little peep through the hinge crack on the door. It wasn't a peep at all but a long, lingering look at this hunk of a man, who had a muscular chest and shoulders, the cutest ass and the prettiest dick she had ever seen. His thighs were doing summersaults with her hormones. She didn't know if it was the alcohol or the lack of sexual activity or a combination of both, but she just wanted to shag his fucking brains out, right there and then.

Michael knew she was there and put on a soap, sponged-filled show of eroticism, making sure that he was arousing himself. He looked at the slightly open door and gave a cheeky little wink and said: 'Why don't you come in and join me? You know you want to, don't you?'

Liz sallied into the bathroom staring at the bronze-coloured, sex on legs spectacle. She dropped the shirt to the floor and began to undress. Her baggy sweat top, sports leggings and underwear soon found their way alongside the shirt, as she revealed her sexy voluptuous figure that she had managed to maintain even after having four kids. Her wanton gaze of lust and passion never allowed her eyes to waiver from his now erect manhood. She stepped into the shower and they immediately embraced.

French kissing, biting and clawing were soon to follow. Suddenly he picked her up by her bum cheeks and she instinctively wrapped her legs around his taught waist and he entered her without further delay. He rested her body weight easily on his love handles and bent his knees slightly so as to manoeuvre his joystick to and fro, slowly at first and then he began to pound her for all he was worth. She cried out, not in pain but in sheer frenzy, until he began to thrust so hard that when they both climaxed together, it was like a ballistic missile in full throttle.

They remained entwined while the water continued to pour over them until he eased her down, gently releasing himself from her hot soft pouch. Without saying a word, Liz stepped out of the shower and wrapped herself in another towel from the rail. She had her back to him at first until she glanced over her shoulder and said, 'I must check the kids. I'll be back in a minute.'

To which Michael replied, 'Don't worry, I'm not going anywhere.'

Liz satisfied herself that her four boys were all still sound asleep and returned to the bathroom. Michael was sitting on the toilet with the lid fully down. He had placed a towel underneath himself for comfort but was still completely naked and most astonishing of all he was still fully at the gallop. She couldn't believe her eyes! She let the towel slip to the floor to join the already untidy heap and once again without saying a word, she mounted him but this time it was reverse cowboy. This time she was the dominating factor. She laid the palms of her hands on his knees so she could control the rhythm of her conquest. He nipped and caressed her nipples and gently bit her back as she slowly began to ride his erect pulsing muscle. Once again, in only a very short period of time they released their bodily fluids and once again remained coupled. It was a bit of an effort in both cases when they decided to stand up to engage in a long French kiss. Michael knew he was living up to his newfound status in the States. He was known as, MCP: Major Chick Puller!

Suddenly Liz came to her senses. She stepped into the shower once more for less than five minutes, before drying herself off and insisted that Michael did the same. She redressed in her sports attire and before they knew it, they were both back at the bar in the kitchen/lounge with Michael wearing the spare shirt, which was ground zero of the whole escapade. They made a little small talk until her parents arrived home about thirty minutes later.

CHAPTER 10

CISSY EXPLAINED THAT ANN was being kept in hospital overnight but would most likely be discharged the following morning after the duty doctor had examined her on his rounds. She also went on to say, Ann wanted everyone to be assured, it was just a silly accident that happened after one too many drinks at the restaurant. Wheelie was staying for another little while just to keep her company and would then take a taxi home. Robbie and Liz would collect her once she phoned to say that she was ready for pick up in the morning and see her home safe and sound. Michael was mighty relieved to say the least, and although Robbie invited him to stay the night, he insisted on going home to be there when his mum arrived back the following morning. A few minutes later he was in a taxi heading for home. He didn't know if he could call it that any more, what with the bloody window cleaner moving in and soon making himself at home.

The following morning Robbie, Liz and Ann arrived at Ann's house just after ten o'clock. Would you believe it? Michael was still in bed! Ann opened the door with her key and although she invited her friends in for a cuppa, they politely declined with the idea that Michael would want to make a fuss of his mum, after all she had been through. After a few moments Ann climbed the stairs to Michael's room. She barged in without apology and demanded, 'Get up and get down those bloody stairs unless you want to be shown the bloody door! Right fucking now!'

It was the first time in his entire life he had heard his mother swear. He was downstairs in his boxers and t-shirt in double quick time. Big as he was, Ann was determined to show him who was boss. She stood in the middle of her sitting room and laid into him like a woman possessed. Michael began to make excuses for his behaviour but Ann was absolutely relentless.

'Shut up, Michael,' she shouted. 'Now you bloody listen

to me. My right cheek is still red in colour and tender to touch. My right eyeball is also bloodshot. The nurse and doctor both told me, had I not instinctively shut my eye when the hot tea was coming in my direction, I would be in a serious condition and would certainly not have been discharged this morning.'

Michael stood there like the big wet shite that he was. He was hoping that his mother would soon calm down, like she used to when he was still at school and even at university, but she was having none of it. She produced a tube of antiseptic cream and eye drops and continued:

'I will need to apply these medications for the rest of the week and I have to make an appointment with my GP for follow up checks until further notice. A fine fucking mess! And you also had the audacity, the bloody audacity, to turn your nose up in front of everyone in the restaurant, when I announced my intention to marry Wheelie. You ungrateful little, no, you, ungrateful big shite! I have put you first and foremost since the day and hour your father passed away. Now that you're up and running it's my turn to invest in some happiness in my latter years. You selfish, arrogant, inconsiderate twat of a son!'

He tried to mutter some sort of an apology but Ann stopped him in his tracks.

'Shut up, Michael, and stop being so bloody pathetic. Keep your eyes and ears open and your fucking mouth shut. Got it? I've known from the day you were born that I made a rod for my own back. Even your late father, God bless him, even your late father would have a go at me in his own gentle way, for not sticking to my guns when you behaved badly. I always gave in to you but no more. No fucking more. Do you hear me?'

The big shite just nodded.

Ann added: 'Now, Wheelie and I are to be married early in the New Year. You will receive an invitation but if you decide that you can't or won't make it then that's up to you. He will move in with me. Do you hear me? He will move in with me, on return from our honeymoon which will be somewhere hot and bloody steamy. He will rent out his little flat and we will both continue to keep our full-time jobs until further notice but we may cut our hours sooner rather than later. I know that you have been earning good money on the music circuit over in the States so you won't need any further subsidies from dear old muggings here. Right?'

She did not give him time to answer.

'Furthermore, I will not be giving you a lift to the airport tomorrow for your return flight. You can pay for your own taxi, for a bloody change! Now, one last thing, there will be no one visiting today as everyone apart from Wheelie are under the impression that we, yes we, are having a quiet mother and son day prior to your departure. I know that you don't normally do verbal apologies very well however I will accept one in writing. I will hopefully calm down as the day goes on but you can pay for a takeaway later and we will leave it at that for now.'

Ann turned away from her son to disguise the hurt she felt for them both and there was complete silence. Complete silence. Avoiding eye contact she made one final statement as he turned to make his way back to his room, 'I still love you, but at this moment in time, I don't like you very much.'

With the festive season behind them once more the McKennas were riding high. The most talked about wedding of the millennium between Ann and Wheelie was scheduled for Saturday 12 January 2012, with their honeymoon to be spent on a fortnight Caribbean cruise. Lenny had made it home for Christmas but as usual spent New Year with his mates in Portsmouth. There was still no mention of anyone special in his life, although Liz and he got a little tipsy on one occasion and she did try very hard to get him to spill the beans but, alas not. Gino and Sharon paid a visit over Christmas but were back at sea again for the New Year. Lou and her husband George were living the dream... Yawn... Sam and Pam were going steady with two guys who worked in the same branch of the local estate agents. Randolph and Andrew... AKA: Randy and Andy!

Ann's son wasn't able to make the wedding but

promised to make up for it on his annual trip home in August later that year. The biggest surprise of all was when Ann proudly announced to all her friends one Saturday night in the Irish Club in Croydon, that Wheelie insisted in doing the honourable thing by paying every penny himself for their wedding and honeymoon, and if Ann didn't like it, he would go on his own. The place was in absolute stitches. He also insisted that she kept her married name that she had for all those years. She would be known as: Mrs. Wishbone-Ferris. Ann and everyone present were absolutely delighted.

'After all,' Wheelie said. 'It's the least I can do, as I am an old-fashioned gentleman.'

Apparently, he had quite a healthy bank account. He had never been out of work since he left school at fifteen and had his own window cleaning business for almost forty years. He was always careful with his money, although he was never backward about being forward, when it came to buying a few drinks.

Liz never gave Michael much thought after their clandestine encounter the previous August. Well, if the truth be known his face, amongst other things did crop up, the emphasis being on the word up, on several occasions, especially coming up to Christmas. They had satisfied each other. As far as she was concerned, he had served a purpose on that fateful night and if the opportunity rose again, she would certainly give it serious consideration. She knew that he would have no regrets as she was just another notch on his love torch, but what a fucking notch, and what a fucking torch.

The baggy sportswear that she constantly wore helped to hide the extra weight that had crept on. She had to buy a bigger size outfit for the wedding and wrap herself up in a pair of control briefs with a high waist, in other words, big fucking, hold-me-in knickers. It wasn't just the overindulgence at Christmas and New Year, it was, yes, you've got it in one, she was five months pregnant!

Ann and Wheelie's wedding was a real blast for all concerned. It was a registry office service with almost one hundred guests. The registrar nearly had a fit when he looked up over his small steel rimmed glasses, and saw the masses squeezing into his office. He said it reminded him of his student days at university, when he and a big crowd of friends tried to break the local record for the amount of people who could squeeze into a Mini Cooper!

The wedding reception was held in the Ambassador, four-star Hotel in West Croydon. It must have cost an absolute fortune but no one seemed to be counting the pennies, least of all Wheelie. Liz had her hands full with her four boys but granny and granddad, Uncle Benny and Aunt Julie where always close at hand. Some of the wedding party, including the bride and groom, made it through to five o'clock in the morning, when they all tucked into a fry-up with bucks-fizz!

Liz knew that she would soon need to let the cat out of the bag but would wait until a few days after the wedding, when the happy couple would be well and truly on their honeymoon. She knew point blank that the baby was Michael's. But how in God's name was she going to explain this one to her parents? What a fool she had been. A well satisfied fool, but a bloody stupid fool, all the same.

She had been on the pill for years, even had a coil fitted, but that bloody coil was so uncomfortable. Even if she missed taking the pill she would always take an extra one, even the morning after pill, all of them. She had taken that many pills at one time she felt like a tube of Smarties. She could shake, rattle and roll! But when the urge came, she lost all sense of control and a state of insanity kicked in, until it was all over and it was too late to rewind. Was she a closet nymph? Well, fuck me pink! Robbie hit the absolute roof when Liz announced the good news! He nearly grabbed her by the throat but Cissy stepped in.

He couldn't help himself when he shouted, 'Another mouth to feed and who's going to help you to take care of it? Eh?'

Cissy was in agreement and nodded her head and then, politely asked, 'Who's the father, Liz?'

Robbie joined in, 'Yes, Liz, who's the father this time? Do you even know who the father is? Eenie... Meany... Miney... Mo. Catch our Lizzy by the toe. When she screams, give her a go. What will we call this one, Mike or Joe?'

Liz sat in silence during the onslaught, which continued for quite some time, but she did hide a little smile, for her dad hadn't realised how close he had come to the truth about the name of the child's father. Robbie was now pacing up and down and eventually Cissy calmed him down with a family measure of Irish whiskey. He sat on the bar stool and stared at the floor. Cissy poured herself a large Vodka and Coke and stood beside her husband with one arm around his drooping shoulders. Liz was nursing a half-empty mug of cold tea. She didn't dare take the risk, asking for a refill. After a prolonged period of silence Liz stood up and said, 'Listen, Mum and Dad. I know more than anything that I've really upset you both, so I'll toddle on home for now and maybe, if you want to, we can carry on this conversation a little later.'

Robbie raised his head slightly and growled, 'Yeah, much fucking later.'

Over the next ten days or so Liz kept herself to herself. Her four sons certainly kept her busy and it has to be said that she was not getting any smaller. As per her previous pregnancies, she didn't show that much until about the six-month period but this bump was much bigger, even more so than the twins. When she and her parents crossed paths and sometimes crossed words over the new arrival, Liz promised them that she would reveal all in her own good time. What she didn't say was that she was waiting for Ann and Wheelie to return from their honeymoon, which they duly did.

Liz gave it another couple of days for them to settle in and then unbeknown to her parents, invited them to her own house to tell them about the impending birth and the part that Michael played in creating the child. Liz thought that it would be better to tell Ann and Wheelie before telling her parents. It may help to ease the unpleasant confrontation between the two couples who had been great friends for years. Ann and Wheelie were delighted to accept their first invitation as a couple to an outing since they had become husband and wife. When they arrived on that rainy February afternoon Liz welcomed them with open arms and a tray full of fancy cakes and a pot of tea. The newly-married couple could well notice the bulge under Liz's sports shirt but did not venture an opinion. They just smiled at each other and sat down on the sofa that Liz had proffered.

Formality soon went by the way-side and Liz began to recite the well-rehearsed scenario, that had gone through her head so many times before but in the end, she just blurted it all out. Of course, she left out the nitty-gritty bits. Ann and Wheelie were gobsmacked! The only thing that Ann said was: 'Please, Liz. Don't take offence but are you absolutely sure that Michael is the father?'

'I'm willing to take a DNA test.'

'That may be the case, if Michael denies that the child is his.'

Wheelie never said a word but knew in his heart of hearts that Michael was indeed the guilty party.

For him to do something like that, on the night he assaulted both he and his mother was right up his street. Ann would be better off without that spoilt overgrown brat! But as they say, life must go on.

The next question on Ann's lips was, 'Have you told your mum and dad who the father is?'

'Not yet. I was hoping to break the news to them with you and Wheelie in tow, so I might have a little bit of support?'

Ann raised her head and looked straight into Liz's eyes and said, 'You flatter yourself, Liz. An unmarried woman with four bastard children already, who wants to put her claws into a tall, handsome, talented young man, with a fantastic future in the world of classical music. We'll need more than just your word for it to be taken seriously.'

Wheelie, who wouldn't normally say boo to a goose, piped up and said, 'Ann! You and I both know what your son is capable of. He's a liar, he's a bully and he's an opportunist who preyed on a very vulnerable and impressionable young single mum, when she was trying to be kind because his own mum had been taken to hospital in a fucking ambulance, because of an injury that he deliberately caused. Never mind the fact that he tried to do me in as well! If we need a DNA test, then let's be having one. I'm sure that Liz will be proved right.'

'Thank you, Wheelie,' Liz said. 'But it wasn't all Michael's fault. We both took our chances and we were both consenting adults, who knew exactly what we were doing, or what we should not have been doing. I've asked for nothing and I want nothing. I just thought that Ann should know that she would soon be a granny, or a grandma, whichever way she wants to put it.'

Ann's anger and defiance began to melt and with a little tear in her eye she murmured: 'I'm sorry, Liz. It's the same old story. A mother always defends her children, good or bad. Please forgive me for my cruel comments.'

'Don't worry yourself, Ann. When my boys grow up, I will probably be guilty of the same.'

A little while later Ann and Wheelie said their goodbyes and drove home. Wheelie kept the conversation light-hearted and even joined in with the song that was playing on the car radio.

Ann was still stunned by Liz's revelation, but hid it well. Her main concern was the McKennas' reaction to the identity of the baby's father. It may well put their long-term friendship to the test.

Liz decided there and then to visit her parents' house two days later, on Saturday afternoon. It would give Ann time to decide if she and Wheelie would be in attendance to offer a little support and Liz was delighted when Ann had told her that they would both be there. Blast off was to be at three o'clock so Liz intended to arrive at half past two, lash the kids into the spare room with a bin-full of toys and sweets to keep them busy. She had already told her parents that she would divulge the identity of the baby's father and she would also like Benny and Julie to be there. She planned to clear the decks in one foul sweep and to hell with the consequences. She hoped that the presence of her four boys in the same house would quell any mud-slinging that may raise its ugly head.

Robbie, Cissy, Benny, Julie and Liz were all seated in the living room, which wasn't used very often, but Liz decided that was where the unavoidable was to take place. All five of them sat in silence as if they were in a doctor's waiting room when the front door bell sounded.

'Who the hell's that?' muttered Robbie.

'It's the parents of my baby's father,' quipped Liz. 'The other grandparents?'

Well, that little wise crack certainly got the other four to look up and pay attention.

Liz then, as brisk as you please, made her way to the front door and welcomed Ann and Wheelie with a little kiss and a hug before signalling to them to shush, by placing her index finger on her lips followed by a cheeky little wink. As far as she was concerned, she had nothing to lose. In the words of one of her mum's favourite songs, 'It's all or nothing'.

As soon as the trio walked into the sitting room the other four stood up in unison and could only muster a wide-eyed gasp.

Robbie asked, 'Is this some sort of joke?'

Liz quickly replied. 'No, it certainly is not. Ann's son, Michael, is the father of my new baby and Wheelie is Michael's new stepfather so that's why they're both here.'

Robbie's face was beginning to contort with rage at the flippant manner in which Liz was behaving, when Cissy defused the situation by offering everyone a nice cup of tea.

'Fuck the tea,' snarled Robbie. No one present had ever seen this mean side of him, not even his brother, who was beginning to have doubts as to whether he could keep a lid on the whole thing.

Ann tried to say some words of comfort to everyone but Robbie was having none of it. He stared at Liz and said.

'Are you telling me that my new, so-called grandchild is the offspring of Ann's son? Some sort of a fucking half-chat? Eh?

Tears began to trickle from Ann's eyes as Wheelie put his arm around her shoulders. Liz didn't say a word. The other three were as totally astounded at Robbie's mealy-mouthed outburst. He added, 'I'm not going to even ask when or where, because you are capable of shagging anyone, anywhere. Have you no scruples whatsoever? Don't you have a fucking conscience?'

Cissy could feel her husband's pain, looked her daughter straight in the eye and added, 'Liz. Have you no shame? Baby number five with four different fathers and none of the fathers anywhere in sight.'

Liz seized her chance for she knew it would come eventually.

'Shame, Mother? Shame on you and your dirty little secrets!'

'What's she on about, Cissy?'

'Don't pay her any mind, Robbie. She doesn't even know what she's saying.'

'Don't I, Mother? What about you, Julie? Haven't you anything to say?'

The atmosphere was certainly reaching boiling point to say the least. Julie and Cissy both were really beginning to feel the heat, when Julie said, 'Now then, let's not allow this whole thing to get out of hand. Come on, Robbie, why don't you and Benny go into our house next door for a drink. Try and calm down a bit and sure we'll look after Ann and Wheelie in here.'

Benny agreed, 'Come on, bro. Just give it a few minutes. You'll feel better after a stiff drink.'

With that, they both ambled out of the room and made their way next door. Cissy signalled for Wheelie and Ann to sit down and asked Liz to put the kettle on. Ann still had tears in her eyes and Wheelie still held her close. Cissy said that she would check on the kids and gave Julie the nod to follow her. After quickly looking in on the four boys, who were still happily playing and munching sweets, they stepped into the hallway and spoke in whispers.

'Oh, to be a fly on that wall,' thought Liz as she had a little smirk, for she knew when to take her chance and what to say. Her mother and Julie would have to come up with a plan to keep Liz from mentioning any more of the unmentionables. They would, rightly or wrongly, have to turn the tide in her favour. Of that she had no doubt.

Meanwhile next door the two brothers were sitting with their drinks saying very little, apart from the odd grunt from Robbie as Benny tried desperately to cheer him up.

'Look, Robbie, come on, it's not the end of the world. One more won't make that much difference, will it?

'That's easy for you to say. She's going to have a fucking half breed and it, yes fucking it, will stand out like a hard-on in a fucking nunnery compared to the other four. They've all got light-brown hair and blue eyes and God only knows what the latest one is going to look like, brown with greasy black fucking hair?'

'Look, mate. Let's not jump to any conclusions. The father is a half-chat, so that makes the new baby, a-half-a-half-chat, a-quarter-chat. I think? Right, so, it might not be that bad. Anyway, there are lots of kids running around like that these days.'

Robbie sneered once again and added, 'Yes you're right, there are lots of kids running around like that these days, but they don't belong to fucking me.'

'Look, Robbie. The baby will belong to all of us. Come on. Let's go back before we have too much to drink.'

On their return to the sitting room next door they found Cissy and Julie fussing over Ann and Wheelie. Giving words of comfort, strong sweet tea and biscuits and they were both absolutely fawning over poor, poor Liz.

'Dear, dear me. What a performance,' thought Liz. 'A night at the fucking Oscars.'

The two men looked at each other as if they had walked into the wrong house. Cissy quickly topped up their drinks and to everyone's surprise background music appeared.

Well now, aided and abetted by Julie, Cissy continued the charade. They were most insistent that everyone should join in the celebration of the new arrival, until they were all pretty much the worse for wear. By that stage they had moved into the open plan bar area where upon, the two conniving sisters-in-law were showing off the four wonderful boys who were now the stars of the show. They were showered with hugs and kisses by the dozen, supported by little corny phrases like: 'Aren't they just gorgeous? Sure, one more, boy or girl will fit right in. It'll all work out in the end. We should be grateful that the baby arrives fit and well. You'll soon be a granny, Ann. And you, Wheelie, I bet you never thought you'd ever be a granddad, eh? Drink up everyone.'

Liz was keeping one eye on her boys and one eye on her scheming mother and aunt. They were a right fucking pair, that's for sure. Her father and uncle were like putty in their hands as were Ann and poor old Wheelie, who was definitely on a roll. Liz took her boys off to bed almost unnoticed and left them all to it. Later in the night she heard the sound of goodbyes, sloppy kisses, big hugs, best wishes, taxi doors, front and back doors and finally, her parents staggering down the hall to bed. The four kids never heard a thing. Cissy and Julie had certainly done the stitch up job of the decade, that's for sure.

A few days later, after long and detailed deliberations, Ann and Wheelie decided that they would not reduce their working hours after all. They would simply retire from work completely, period. They both realised that the dust wouldn't settle anytime soon regarding Liz and the new arrival. The bad feeling about Michael being the father was of much greater concern but Wheelie assured her that once the baby arrived Robbie would come round. Ann smiled and was so grateful that her husband had become her rock in such a short period of time. She loved him to bits. He would explain to the McKennas, that they now had the bug for cruising and that's what they intended to do, while they still had their faculties or until either of them popped their clogs.

Ann couldn't help but smile with relief as her man always seemed to have the answers these days. In his own words: 'There's no such fings as problems any more, just solutions, my love.'

The McKennas met in the board room at the head office of MKE Ltd. It was almost the end of February 2012 and Ann's position of personnel director needed to be filled before her departure at the end of March, just in time for the new tax year. Lou would fill the post but would still oversee the smooth running of head office. Sam and Pam would take it in turns to make themselves available two days a week to learn the job of office manager, and hopefully one of them would take the reins from Lou in the not-too-distant future. Lou was over the moon with her hard-earned promotion and had often wondered why it had taken so long. After all, Ann was getting on a bit. Lou just knew that she was born to be a director, even a managing director? None of the twins were particularly keen on Robbie's plan but he insisted that if they wanted to progress in MKE they would have to learn new tricks. He stipulated:

'No more fucking outsiders, end of fucking story!'

Meanwhile Liz informed everyone that the baby was due in early June. When Ann had given her son the news of his offspring over the phone, he denied it ever happened. He accused Liz of being a gold digger.

'She knows full well of my potential in the world of classical music. She knows full well of my talent. She knows full well that I will soon be on my way to the Boston Philharmonic Orchestra. She knows full well what a catch I am... She knew full well what she was doing.'

That one little slip of the tongue sealed his fate, 'She knew full well what she was doing?'

Ann began to roar down the phone.

'Stop right there! You lying fucking toe-rag. If it didn't happen, how come she knew full well what she was doing? How do you know what she was doing? And how come she knows full well all about your future, when you've hardly spoken but a few words over the years. What was it you once said? "She was easy meat".

'I remember full well, threatening to wash your mouth out with soap when you bloody said that. Remember? Bare-faced liars need a good memory and yours is fucking shite!'

There was silence from Stateside and then Ann insisted that on his return in August that year, he would be subject to a DNA test. Silence once again, followed by the tone of Stateside, hanging up.

Wheelie muttered under his breath, 'Absolute, big fucking wanker, of the highest degree.'

Ann said, 'I bloody heard that, and I fucking agree.'

The changes at MKE head office seemed to go according to plan, however the twins had to be pressured into Robbie's plan almost on a daily basis until he wore them down. He seemed to have acquired a sense of dictatorship in the weeks that followed Ann's departure. She and Wheelie were lapping up their newfound freedom and although they were booked onto another cruise in September, this time for two weeks around the Mediterranean, they had mini-breaks and days out all over the country. Ann insisted that they were not to be too far away when their first and possibly their only grandchild arrived in early June. She found it hard to imagine Michael committing to anything apart from himself.

By the middle of May, Liz had grown to the size of a small country. Back pains, stomach pains, thumping headaches and undependable bowels made life very difficult. Cissy, Julie and sometimes Benny were there to help but Robbie gave the whole situation a wide birth, to coin a phrase. Cissy found the need to stay overnight at Liz's house on many occasions, such was the discomfort and stress that this latest pregnancy had brought with it. Liz couldn't get her head round the fact that this time it was all so different. The previous four came and went like a dream. Her GP, who was from Dublin, remarked that she was able to fart them out with little or no effort but this time it was like the pregnancy from hell. All the check-ups revealed nothing except it was going to be a big bundle when it arrived. In the past Liz never worried whether it was going to be a boy or a girl, but she knew on this occasion it was going to be a big payload being delivered by mother nature. She sensed that it would be a mammoth task with a great deal of blood, sweat and tears.

When she was lying down during the bouts of discomfort, she felt just a little afraid, although she told no one, especially her father. He would just say that it was God punishing her for all the trouble she had brought upon him and her mother. He would also harp on about how well her brother was doing in the Navy. He also praised her three cousins who were forging great careers in the family business when all Liz could do was part her legs. She never before in her life felt so distant from her father. Would they ever be close again? She doubted it. But hey, who could blame him?

By the 15 June, Liz had still not delivered. She had been in and out of hospital with false alarms that often, the nurses had nick-named her, 'False Alarm Liz'. But on the morning of the 16 June when she arrived once again by ambulance, the doctors decided that she would not be going home until the baby finally arrived, which they believed would be sooner rather than later. Once again, she was examined thoroughly but this time it was not good news. The baby had manoeuvred itself to a sideways position with head uppermost and because of its size, a caesarean section would be the safest option. Liz was in such distress that the anaesthetist put her under. Her parents were asked to sign the consent form before the procedure could be performed. This was the first time Robbie had shown any emotion. He began to tremble at the thought of them cutting his daughter open. The surgeon assured them that all would be well but they needed to act immediately or complications may arise. When Liz finally came to, she was in the recovery room. She glanced to her left and there in a cot was the most beautiful baby she had ever laid eyes on, beautiful and rather large to say the least.

At the end of the bed stood a nurse with a very reassuring

smile who asked, 'Would you like to hold your new son? He's a well-built boy who's strong and healthy. He weighed in at twelve pounds exactly, on arrival.'

Liz didn't need to be asked a second time. As she pulled back the wrap from his head and shoulders she could only gaze in wonder at her fifth son. Meanwhile, Robbie and Benny were sitting in the waiting room along the corridor from Liz while their wives had gone to pick up tea and biscuits from the cafe. All four had been close by, all the way through the birth. At one stage they thought they were going to lose them both. The two couples had also gazed in wonder at the new arrival while Liz was still sedated, for he was not at all what they had expected to see. He had light-brown hair and blue eyes just like his four brothers. His skin, although very slightly darker than his siblings', would not necessarily make him stand out in a crowd. This brought a great big smile and an even greater big sigh of relief from Robbie.

'You know something, Robbie? You'd never know, would you?'

'You're dead right, Benny. You'd never know, would you?'

'Not unless you knew, Robbie, but who's going to know, that doesn't know, who needs to know?'

'You're dead right, Benny. If you didn't know, you wouldn't know so, who gives a fuck who doesn't know?'

'We all know, Robbie, but that doesn't matter right now. The only thing that matters is that they are both doing great, right?'

'You're absolutely right, Benny. And most important of all, you still wouldn't know if you didn't know.'

'You know what I know, Robbie?'

'No, what do you know, Benny?'

'Fuck the tea and biscuits, Robbie. We're going to wet the baby's head, that's what I fucking know. Know what I mean, Robbie?'

'I know exactly what you mean, Benny.'

When Cissy and Julie returned to the waiting room their

husbands where nowhere to be seen but a small scribbled note was pinned to the small message board on the wall by the door. It read:

'Robbie and Benny have gone to put the kettle on, in the nearest pub! Don't wait up!'

The McKennas were as close as ever. That's for sure.

After a few days' convalescence, Liz and the newborn arrived home to big cheers and even bigger smiles from her four sons who couldn't and wouldn't wait, to give their baby brother a big hug. Of course, Cissy and Julie were in support, with promises from Robbie and Benny that they would be there as soon as work allowed. The whole scene around the house was that of complete mayhem but nobody seemed to care. Unbeknown to anyone, Liz was so relieved that her newborn, who she had decided to name Michael, looked so much like his brothers. Her dad was right. There would definitely have been a problem later in life, especially at school, if he had looked more like Michael senior. She understood now exactly where he was coming from and she forgave him for all the nasty things that he had said before the birth. He was understandingly angry with her for putting herself in such an uncompromising situation, which could well have ended in tears for everyone, not least of all her five sons.

On Saturday 25th of August, another McKenna hooley was had, after another McKenna christening service. It was decided to have it in around the two McKenna homes, just like at Christmas and because of the great weather they had a bouncy castle in Robbie's back garden. They could keep the guest list exclusively for family and close friends. If they had it elsewhere then the possibility of gossip gatecrashers, with their snide remarks about the arrival of Liz's fifth son and the lack of another father would be avoided. Ann and Wheelie were over the moon that they had both been invited and Ann was beside herself with pride as she posed with baby Michael for photographs. Wheelie had a permanent smile from ear to ear, ably assisted with the large amount of alcohol he managed to consume throughout the day. At about four in the afternoon while the party was in full swing, Ann's mobile phone rang. On first glance she could see it was her son Michael's number. She quickly found a quiet spot in the garden, away from all the commotion and answered his call and without giving him a chance to speak, she gushed:

'Oh Michael, I'm so glad you called. I knew you would. Wait until you see your son. You will definitely have a change of mind about not having anything to do with him when you see just how beautiful he is.'

'I'm sorry, Mrs Wishbone... I mean Mrs, Ferris... I mean... This is Michael's roommate Morgan O'Neill. I'm from South Carolina. We share an apartment?'

Ann cut in, 'I know who you are but where is Michael?'

'I'm sorry, ma'am—'

'Oh for pity's sake put my son on this phone right now!'

'I can't do that, ma'am. He's been in a car accident... Early this morning. He was taken to the hospital. That's where I'm calling from right now. I'm sorry, ma'am, but he didn't make it.'

'What? What are you saying?'

'Michael died as the result of his injuries, ma'am. I'm so sorry, ma'am.'

The line went quiet.

'Hello, ma'am. Are you still there?'

Cissy found Ann lying face down and thought she had fainted because of all the excitement, until she picked up the mobile phone that was next to her on the grass.

In the following few days Ann was busying herself organising flights for her and Wheelie to Boston. Formal identification of Michael's body and his repatriation to Croydon took longer than anyone could have anticipated. Autopsy and accident reports and the necessary transportation of Michael's coffin seemed to take forever but Ann soldiered on. She was more than pleased that there was no trace of alcohol or drugs in his system, contrary to common belief among those in authority in Boston. Michael was alone in the car and had driven that mountain road to and fro on many occasions while visiting his girlfriend Celina. Her family had a small cabin that she and Michael would sometimes escape to when it was free. There was no sign of skid marks at the point of leaving the mountain road and he would have been killed instantly on impact at the bottom of a deep ravine. The reason for his early return to Boston that Saturday morning was that he was performing with three of his fellow students, at a formal art exhibition at eleven o'clock in the city centre. The general census of opinion was that he lost control of the car due to being momentarily blinded or possibly falling asleep at the wheel in the strong early morning sunshine. The unofficial finding was 'accidental death.' This would be most likely confirmed by the verdict of the official inquest, which was to follow in due course.

Nearly four weeks passed after Ann's return. She managed to get her son home for his funeral, which was attended by many locals and the greater family circle including his girlfriend, Celina who had travelled from Boston on her own. Robbie, Benny, Cissy and Julie were amongst the mourners, but Liz decided to give it a miss. She stayed at home that Saturday morning enjoying the company of her five sons, paying particular attention to baby Michael. She thought that it was a strange coincidence that Michael was killed on a Saturday morning and was also laid to rest on a Saturday morning. Out of her five sons, the youngest was the only one that had any chance of knowing his father, and now he was dead and buried. It could certainly be a cruel world, but keep the head up and meet what tomorrow brings and get on with life.

CHAPTER 11

WITH CHRISTMAS NOT FAR AWAY, the McKennas were as busy as ever. Liz had several follow up appointments with the hospital and her local GP. The complications that had arisen prior to and during the caesarean section, resulted in the surgeon making what may have been a life and death decision. To ensure both baby and mother came through it alive and well he found it necessary to remove her uterus. This meant that she would not be able to have any more children. Liz accepted this from day one but the medical team needed to emphasize the necessity of that decision and satisfy themselves that there would be no come backs from Liz or any of her family. Belt and braces for everyone concerned. When Robbie realised what this all meant for sure, he couldn't help but make a wry comment to Benny:

'No more surprises for me, bro. Eh?'

Benny smiled and replied, 'For sure. I think five is more than enough. Eh?'

Cissy and Julie also had wry smiles on their faces. No more babies meant there would be no more blackmail scenarios to worry about. They were planning their next adventure in a large country house near Guildford in Surrey. Daphne Delores de Courtney had been in touch again and her husband Simion was just dying to see them both. Preparations were under way for a tryst early in the new year. Another weekend away at a country hotel for both wives, sometime towards the end of January 2013, after a busy festive season it would do them the world of good. They would book into the said hotel on a Friday and return home on the Sunday, having spent Saturday night languishing in the very large Surrey residence of the de Courtney's. No holds barred.

June 16th was Michael's first birthday. Steven was now over eight years old, Connor six and a half years old with Ryan and Anthony over four years old. They had a similar get-together as they had done for Michaels christening, all round to the McKenna family homes and yes, with another bouncy castle. Robbie and Benny were bouncing away almost as much as the kids. On this occasion some of their friends from school were there which bolstered the numbers up considerably, but all the adults mucked in and the afternoon just flew by. Lenny made the trip up from Portsmouth as he had returned from his posting in Gibraltar the previous year and was promoted to petty officer second class. Hopefully he would be on the move again the following year, attached to the US Navy in Miami Florida. Further promotion was definitely on the cards. What a life.

Meanwhile, cousin Lou was so far up her own arse she stunk of shite but Sam and Pam were planning a double wedding for 2014. The twins were still great friends with Liz and absolutely adored her sons. Ann and Wheelie paid frequent visits to Liz's home and made equal fuss of all five boys. But poor old Liz was sometimes getting near the end of her tether. During school term Michael was the only son at home in the mornings. Steven and Connor were at primary school all day, Ryan and Anthony were at pre-school until noon but there still didn't seem to be enough hours in the day to have any Liz time. She was twenty-eight years of age and she felt permanently worn out. She also knew that most of the time she didn't look her best. Who would take a second glance at a single mother with five kids? But as she had often heard it said: 'You made your own bed, so you can lie in it!'

Christmas Day that year would prove to be much more of a mad house than usual. Contrary to all previous years, Liz decided that it was time for her and the boys to spend Christmas Eve in their own beds, as it would be a great idea for her sons to waken up in their own house on Christmas morning and not at their grandparent's house. Selfish or not, she wanted the whole exciting episode of jumping out of bed and unwrapping their presents, to be shared just between them in their own home. They would join the remainder of the family in their own good time and stay over until Boxing Day. Her dad would have to stay off the drink until he arrived in his car to help Liz to transport the boys from her house to his, making use of both cars.

However, there was one extra guest on that particular year. It was a nephew on Julie's side of the family who in fact had been in the same class at school as Liz's brother Lenny. His name was Davy Beggs. Liz remembered that Lenny and his mates used to call him Daft Davy. He wasn't the sharpest tool in the box, just a complete tool. He had been on brief visits before but Liz always seemed to miss him. He wanted to see for himself how the other half of the family celebrated Christmas, as Robbie and Benny had always boasted that they threw the best family Christmas party in Croydon and it has to be said, he was not disappointed. He gave a lot of time to Liz's boys and could sing along with the karaoke as good as anyone else. His greatest feat of the day was jiving with Cissy and Julie at the same time. He had them bouncing all around the floor, sometimes in different directions. The cheers and hand-clapping by young and old were second to none. Although he had that scruffy, shaggy look, his dark curly hair and blue eyes made him slightly interesting if not a little attractive. He had the knack of growing on people.

The following morning, he made time to speak to Liz on a personal note. He showed genuine interest on how she made ends meet and how as a single mum she managed to keep house with five active boys to look after. He asked about her social life or lack of it. Did she still have to depend on her parents to help out with holidays, oh yes, and the car? He asked a very pertinent question: Had there ever been a time when she didn't have to depend on her parents for hand-outs? Liz gave a very, embarrassed shake of the head. She smiled and thanked him for his concern and he assured her that if she ever wanted to turn her life around and gain her independence back, then he would be willing to help out. She wasn't too sure how he could do that but she said that she would bear his very kind offer in mind.

In the New Year of 2014 Steven and Connor both asked

their mum if they could take up after school activities, such as music lessons. Liz was slightly taken aback at first but they explained that a music tutor had given a demonstration that afternoon and they thought that they would like to try it out. Steven wanted to learn the guitar and Connor wanted to learn the banjo, both of which were taught by the same man. They gave her a short note from the school giving times and fees. They would begin with one, forty-five-minute lesson per week and then progress to two lessons per week depending on the standard achieved. The school had secured a grant to help with the cost, which reduced the fee to £5 per lesson per pupil. The tutor, Mr Patrick Joseph McGrath, would supply mini instruments that were suitable for children for lessons at school and practise periods at home, depending on how many pupils responded. Liz knew straight away that she couldn't afford the cost but knew that once again if she asked her parents that they would agree to cover the fees. It was just that she was always asking them to provide the extras in life but if that was what the boys wanted to do then, she would have no option but to approach them with cap in hand, once again. She knew that they would say yes without a second thought but it was always a bit of a chore to have to ask.

The brothers took to their newfound hobby like ducks to water. The tutor liked to be known as PJ by the school staff and his pupils. His easy-going methodology paid dividends, especially with Steven and Connor. In no time at all they were playing simple tunes and accompanying each other and were attending two lessons per week. Robbie and Cissy were more than pleased that their money was well spent and were already making plans for the boys to demonstrate their skills at the next hooley, whenever that might be. Liz would sometimes just sit in awe, watching them practice in the sitting room of their home.

Patrick Joseph McGrath (PJ) was born and raised in the centre of Dublin in an area known as Marino. He was the only son of Paddy and Biddy McGrath who had lived in and around Marino all their lives. Unfortunately for mother and son the father, although a hard worker thought he was a hard man, especially when he had rendered himself drunk. At six-foot-tall he could handle himself but he wasn't always on the winning side, which then made Biddy the subject of his anger and frustration when he arrived home. She was too small to fight back and her son PJ witnessed many an argument resulting in his mother being physically assaulted. Paddy always punched her in and around her torso so that no one would see the extent of her injuries. PJ promised himself from a very early age, that when he got big enough, he would certainly give his bastard of a father his comeuppance. Then, divine intervention stepped in. When PJ was sixteen years of age his father suffered a massive stroke resulting in home confinement. On the rare occasions he went out it was by means of a wheel chair pushed by the ever-loyal Biddy. PJ never got the chance to set the record straight with his bully of a father. The good Lord got there first.

Biddy's sister, who was a former entertainer in the theatres in and around Dublin, had married and moved to London. Her full name was Karagh Marie Flannigan but from a very early age was known as Kaz, as was her stage name, Kaz Flannigan. She had married an entrepreneur known as Reginald Archibald Coulter, who had many various business interests. His pride and joy was the entertainments company he owned which was based in London. He commuted between London and Dublin on a regular basis thus, the meeting and courtship of Kaz was inevitable. They lived in a three-storey town house in West Croydon. The ground floor was a spacious apartment with two bedrooms (master en suite), a large open plan kitchen/dining room and a family bathroom with a small back garden. The two upper floors contained two large bed rooms with a shared bathroom on each. These rooms were permanently let to budding young female entertainers who mostly worked in and around the West End of London. Kaz insisted that they would only let to women as she knew only too well that men, young or old were not to be trusted to keep any humble abode clean and tidy, least of all hers.

Because Kaz and Reggie married later in life than most, and he was also five years her senior, they decided not to have any children, however, by giving the youngsters a helping hand in the entertainments industry it would more than make up for it. So, with her brother-in-law incapacitated in Dublin, she felt sure that young PJ would succumb to her many previous invitations to come to London and further advance his music studies. He had been concerned in the past about the welfare of his mother if she was left alone in the house with his father, but now, as Kaz put it, the world was his oyster. Biddy was more than pleased when PJ finally took up Kaz's offer and enrolled in the London Academy of music based in West Croydon Campus. Visits home would be arranged several times a year by good old Auntie Kaz, who insisted that PJ call her... Kaz!

Twelve years later he had a very successful music school based in his aunt's large sitting room, which she rarely used and had converted to suit his purposes. He was also very sought after in the clubs and pubs in and around the London's West End and Reggie's accountant looked after the money side of things. PJ was extremely proficient in a number of instruments, in particular guitar, banjo, button accordion and the bodhron (Irish handheld drum). He could also belt out a song or twelve. At the age of twenty-eight, he had remained single. He would use the excuse that no one could ever match up to his mother, who at this stage was widowed for nearly five years. When his father died, he thought, 'Mammy's got peace at last. God love her.' And so, it came to pass that he was to become Steven and Connor's music tutor.

By this stage Kaz was recently widowed and had inherited Reggie's estate in full. His only other surviving relative was his older brother, Bernard Bartholomew Coulter, a semi-retired barrister who had inherited and lived in the large sprawling family home in Suffolk. Kaz was in the process of selling off all of Reggie's business interests but still enjoyed letting out her upstairs rooms to 'the stars of tomorrow'. He also left her a substantial amount in his life insurance and in his savings account. She was more than happy to support PJ in any way he would let her. Sometimes she had to put her powers of persuasion to the test, by assuring him that any monetary assistance by her was recorded and was, in fact, a very sound investment.

Liz made a most determined resolution for 2014. She would begin a very strict diet and exercise programme. She had enrolled into the mothers and toddlers club at the local gymnasium and with about a dozen or so other conscientious objectors to unwanted weight gain and the, through-other fashion look, decided it was about time for a complete make-over and turn themselves into something a little more glamorous. After about four weeks or so, almost half of them had kicked it into touch, but those who stayed the course could certainly see that their hard work in the gym and the strict diet were beginning to make a difference. They nick-named themselves: 'mums with tight tums and bums'.

Liz's target date to show herself off was the end of term music concert on the afternoon of Wednesday the 16 April, just before the Easter break. Steven and Connor were taking part although all those performing would be accompanied by their music tutor. PJ wanted to make sure that they all had a good crack of the whip and with him on stage beside them it would hopefully alleviate any last-minute nerves. Liz was looking forward to meeting PJ, as her two boys never stopped talking about him. When she arrived at the school assembly hall with Ryan, Anthony and Michael in tow, Cissy and Robbie were already there. Benny and Julie couldn't make it due to work commitments but the place was packed in no time and it was difficult for those who arrived a little later to get a seat.

Mrs Simpson, the head teacher, gave a short introduction to the proceedings, which were to last a little over an hour, and then PJ took the stage. He ran through the single-page printed programme, a copy of which was placed on every seat beforehand and explained that each of the acts were still in the early stages of mastering their instruments. A concert such as this would take place at the end of each subsequent school term, to demonstrate the marked improvement in their musical endeavours and thus encourage others to take part. He also explained that some of those taking part had decided on using stage names for today's performance and hopefully none of their parents or guardians would object.

Liz was busy settling her three boys when Robbie said as loud as you please:

'Our two are billed as Steve and Con McKenna!'

Liz nearly dropped Michael and gasped, 'Steve and bloody Con. What's that all about?'

Cissy couldn't help but laugh and added, 'Ah Liz, will you leave them alone. Sure, it's only pretending. It's not as if they are going to change their names overnight.'

Then all three adults burst out laughing and settled down to enjoy the show, each with a young McKenna on their knee.

When Steven and Connor were introduced by PJ they were number four on the programme. They sauntered onto the stage without a care in the world. They sat on two stools to the left of PJ and they all began to play without saying another word. Not only did the boys play well, they even sang the chorus of their second offering to the surprise of the audience.

And they were the only performers throughout the concert that sang as well as played their instruments. Afterwards, everyone was invited to stay behind for tea and biscuits and speak to the school staff, as well as being introduced to PJ, the maestro himself.

Steven and Connor grabbed their mum, a hand each, and practically dragged her across the hall to meet PJ. Well, when he saw Liz, he was taken aback to say the least. Ryan, Anthony and Michael soon followed with the help of their proud grandparents. Liz held out her hand and said hello but for a brief moment PJ was speechless, then he came to his senses and began to warble incoherently, which resulted in

Liz covering her face with the same outstretched hand, to hide the little giggle she tried so hard to suppress. PJ had only one thought in his spinning head: 'She is drop-dead gorgeous.' His boyish good looks, short blond hair and brown eyes were more than just pleasing to say the least, not that Liz had the chance to notice, what with five kids in tow.

Robbie and Cissy couldn't thank him enough for the unbelievable progress he had made with Steven and Connor. Liz was equally complimentary, but PJ heard very little; he seemed to answer as if he was on auto pilot and tried hard not to stare too much at Liz. It was difficult for the other families to get a word in but they managed it somehow. Poor old PJ thought he was on a never-ending merry-go-round and he bloody loved it! He had to keep blinking his eyes so as not to make it too obvious what he was going through. Love at first sight!

When the McKennas were leaving, Liz made time to shake PJ's hand and thank him once again. He tried to avoid eye contact but to no avail. He smiled and said that he hoped that they would meet again sooner rather than later, but Liz thought that he was just being a little over polite, although she did realise that she had an effect on his persona that afternoon. She returned the smile and once again thanked him for all his hard work and then left. He felt as if he was in-between limbo and heaven.

The music lessons for the two brothers progressed at an alarming rate and their home resonated with guitar and banjo practice almost every night after homework was completed. Liz didn't mind, as she could easily monitor their improvement from down stairs as the boys played upstairs in their bedroom. The other three brothers listened and clapped their hands with abounding enthusiasm and never tired of stamping their feet with the odd yahoo thrown in for good measure, usually screamed in the wrong place but no one seemed to mind. During the school summer holidays Steven and Connor maintained their high level of progression at PJ's music school in his Aunt Kaz's front room in West Croydon, which was easy to get to by car.

Liz would normally take them and wait to bring them back home again. She really enjoyed the cups of tea and stimulating conversations with Kaz as she listened to her Steven and Connor's musical endeavours in the back ground. Cissy and Robbie took turns to keep an eye on the other three brothers.

Summer holidays that year at Bognor Regis for Liz, her mum and dad and her five fine sons came and went with the usual bang. The business interests of the McKenna family were still going from strength to strength. They had survived the credit crunch much better than any of the other family businesses in and around central London, by far! The best decision that was ever made was when Robbie stood his ground in 2007 and refused to spend any money on acquisitions and not rush head into what would undoubtedly have been financial suicide. They were being canny with any business ventures and to date Robbie always had the final say, and because of that rationale, doom and gloom were still held at bay.

The double wedding of the millennium in August for her cousins Sam and Pam was exactly that. It was nothing short of a showpiece affair with every man and his dog invited, including senior members of the local council. The service, venue, music and lashings of food and drink were second to none. Both brides insisted that Liz bring her five sons with her and God help anyone who made any snide remarks. Also invited were a large number of the relatives from Omagh in Northern Ireland which included Davy Beggs. Lenny still called him Daft Davy when he was out of earshot which brought a little giggle from Liz but she thought he was okay once you got to know him, and Daft Davy wasn't that daft, as he engaged in small talk with Liz at every opportunity throughout the wedding celebrations. He was great with her boys and even got Liz up for a dance now and again, even a sly slow one, up close but not too close, as he knew his plans involving Liz were not to be rushed. It may take a slow and tedious period of time but he knew he had to be patient, for now.

The day after the wedding Davy even made time to call at Liz's home and once again made a great impression on her five sons. He helped around the house and was full of praise for the impromptu concert that Steven and Connor performed around the kitchen table. He also brought with him an abundant variety of sweets and a box of chocolates for Liz. She nearly had a little tear in her eye. When he left after about two hours they embraced and gave each other a peck on the cheek. He promised to return the following day and take them all out to lunch at McDonalds. Well, she thought that the whole episode was too good to be true, but true to his word he turned up the following day at twelve o'clock driving Robbie's car and between him and Liz transported the five brothers to lunch. Steven and Connor insisted in travelling with Davy, there and back. Once again when they parted at her front door, Liz and Davy embraced, only this time they gave each other a peck on the lips. He was flying back to Belfast and then a car ride home to Omagh that night but they had exchanged phone numbers throughout the afternoon and promised they would stay in touch. Once again, Liz nearly had a little tear in her eye.

Although Davy and Liz had exchanged phone numbers it didn't take long for them to correspond using the email system, with the content always very cheery and on occasions containing the odd innuendo. Davy always mentioned her sons and inquired in detail about Steven and Connor's progress in their music lessons. When the festive season came round once more Davy orchestrated another invitation from Benny and Julie. He arrived on the afternoon of Christmas Eve. He borrowed Julie's car and via the large toy shop in the centre of Croydon, hurried to Liz's house with a present for each of her five sons. After a great deal of hollering and whinging from the boys, Liz agreed with Davy that the Christmas presents that he had brought and only those, may be opened that evening but only after they had eaten their dinner. Well, needless to say the food disappeared in less than five minutes, and then there was wrapping paper and torn cardboard boxes all over the kitchen table and kitchen floor. Each expectant little pair of hands revealed an upmarket battery-operated dumper truck, pertaining to the age of each of the boys. They would all alter course when they came into contact with an obstacle e.g. a table leg, a door or sometimes a wall. Liz gave Davy a little peck on the cheek, followed by a little embrace and all five of her sons gave him a big hug and in the case of Michael, her youngest, a big slobbery kiss was added.

When bath time was over the boys were bedded down but Liz knew it would take some time for them to fall asleep. Davy decided not to stay too late as tongues might wag the following day at the McKennas' festive bash. When he arrived back at Benny and Julie's house, Robbie and Cissy were there, enjoying a few drinks and a snack. Davy was coerced into giving a full report on the afternoon's activities and did so without fear of conscience. He knew all four of them far too well.

The usual McKenna forty-eight-hour celebrations went just like every other year … With a bloody big bang! Liz and Davy stole the odd little peck, the odd little kiss, but always out of sight, which has to be said, was not easy. Not even for devious Davy.

Lenny drove up from Portsmouth, Wheelie and Ann, Pam and Sam and their husbands all joined the fun-filled non-stop party atmosphere. Liz's kids absolutely thrived on this annual family gathering. And lo and behold, Lou and her toffee-nosed husband made a brief appearance on Boxing Day. Davy was on his way back to Omagh via the usual transport links on the 27th December. This gave him the opportunity to use Robbie's car to assist Liz to ferry her kids back to their own house on the evening of the 26th December. Liz's dad was over the moon, as it meant he had no driving to do that day and could carry on the movement with his alcohol consumption.

When Liz and Davy finally got the kids to bed they both settled down on the sofa for a large mug of tea, accompanied with a biscuit. They smiled and exchanged pleasantries and then indulged each other in their first full-blown kiss, with no holds barred. Tongues darted from mouth to mouth and they were soon fumbling with the buttons of their shirts. All of a sudden, Liz pulled back and became quite emotional. She rested her hands on his shoulders and began to shake her head and then whispered:

'I'm sorry. I'm sorry, Davy.'

'What are you sorry about, Liz?'

'I can't do this.'

'What can't you do, Liz?'

'I can't do this, Davy. I can't do this.'

'I don't understand. What are you talking about? Aren't you enjoying this time alone together? Liz, talk to me.'

'I didn't mean to lead you up the garden path, Davy. We can't have any sort of relationship. What with only seeing you a couple of times a year. There's no future in it and I won't be your part-time fuck-buddy. I'm sorry, Davy. I can't be your London shag. I've been used too many times in the past. I think you should go now.'

'Can I finish my tea first?'

He didn't wait for an answer. He stood up, drank the lukewarm tea and said, 'Don't worry, Liz. You didn't lead me up any garden path. I understand where you're coming from. I'll be on my way. See ya.'

With that said, he left the house under his own steam, leaving Liz on the sofa. He gently closed the front door behind him and drove the short journey back to Benny and Julie's house.

He couldn't help but think to himself:

'It's not over yet. Patience is a virtue. Time and patience are on my side. My time will come... Eventually.'

A little while later, Liz gently sobbed herself to sleep.

CHAPTER 12

The New Year of 2015 came and went. The business activities of the McKennas took a slight stumble, but true to form Robbie guided the company through the minor hiccup and onward to further success. Apart from Michael, Liz's other four sons were attending full-time schooling. She continued to attend her slimming club and had also progressed to a more advanced fitness class with two of the remaining mums from the gym. Correspondence between her and Davy continued, but less frequently than before. He was always careful in his wording and always asked about her sons. He also said he may not return to London in the near future, but he would give it a year or so and he would once again look her up. Liz was quite happy with the idea.

Steven and Connor were going from strength to strength regarding their music and guess what? Ryan and Anthony began their first music lessons with PJ in the January school term, paid for by the ever-doting grandparents. Liz invited her mum and dad, Benny and Julie, over to her house for an impromptu performance from the two proven musicians at the end of February. This was to be followed by the surprise revelation of the two potential musicians! After a most impressive performance from Steven and Connor, and while the adults enjoyed a large pot of tea, Ryan and Anthony left the kitchen and waited for their mum to announce them. Liz stood by the kitchen door, which was slightly ajar, and called out: 'Look what Ryan and Anthony brought home from school the other day? Okay, boys. In you come!'

Well, in through the door the young pups waltzed, each holding a mini button accordion which was secured with shoulder straps. They played the first verse of 'The Wild Rover' in unison ... Well, not totally in unison. The melody was just about recognisable, but when Steven and Connor joined in with the guitar and banjo for the chorus, it sounded a lot better. Second time around, all the adults sang along and rounded off the performance with a standing ovation. Tears all round, to say the least. Robbie could hardly contain himself but he took a deep breath and said in a matter of fact tone: 'Well, I'm just glad our hard-earned money is not being wasted!'

The McKennas were as close as ever. That's for sure.

In August that year Lenny was posted to the US Navy in Miami Florida for three years and to everyone's delight was promoted to the rank of petty officer first class. He explained that he would not make it back for Christmas that year but would definitely make it back the following year. He also reminded everyone that visitors to Miami from the family circle would be well looked after as they were in recent years, when he was posted to Gibraltar.

At this stage, Liz's youngest was over three years old and was attending pre-school each morning from 9 am until noon, Monday to Friday. Initially Liz just lazed around the house each morning. It was the first time in more than ten years that she actually got some time to herself, even if it was only three hours each week-day. After about a fortnight she decided to put this newfound free time to good use. On the advice of her keep fit instructor, who also gave her a balanced fitness programme she decided to exercise Monday, Wednesday and Friday mornings after she dropped off Michael at pre-school. She intended to walk three miles on each occasion, stopping every now and then to carry out basic fitness exercises. Apart from the local park there were many other suitable locations to get down and get with it. This enabled her to vary her route whenever she had a mind to. In a very short period of time Liz could really feel the benefit of her labours. One of the other mums from the gym decided to join her, which made the whole idea much more appealing. No pain, no gain, proves much more enjoyable when you have company and it has to be said, a little bit of friendly competition does no harm whatsoever. Now that Liz had four kids attending music classes each week it meant that on school holidays they were continuing their tuition at PJ's. Only Michael was left at home on those days and he was the easiest child in the world to look after. That easy, in fact, that Robbie volunteered on almost every occasion.

Liz and Kaz's little get-togethers were now twice as long as before while PJ diligently carried out the task in hand with the four boys. He took them all at the same time so as to mix and match the various sounds as a quartet. PJ had noticed how trim Liz had become, although he had always found her attractive, but now she had this gorgeous aurora around her (as per the animated character, Princess Aurora). An invisible self-assurance and a permanent glow which made her without a doubt, the sexiest yummy mummy he had ever seen. His feelings for her had grown not just because of her fitness regime but because he had gotten to know her better and better as they met more and more at his home music studio. It got to the stage that when Liz and the boys left after their two-hour stint, he couldn't concentrate on anything, much less another pupil. In fact, he got that bad, he ensured that they came immediately after lunch and then poor old PJ had to take the rest of the afternoon off.

Kaz knew exactly what the problem was, but she had no idea how to help her nephew. She always thought something like this would happen when he was younger but surprisingly it didn't, until now. Liz and PJ were both thirty years old but she didn't seem to realise the effect she had on him, or maybe she had an inkling but decided to ignore it. PJ on the other hand had it bad. When Liz arrived with her sons or just before they were due to arrive, PJ was just like a little puppy dog. However, it did not deter him from giving the boys great value for money for he began to realise even with the young twins joining in, there was a lot of talent just waiting to be tapped. Of that, PJ had no doubt, whatsoever.

When the festive season was on the horizon Liz came up with a devious plan. She realised that if it was to work by Christmas then she would have to promise her mother and Julie that this would be the last time she would bring up the subject of their sordid sex lives. Her plan was that they should all agree that a people carrier for Liz and her boys would be a viable asset for everyone concerned. All Julie and Cissy had to do was convince Robbie and Benny that it would benefit everyone in the family, especially when transporting the boys en masse. One vehicle would suffice on every occasion. School, music lessons, even on holidays. What's not to like?

'Just like that,' said Cissy.

'Yes, Mother. Just like that.'

'You've got a bloody nerve. Who do you think you are, Liz? Eh!' snapped Julie.

'I'll tell you exactly who I am, ladies. I'm the one person who could turn your nice comfortable lives upside down in less than five minutes. Do you two think for one minute that Uncle Benny and Dad wouldn't kick your arses out of the house, as soon as they got wind of what you have been up to for most of your married lives?'

Cissy piped up, 'You wouldn't dare!'

Julie joined in, 'What proof do you have, Liz? Eh!'

'Oh, didn't I tell you? Must have slipped my mind.'

'Don't fuck about, Liz,' snarled Julie.

'I kept all the info from your secret phone, ladies, from all that time ago. I also sent the damning photos to my phone, just in case like, you know. Just in case I needed one last favour.'

'You two-faced little bitch,' shouted Cissy.

'Holy fuck, Mother. You're calling me two-faced? Why don't you two ladies have a good look in the fucking mirror. Pay up or else.'

'Or else what,' sneered Julie.

'Or else, I'll send all the dirty laundry I've got on you two to both Dad's and Benny's phones. Not straight away, like. I'll let you both sweat for a day or two, or maybe a week or two and then it'll hit you two like a fucking bomb blast.'

Julie and Cissy looked at each other, wide-eyed and mouths gaping. After a brief silence Julie whispered something into Cissy's ear. They both nodded to each other and then Julie said, 'Alright, alright. You scheming little bitch. You can have your people carrier by Christmas.'

Liz smiled and said, 'A brand-new one. Nothing second hand.'

Both guilty parties frowned simultaneously and once again nodded in agreement.

'How do we know that this will be the last time you will blackmail us,' asked Cissy.

'You sort out the new vehicle, convince Dad and Uncle Benny that it's going to be a Christmas gift for me and the boys and once I have the keys, then I will hand my phone over to you two. You can delete or transfer any incriminating evidence to one of your phones. Simple as that. Okay?'

'But what if you've already transferred the information to another phone that we don't know about,' asked Cissy.

'Mother, would I do that to you?' Liz smiled once again and added, 'You'll just have to trust me, won't you, ladies? Take it or fucking leave it. End of fucking story.'

Would you believe it? In early December Liz had the keys of a brand-new people carrier and she and her sons couldn't have been happier. She didn't have any other incriminating evidence on her mother and Julie, but it was nice to know that they didn't know that. And the story that the sisters-in-law conjured up had the two brothers convinced that it was they who had come up with the whole idea in the first place. You couldn't make it up.

By Easter 2016, Liz had turned her whole life around. She was totally independent regarding transport for her and the kids, and her fitness campaign was paying dividends. Wherever she went, whether it was school, the gym, shopping, music lessons or to the McKenna head office, she had everyone's attention. In particular, the roving eye of every full-blooded male, young and old. And Liz revelled in it. The only downside was that she didn't have a man in her life. She quite rightly, had lost all faith in men except her dad and her uncle. Oh yes, she must not forget about her good friend PJ. Liz knew that he was besotted with her but in a nice way. They had been out on the odd occasion for a few drinks but he always made sure he got her home safe in a taxi and they never stayed out late. He had realised from the very start of their socialising that it was purely platonic and he didn't mind. He just enjoyed the pleasure of her company under any circumstances. Plain and simple, but he could always hope. Couldn't he?

Liz had toyed with the idea of making herself available for online dating, but who the hell would want a stable relationship with a single mum with five kids, and who would do the baby sitting? It took all the powers of persuasion to get her mum or dad to volunteer when she had been out with PJ and that was only because everyone thought he was the perfect saint. Well, he bloody was, wasn't he? But the internet did come to the rescue in the guise of her small but vibrant selection of sex toys. She may not have had sex for some time but she made sure she still enjoyed an orgasm. It was a lot better than what her mother and aunt did to get their rocks off.

But the one outstanding pleasure she had was the company of her five sons. She absolutely adored them, and would do nothing to jeopardize their happiness. They in turn gave a lot of happiness in return especially to their grandparents and Uncle Benny and Aunt Julie. Warts and all, her immediate family made sure that none of the boys wanted for nothing. The annual holidays and the little extras at school were still at the behest of her parents. Liz had no way of changing her circumstances so as to afford those little luxuries herself, but she must remain grateful for small mercies. In the words of her toffee-nosed-cousin Lou, 'If she had kept her legs closed instead of being open all hours, she wouldn't have found herself in such a precarious position!'

Another year of success for MKE Ltd was becoming very apparent as 2016 progressed however; the result of the Brexit Referendum in June that year almost put a spanner in the works. MKE Ltd trusted Robbie to steer them through any rough patches. True to form, they stuck to their guns throughout 2016 and didn't panic. Robbie always had an ace up his sleeve. The two brothers were up and down the country with their beloved darts tournaments and Cissy and Julie still had their illicit weekends away for the usual spa breaks. Nudge-nudge. Wink-wink. The family holidays were going from strength to strength as Liz's boys were getting that little bit older, they were easier to entertain and in a lot of cases could entertain themselves. And let's face it, Butlins at Bognor Regis was ideal for all of them.

But you know, although Liz was very grateful for all the assistance her mother and father provided and Benny and Julie as well, she couldn't help feel a little bit like the poor relation. Her brother Lenny was having the time of his life in the Royal Navy, Pam and Sam were becoming proper businesswomen in their own right, each with a fantastic husband who also had a successful career, and last but by no means least, snotty Lou and her dickhead of a husband were definitely living the dream. Even her best friend Sharon and her fiancé Gino were still travelling the world on top class cruise ships and being paid handsomely for doing so.

No matter how much Liz loved her sons, every so often she would reflect on the silly, naive way she conducted herself in her younger years. Well, maybe not when she thought back to her date rape. She still had flash backs of that awful night but then again, could she have had, a little more fore-thought and managed to avoid the violation she had to endure? At first she blamed Lenny for having a relationship with her first love, Ed, then she blamed and continued to blame her mother and aunt for their infidelity, year after year after year. She was totally convinced that Cissy and Julie didn't have even a hint of conscience between them, but she was in a bed of her own making and that didn't look if it would change any time soon. Then in January 2017 circumstances looked as if they might change. A few days after New Year all the close family were summoned to Benny's house for a very important announcement.

On 1 May that year, it would be Benny's sixtieth

birthday! Wow! He was planning to celebrate it in style with the festivities taking place over the entire May Day Bank Holiday weekend. Family and friends from near and far would be invited at various times, on various dates and locations so it was essential that everyone keep that weekend free. More detailed information would be forthcoming in plenty of time before the birthday event and the whole caboodle would live up to the usual hijinks of the McKennas! Liz's cousin Davy had been in touch shortly afterwards to say he would like to come over to London a day or two early for Benny's birthday bash and maybe they could spend a little time together to catch up on the general things in life. He also added that he may have a plan suitable for the future, for her and the kids but they would need to discuss it in private. Liz was intrigued and agreed almost immediately, much to Davy's delight.

Meanwhile Cissy and Julie were making their own preparations for the upcoming event, but also an event of their own. They both realised that they would be the organisers for Benny's sixtieth and all the running about before, during and after everyone had gone home so, they sat down over a few drinks one night when their husbands were out attending a darts match at the Eagles Nest. As there were two bank holidays in May they decided to have a spa break on the second one. No problems there as the two brothers would be more than supportive, after all the hard work the girls would put into the birthday celebration weekend. Sure, how could they object? There was never a hint of doubt in the past regarding the spa weekends so lead on MacDuff. They both settled down at Julie's kitchen table with slow background music playing on the CD player. As Cissy poured their second large Vodka and Coke Julie said, 'I have an idea that might well blow your socks off, or should I say, your knickers off?'

Cissy smiled and returned to her seat close to her partner in crime.

'Pray tell?'

'Well... On our next trip to Guildford, instead of taking

part in the usual frolics on the Saturday night, why not save ourselves for something really special on Sunday night?'

'Oh, Julie... What do you have in mind?'

'Well... The money we pay for DD's erotic get-togethers is money well spent, and her husband Simion always surprises us with an array of unusual entertainers. The drinks and food are always top class but there are more and more punters showing up and sometimes it results on certain unwanted attention. If you know what I mean?'

Cissy nodded in agreement and said:

'I do love woman on woman, especially in a group, but if I want male intervention, I want it to be slow and sure and not just a last-minute climb-on.'

'I agree entirely, Cissy, so with that in mind I propose we make DD an offer, for a private liaison of our own creation.'

'Now, Julie, you know that it won't come cheap.'

'I know that but we have an abundance of spare cash in our secret bank account and a ton more in our safety deposit box, so why don't we push the boat out and go for the fucking jackpot? After all, if it all goes according to plan, we can make further plans for the foreseeable future.'

'What brought this to mind, Julie?'

'Well... It's only when hubby mentioned the big six-o that I realised that you and I are both fifty-eight years of age this year! We still look good for our age but the competition in Guildford is becoming increasingly difficult, so I think at our age we should break out of the norm, and ensure all the meat on all the bones is all ours. We no longer share or wait to share with anyone else.'

'So what you're saying is, we are going to be the cats that get the cream.'

'More like the pussies that get all the cream!'

'Okay. You've obviously given this a great deal of thought, Julie. Give me an outline of just what you've conjured up.'

'Well, Cissy... How about a couple of twenty-five to thirty-year-olds, good-looking young studs to join us, once we've warmed each other up?'

Cissy's eyes and mouth opened in unison as Julie continued, 'Nicely shaven chests. Suntanned all over. Oh yes... And nicely shaven down below with plenty of flavoured oil... I know our mutual dislike for too much pubic hair on the male or female anatomy, so smooth all over is an absolute must.'

'You know, Julie... I can just imagine each of us with a nice young stud for dessert.'

'No. No. No. Cissy. Not one each. I said a couple. Two each!'

Daft Davy arrived in West Croydon on the Wednesday before the bank holiday at the end of April that year. This gave him a two-day buffer zone before the birthday festivities kicked off on the Friday. Liz had already arranged for him to call round to her house to join her and the boys for their evening meal. He brought the obligatory bags of sweets for the boys and a lovely bunch of flowers for her. He also helped with bath time and the five sons duly entertained him for about half an hour before they were all dispatched to their bed rooms. Even Michael, who at just over five years old joined in with the bodhran. Davy and Liz settled down in the sitting room with a bottle of white wine. It was an expensive brand that had been on special offer in Belfast International Airport, and Davy just knew it would be an essential aid to put Liz in a relaxing mood, as he slowly nit-picked his way through his devious plan. His manner and demeanour had been tried and tested on many occasions before and he was quietly confident, in an unassuming arrogant way, that it would work again, so long as he didn't rush things. If sex was to play a part in their future relationship then that was all well and good, but for now that would have to wait. The priority was to get Liz on side... And then, the conniving bastard that he was, would clean up by mesmerising her kids with all the up sides of future adventures... In Omagh, Co Tyrone, N. Ireland.

Davy's plan of action was, he would invite Liz and her five sons to Omagh for part of the school summer holidays.

He was living in a large four-bedroom detached house on the outskirts of town with a large front and back garden. He had never married and had no access baggage from any previous relationships. There would be more than enough room for everyone and there would be no strings attached. Liz was all ears... So far so good. Now, the usual summer holiday with Robbie and Cissy could still be on the cards at the beginning of the summer which would still leave plenty of time for the proposed trip to Omagh. For say, three or four weeks? Davy was so convincing that Liz almost said yes straight away. Davy's smarmy charm and the wine were definitely working overtime. Then Liz took a deep breath and sat back on the sofa, to cool down as she was becoming very hot and bothered. She was already letting her heart run away with what little common sense she may or may not have possessed at this period in time. Davy added that he would cover the cost of the return journey by car from West Croydon to Holyhead, then the ferry to Dublin, followed by a simple two-hour journey to Omagh.

'Listen, Liz. You're an experienced driver in that people carrier of yours. The boys will keep you well-entertained throughout the journey. You know they will.' He hesitated and then added, 'Just think of the adventure for the boys, and you. It will be the first time in your life that you would be totally independent.'

'It sounds great, Davy, but what about spending money. After all, Mum and Dad will have paid for the usual holiday at Butlins, so I can't ask them for more money to go to Omagh for three or four weeks!'

'Listen, Liz, I've got it covered. You know that I work from home in a port-a-cabin at the side of the house... Well you can work for me by helping with my courier firm. Especially at that time of year I could do with a bit of extra help.'

Liz sat wide-eyed as Davy poured her another glass of wine, making sure to pour himself just the tiniest drop.

'Look, Davy... It all sounds great. Almost too good to be true.'

'That's because it is, Liz. Look, let's have another drink to give you time to think. Just sit back and relax. Just you sit back and relax, Liz.'

He also sat back and gave a pleasant little smile of gratification. He knew full well that the seeds were well and truly planted. No more for now. Just leave her in a little while and let her sleep on it.

Tomorrow would be another day. A day in which he would proceed with the coercion of her sons. That would be the easy bit. He kept reminding her. Yes. She needed more time to think. Just a little more time to think.

After he left, Liz poured herself another glass of wine from the bottle that she had stashed in her cupboard in the kitchen. A hand full of ice to enhance the flavour was needed. She sat for quite some time on her own as the boys were fast asleep. They had always been good sleepers. They could sleep anywhere. No probs! They also found it easy to make new friends and would always be up for a musical interlude. Anytime. Anywhere. The following morning, she woke up with Omagh on her mind. No mention of this to her sons. It was far too early yet. The mere mention of holidaying in cousin Davy's house would cause quite a stir. She needed more time to think, to work out all the travel details. More time to think. How to break the news to her mum and dad, yes… She needed more time to think it through.

Over the next few days, Davy, using the birthday festivities as a natural diversion, plied the boys with stories of laughter and adventure about his home town of Omagh but nearly always when they were adrift from the remainder of the family and friends. The weather was fantastic so a lot of his time spent with the boys, in one or other of the gardens at the family homes. No one gave it a second thought. It gave Liz a bit of breathing space for once, and her parents and Benny and Julie were more than pleased that Davy was showing such a lot of interest in the five young desperados, as they had become known over that particular weekend. Davy always made sure that he didn't drink too much during the day so he could drive Liz and the boys safely home and arranged for a taxi for the return journey. He saved his partying for the night-time sessions. But he always made sure at every opportunity to give a sly private mention of the Omagh trip to tipsy Liz. The more he winked and smiled the more she began to feel that it could easily happen. Just a bit more time to think. She hadn't realised that she got that little quip from Davy. What a charmer!

When bank holiday Monday arrived the family circle and close friends were heading for the Eagles Nest for a lunch time session, which would undoubtedly develop into an all-day event. Most of the die-hards were still going strong with Robbie and Benny leading the way. Liz decided to give it a miss as the kids were up for school again the following morning. Davy decided to make a surprise visit and arrive with an armful of chocolate bars, as if they hadn't overdone it already over the weekend. But nevertheless, Liz was pleased to see him and the five boys were jumping with joy to see cousin Davy, especially as he was overladen with their favourite treats. Once they settled down in the kitchen to devour their tasty sweets, Davy motioned Liz into the sitting room out of ear-shot and in almost a whisper he asked, 'Well, Liz. What do you think of our plan about Omagh?'

Liz paused for a few seconds and said, 'Look, Davy, it sounds like a really great idea. I would love to go and the boys would love to go.'

'Then what's the problem, Liz?'

'First of all, how do I tell Mum and Dad? Second of all, I don't like the idea of you footing the bill for our travel expenses. I do like the idea of working for you, so I can help to pay my way if... If we get there. But—'

Davy stopped her in mid-sentence and said, 'First of all, I've told, no, not told your mum and dad. I just mentioned the idea and told them, that you and I had just brushed over the idea of a trip to Omagh. We were having a few drinks in private at their house. You understand? I hadn't said that I had actually asked you yet, which is sort of half true. I told them I was just sounding them out to see their reaction.'

Liz cocked her head to one side and said, 'And?'

'Well now. They think it's a great idea. They think it would be a great adventure for the boys and also give you a bit of independence! Especially the bit about you working for me while you're there!'

'What about the cost, Davy?'

'Well now. They both immediately offered to pay the bill, without question! In fact, they insisted that they pay the cost of the return journey. So, it's not if, Liz, it's when. Don't you think? Liz? Liz?'

There was a short pause and it looked like Liz was going to say something then... Nothing... Then...

'Right, Davy. We're fucking going. We're fucking well going. Yes, we're fucking well going!'

He whispered, 'Let's not tell the boys just yet. Not until everything is in place and that won't take long. Trust me, Liz.'

After the dust settled and Liz recovered her composure, Davy phoned for a taxi to take him to the Eagles Nest to join the party. When he arrived the sing-song had already begun and a very talented duo with guitars were leading the way, from their normal position in the far corner of the very busy bar. He managed to squeeze into a very small but vacant stool between Robbie and Cissy.

'Well?' They both said in unison.

'Well now. It took a bit of persuasion but, with a great deal of perseverance on my part, I finally talked her into it.'

Robbie and Cissy were chuffed to bits that their joint plan with Davy had actually worked. They were over the moon. Why hadn't they thought of it before? Liz and the kids would have a great time! Robbie shouted to Big Frankie behind the bar, 'Frankie boy! Keep the drinks flowing and by the way, this man here, this man here is not allowed to spend any money this fine day. His money is no good today. Okay?'

Davy settled himself in for a freebee afternoon. Once again that sneaky little smile began to form on his face.

Slowly at first and then it stretched from ear to ear. He loved it when a plan came together... That's for sure.

CHAPTER 13

THE TWO-WEEK ANNUAL HOLIDAY AT BUTLINS with Robbie and Cissy went with a bang! Liz and the boys had only a few days to get sorted out prior to their great adventure in Omagh. They were booked onto the 2 pm Holyhead to Dublin ferry on Saturday 29 July. It would arrive in Dublin at about 5.15 that afternoon, where it was agreed that Davy would meet them to take over the driving seat from Liz. Although she had every confidence in her driving ability to complete the journey in full, her parents were concerned that it may be two hours too far. After all, she and the boys would be up very early that morning to ensure that they had sufficient time to make the five/six-hour journey to Holyhead. This time line would allow for rest periods for food and toilet stops. Davy agreed with Robbie and Cissy and was dropped off at Dublin Port by one of his drivers while carrying out a delivery in Bray which was only a few miles south of Dublin. Everyone's a winner.

Well, after the hubbub of whoops and jeers from the five boys, Davy eventually got behind the wheel and off they all went on the last leg of their journey, Omagh bound. Davy's house was every bit as impressive as he had made it out to be. Every mod-con that anyone could wish for was there. Liz couldn't believe her eyes and the boys were over the moon. All five sons immediately undertook a trail of investigation into every nook and cranny of the large detached four-bedroom house with two very large front and back gardens. There were two fairly large trees in the back garden. The ground was half patio, the other half was well-trimmed grass, surrounded by a six-foot wooden fence with open countryside in all directions. Out front, two smaller trees with a bushy hedgerow bordering the neat lawn with a parking area for four vehicles. The house was set-back approximately fifty yards from the A32, just under a mile south-west of Omagh.

Where could they hide, or where they could make a den, indoors and outdoors, it was great fun. Poor old Liz and Davy were left to carry in the large array of luggage for the four-week stay but they didn't mind as the boys were already having the time of their lives, but Liz insisted on one thing. Once they were all reasonably settled it was FaceTime with the grandparents. Liz hardly got a word in, what with each of the boys, in age order, from eldest to youngest, giving granny and granddad a detailed version of the day's events. At each of the rest stops to Holyhead Liz had kept her parents up to date on their progress by texting while her sons were busy eating or going to the toilet. Steven and Connor had been a great help with their three younger brothers throughout the entire journey. Robbie and Cissy were relieved, to say the least, that they had all arrived safe and well and without incident. After FaceTime Robbie and Cissy looked at each other and smiled with relief.

Robbie said, 'Told you. I knew they would be just fine and dandy.'

Cissy agreed, 'Sure you did.'

That first Saturday night in Omagh was a hoot. Everyone had settled in nicely and tucked into good old fish and chips that were delivered by one of Davy's drivers. This was followed by an hour of music and laughter around the large kitchen table before the three young ones were off to bed. Steven and Connor were allowed to stay up a little bit later but that notion soon wore off as they had to give in to their drooping eyelids due to the long day of adventure. Liz wasn't long behind them and Davy, well, Davy poured himself a very large measure of Bushmills Whiskey. He lay back in his favourite, large armchair and smiled. Yes, everything had gone like clock-work. He only had himself to thank. But now, who else could take the credit for such a well-executed plan? Only himself!

The following morning was a slow start for everyone except Davy. He had started work at seven o'clock from the port-a-cabin at the side of the house. Liz made her way downstairs just after nine and the boys joined her in the kitchen in dribs and drabs for breakfast. Davy had thoughtfully bought an array of breakfast cereals based on what he had seen in Liz's house in West Croydon. Liz was sipping a mug of tea as she lovingly watched her two eldest help the three youngest, although Ryan and Anthony, who were now just over eight years old, were becoming more independent by the day but dear little Michael who was just over five years old just loved to milk it, as the baby of the brood.

Davy popped in for a cup of tea and a few slices of toast soon after. Liz was surprised that he was working so early on a Sunday morning, much less working on a Sunday at all, but Davy explained that as he was running his own business, he had to take any and all work as it came in, which he boasted was the secret of his success. He had five small vans and one large one on the road at various times of every day and on many occasions late into the night, no job too big and no job too small. All liveried with 'Omagh Reliable Services Ltd'. Courier services in this part of Northern Ireland were much sought after. There was a high demand for local deliveries regarding prescriptions, cigarettes, alcohol, takeaways and furniture, or even moving house! If he needed a larger van than the one he had, his mate would lend him one, at a price.

He also had several contracts for lock-ups/open-ups. He was contracted to lock up various premises each evening and open up the same premises each morning. These included various office blocks in and around Omagh, parks and playgrounds, public conveniences and would you believe it, two grave yards! He picked up and delivered goods to and from Belfast International Airport, Belfast City Airport and was also subcontracted to various national courier companies throughout the six counties of Northern Ireland but also other locations in the South of Ireland. These included the counties of Monaghan, Cavan, Sligo, Donegal, and sometimes as far south as Galway, Limerick and of course Dublin. He planned to expand his business by increasing the size of his fleet of vehicles in the not-too-distant future, in the next year or two. He just needed to build up his capital a little more, but the way business was going it was definitely on the cards. He also explained that he did have two local mums that worked on a job-share basis for him in his office (port-a-cabin) but at this time of year they both like to take holidays with their families, so with that in mind Davy said, 'Right then Liz. You can help me out over the next four weeks or so as a stand-in for them. They'll be away a fortnight at a time. Easy-peasy, lemon-squeezy. Yeah?'

Liz looked him square in the eye and asked, 'When do you suggest I start?'

'Tomorrow morning will do fine.' Before she could get another word out he added, 'Suzie will be in this afternoon for a few hours so she will give you the general run-down of how things work and the same again tomorrow. By Tuesday you will be working the morning shift. And don't worry I will be here with you for the first week to steady the ship, so to speak.'

Liz rested her forehead on the back of her right hand and said one word. 'Fuck!'

'Oh, and by the way, Liz. Don't worry about the boys. I've a friend of mine who will pop round and pick them up after lunch time tomorrow and take them for a spot of sight-seeing in your people carrier. He's insured to drive anything on wheels, and then after that you and I will sit down and make a plan for you and them for the rest of the week.'

She just looked at him and started laughing.

'What are you laughing at, Liz? I will help out as well, each time you want to take them anywhere. Trust me. All will be well.'

The next morning at seven o'clock, Liz and Suzie were greeted by Davy. He spoke very little and relied on them both to get on with it, much to Liz's surprise, but she needn't have worried as Suzie was extremely proficient and also very easy to work with. To be honest, they got on like a house on fire and Liz took to her newfound employment like a duck to water. Davy knew she would.

Suzie took time and patience to instruct and train Liz in the very simple method of the office controller, because that's exactly what the job was. To control, record and manage all communications, which were done by mobile phones to and from the office. There was a simple format to follow that was written down in full on an A4 plastic laminate card. In no time at all, Liz was answering the phone with little or no problems, much to Suzie's delight and Liz's relief. The morning went like a flash. By midday, Davy waltzed into the office with two mugs of tea and a small plate of biscuits for the two hard-working ladies. Liz was full of herself. She and Suzie had been going at it for five hours with only two short spells for a cuppa which, on each occasion, they never finished. She had regained all that long-lost confidence and she was pretty sure that by the end of the week, she would be like a good old pro in her newfound employment. Suzie also explained that when Gertie, the other part-time controller, returned from holiday, Suzie would be away for the same period of time. She added that Gertie was a very easy person to partner in the control office.

It transpired later in general conversation that they were both paid well above the minimum wage, for obvious reasons. Most days, they were extremely busy, with very little time for a break, and silly mistakes were not taken lightly. Although it has to be said that Davy knew exactly when to intervene and help out. His drivers were also well paid. He had the same crew for nearly two years and not one of them had ever let him down.

Throughout that morning the boys were busying themselves with the various gadgets with Davy's TV set, amongst other things. And Davy made sure they had some sort of breakfast before they raided the biscuit tin. After the five brothers had lunch, which was prepared by Liz, Davy's mate Alec arrived to pick them up for an afternoon excursion and the six of them were gone in a flash. Liz and Davy finished their sandwiches and mugs of tea when he decided to show Liz the garage at the other side of the port-a-cabin.

He activated the metal roller shutter at the front of the garage by depressing a small fob on his key ring thus revealing the following: a brand-new five-door 2017 Vauxhall Astra. It was blood red with a black roof and Liz could tell by his elongated description of the vehicle, that it was his pride and joy. To the right of it was what he called his little run-a-round, a Nissan Micra that was used for local errands near, and not so far, by him, and in time, he thought that when Liz got used to the local area that she may or may not be trusted to carry out those little errands.

Liz felt herself blush just a little at the trust and confidence that Davy was showing her in such a short period of time, but as they say, blood is thicker than water. When they returned to the office he instructed Suzie to sit back and enjoy the sandwiches that Liz had made earlier, which were still sitting on the table behind her, along with a tepid mug of tea.

Suzie smiled and said, 'Your wish is my command, Davy.'

She then produced a bottle of orange juice from the fridge beside the table and watched in anticipation the results of her new friend's ability to master the controller's job, but she knew that, rather than throw Liz in at the deep end at this early stage, Davy would sit down beside her and they would work as a team. To Suzie's delight, Liz did just great, better than she could have hoped for. After an hour or so there was a slight lull in the proceedings and Davy turned to Suzie and said, 'Well done, girl. I think that you certainly pulled the cat out of the bag this time. Your training technique is getting better and better!'

Liz turned to face them both and shouted, 'What about me, then?'

Davy smiled and in a very sarcastic manner added, 'If you hadn't passed that test first time, then good old Suzie here would not be getting her good old training bonus. Yes, ladies, there's method in the madness!'

Meanwhile, in a rather large house about five miles south-east of Omagh, in sprawling grounds, two great friends were settling down to a pot of their favourite coffee prepared by their favourite cook, cleaner and bottle washer, a spinster who was sixty-five years old: Mona Lisa Mc Kibbin, known to all and sundry as Mo. The top selling record of the early fifties, by the one and only Nat King Cole, had been her late father's favourite ballad and he couldn't help himself, against his wife's misgivings, of naming their only child Mona Lisa. For obvious reasons, some of her neighbours in her senior citizen accommodation, in Omagh town centre, lovingly referred to her as, Mona Lot.

The two friends had known each other since their first year at Royal School Dungannon, Co Tyrone and then at university, before both were headhunted by the same finance company in the City of London. They had majored in accountancy and achieved high levels of proficiency in that discipline throughout their time in London. They were both now thirty-two years old. James Roland Montague was the sole owner of the property while John Phillips was his trusted companion. It was obvious that James came from a privileged back ground and was a boarder at RSD, whereas John, who came from a working-class family, was a day boy. James was an only child while John was the eldest of two brothers and one sister. All his siblings were working and making homes for themselves in and around London. His father suffered a fatal heart attack not long after James' late father had died. John's mother was now a resident of the same senior citizens' accommodation as Mo.

The Montague family tree dated back to the plantation of Ulster in the early 17th century. A lot of the family estate had been sold off after his late father's death, Thomas Eustace Montague, five years earlier due to ongoing debts that had been inherited from previous generations. James felt that they were always in debt to the bank and had for several generations been paying what can only be described as extortionate interest rates to unscrupulous money-grabbing bastards, who were in the guise of dependable and loyal financial advisors. His mother had pre-deceased his father by ten years, which led to his father's downfall of excess drinking, gambling and throwing good money after bad, to the said cronies that James had dispatched on his inheritance. However, this made a substantial dent in the family coffers which in turn restricted James in indulging in the lavish lifestyle he craved.

His best friend, John Phillips was the most proficient accountant he had ever encountered and without him, James would never have achieved his unexpected results at university. So, after careful consideration, James offered John a position as his financial advisor when the dust had settled with the family estate. It wasn't long before John created a business plan that would be easily implemented. It took two years after the death of James' father before property sales were complete and all debts settled. Apart from the six-bedroom family home, there were about ten acres of grazing land that had been let out to two local farmers. The trust left to James by his father was yielding a healthy return for investment.

There was a small fledging delivery service in Omagh that needed an injection of ready cash sooner rather than later, and it wouldn't cost much to make a steal. The owner in question would have to agree to sell everything but the name and he would become a salaried manager but, for all intents and purposes, everyone else would assume that he still owned the business. He would deal with John and John only thus, creating a silent working partnership with the new owner. The business would move from a makeshift garage and run-down port-a-cabin in the centre of town to another location south-west of Omagh, on the A32, Davy's current address. It took a further two years and a lot of hard work from both Davy and John before the venture moulded into a profit-making enterprise.

But, not so quick. You see, while they were working in London, James and John had delved into the drug scene. They had made many good contacts both buying and selling but needed some sort of front to set up their own organisation and then make good and eventually, make big money, resulting in the lifestyle that James thought they both deserved, especially James.

One of the main contacts on the drug scene in London was a very well-educated Dubliner called Pascal Murray. He was a self-made successful businessman who had lost his fortune when the worldwide credit crunch struck in 2008. The only thing he was able to hold on to was the large family home situated north-east of Dublin on the Howth peninsula. He was in his mid-fifties with a wife and three grown-up children, who kept his private life to himself. The secret of his criminal success was to keep his head down and not to blow too much money in other people's faces. No one knew how much money he lost, not even his close family. As far as they were concerned, he had suffered minor losses but had redeemed those losses over a period of time and was now a financial advisor for an exclusive list of clients. It was he that James and John approached on one of their many trips to London. After a boozy lunch in an upmarket bistro in Mayfair a deal was struck between the three co-conspirators.

Pascal would arrange for the drugs to be brought in from mainland Britain. Mode of operation was on a need to know basis. James and John didn't need to know. When they had offered a hint of concern about being excluded from that part of the plan Pascal immediately said, 'Take it or leave it! There are plenty of other takers!' After a short pause he added, 'Listen, guys. We've known each other for years. I trust you and you trust me, yeah? The less anyone knows, the better for everyone concerned. Okay?'

Two weeks later, James and John were at their first pick-up point north of Dublin. It was a quiet Saturday afternoon when they found themselves in a layby just outside Swords close to the M1. A small white van pulled up behind them and the middle-aged driver studied the make and licence plate of their car. Satisfied that this was in fact the correct vehicle, the middle-aged man, wearing a hoodie with the hood pulled well over the top of his head and downwards, almost covering his eyes, approached the waiting car. He opened the passenger door where James was sitting, and placed an over-the-shoulder duffle bag into his lap and scarpered in a flash. The two friends glanced into the bag and scarpered just as quickly back to Omagh. Not a word was spoken until they were at least an hour into the journey and then they both erupted in laughter. Almost uncontrollable laughter.

Over the subsequent weeks there were another two pick-up points inserted into the operation. No pick-up point would be used twice in a row. Means of contact would be a pay-as-you-go mobile phone. When the vehicle from Omagh was about fifteen minutes from Swords they would contact the Dublin base. Then and only then would the relevant pick-up point be divulged. Apart from Swords the other two pick-up points would be just outside Malahide and Portmarnock, all on the east coast and all, north of Dublin. On each and every occasion everything went like a dream.

On their return to the Montague family home, the two friends broke off from the A5 a few miles south-east of Omagh and continued the last few miles along the back roads until they stopped at an old metal gate with a sign which read, in large black letters on a white background:

'Private Property. Admittance Strictly Forbidden.'

James alighted the vehicle and unlocked the heavy-duty lock and chain securing the gate in position and John drove through, then along a small dirt track for about 100 yards until he stopped alongside a small log cabin. By this time James had relocked the gate and they both stepped inside the cabin.

In the glory days of the estate it was used by the game keeper. It consisted of a small sitting room, galley kitchen, a small double bedroom and a toilet and shower room. All power had been switched off as it had not been in use for a prolonged period of time, but the two cohorts were now using it as a base for their illegal activities. An old-fashioned paraffin lamp was their only means of light but it served their purpose just dandy, bolstered with a small battery-operated blow heater. They had a hiding place under the floorboards under the old dusty bed. The drugs were kept there prior to break down and packaging, which was done inside the cabin in daylight hours and then dispatched to the relevant customers by John, far and wide. On no account were the drugs to be brought into the house. In order to keep up with demand James suggested that John should enlist a local go between in the guise of Davy and ORS Ltd. It was the perfect front. All the employees were dependable and because of the substantial success and growth of the company over the past two years, no one would be in the least bit suspicious with the increase in turnover. The drugs were broken down into manageable amounts, not too much, not too little, but enough to keep the customers wanting more... And more.

Davy of course would be on a nice little extra earner with a bonus thrown in now and then to keep him sweet. As long as no one succumbed to splashing the cash in the local area. Save it for the away trips or home improvements. The staff at ORS were all well-paid and had proved extremely loyal and dedicated to their employer. They all knew of course, that Davy couldn't have achieved the extraordinary success on his own and that there had to be a big fish supplying the money and the back-up. They had all encountered John at one time or another, especially when he and a local accountant arrived at the end of each month to bring the company paperwork up to scratch. But no one cared as long as ORS continued to be successful for the distant future. At least two of the drivers had been trained in the event that a stand-in would be required for Davy on days off or holidays. The two controllers were always on the ball and now with Liz as a potential future addition to the set-up, albeit if and when she was well and truly encompassed into the devious plan for the not-too-distant future, everything seemed to be ship-shape and Bristol fashion.

It wasn't long before Davy was trusted with the three pick-up points for the drugs. John had supervised him on several occasions before letting him loose on his own. He followed instructions explicitly and had impressed the Dublin base when there were last-minute changes. He was also instructed to take the same route to the log cabin hidden in the small copse in the estate. The gate would already be opened on his arrival and relocked on his departure. He only dealt with John and at this stage had never even clapped eyes on James. Another step in the direction of paramount security was that the dealership from which ORS leased its vehicles would also lease a run-around for use in the pick-up points for the drugs. This vehicle would be changed every six months or so depending on the number of trips to Dublin, which were slowly increasing.

Thus, the Nissan Micra that Liz saw in the garage when Davy was giving her the tour of his mini empire. Oh yes, although the drugs would always be contained in some sort of duffle bag, another security devise was introduced. The cargo, or gear, as the drugs became known, were placed inside a sealed bag within the duffle bag, secured with a numbered security tag which was recorded in Dublin and ratified in Omagh. This was belt and braces for both sides of the operation, which had become slick and professional. Everyone was a winner. Of course, James and John used a similar strategy for their end of the business.

Davy's distribution route was covered by various drivers in ORS who either didn't know, or didn't want to know what was in the sealed bags that they were delivering, all around the country. As far as they were concerned, they recorded them unto their handheld device and made sure the customer signed on receipt. Mostly to small business premises, for further distribution in the ever-growing network. Some of the delivery points were private residences, who preferred an un-liveried vehicle. Collection of monies from the customers was seven days after each delivery which was done by Davy, either in the Micra or sometimes in his own car. On the Monday of Liz and the boys' second week in Omagh Davy began to sow the seeds regarding Liz's future in the illicit activities. After her morning shift, Davy arranged with his mate, Alec, to once again volunteer to take the five boys to the local swimming pool.

'Tell you what, Liz. I've got a few things to do this afternoon. Why don't you keep me company?'

'Okay, Davy. What have you got in mind?'

'Well, it's like this, Liz. Most days of every week I have to collect payment for services rendered. Some of our customers like to pay cash. You know. To keep some of their money making off the books. Lots of people do it these days.'

'Don't I know it, Davy? I've watched Mum and Dad, Benny and Julie doing that all my life! Sure. Okay. I'll come with you.'

Davy continued, 'Some clients pay by bank transfer straight to our accountant, who deals with all the money aspects of ORS. When I've collected the cash on any particular day it gets picked up on that night by John, who sort of runs things for me behind the scenes. I can't do everything myself. You understand?'

With that said, Davy jumped into his private vehicle and Liz duly jumped into the passenger side. Davy was full of it. Driving around the local area in his up-to-date flash car with a good-looking dolly bird beside him. He was never at any location for more than a few minutes and always carried a fairly large brief case secured with two combination locks, one each side of the carrying handle.

On returning to the office that afternoon Davy placed all the thick brown envelopes containing the cash into the safe under the controller's desk. Suzie, who was on duty didn't bat an eyelid as Davy struggled under her legs to gain entry to the safe. He quite enjoyed that part of the exercise. He then asked Liz if she fancied a cuppa, not there in the office but in the kitchen in the house. It would be a little while before Alec brought the boys back from the swimming pool. Davy had given him enough money to take them to KFC afterwards. He wanted to talk to Liz in private.

As they both settled down at the kitchen table with their mugs of tea Davy said, quite nonchalantly: 'How would you like to earn some extra money, Liz? It won't be a lot at first but in the next three weeks you could help me out with the collections. On some days I need a helper to get round them all.'

'But, Davy, how would I find my way around the different locations?'

'Don't worry about that. I'll guide you round and when you think that you're confident to go on your own I'll also supply you with a small portable sat-nav.'

'But what car would I drive?'

'Listen, Liz. I can put you on the insurance as a temporary cover. You could use the Micra or even your own car if you like. It's worth twenty pounds a pick-up!'

'How much?'

'Twenty pounds a pick-up, and you could do four or five on any particular day which would make my life a lot easier, because on some days I could have more than twice as I had today.'

Liz was now deep in thought. She was depending on the part-time work as a controller to help finance her four-week stay in Omagh, but if she could earn up to £100 for an afternoon's work once or twice a week, she would feel an awful lot more independent. Before she got a chance to answer Davy said, 'I'll tell you what. I've more collections tomorrow afternoon. We'll take the Micra with you at the wheel and have another jaunt out. What do you say, Liz?'

She didn't have to say anything. It was done and dusted.

Over the next few days Liz and Davy proved to be a bespoke duo and she loved every minute of it. She knew that what they were doing wasn't totally legal, but it reinstalled an excitement she had not experienced in a long, long time. She was in control of her own destiny. She did it of her own accord. She was in control for the very first time in her adult life. It wasn't long before she went out on her own, with the help of the portable sat-nav. She was beginning to get high on the adrenaline and on a few occasions felt a tingle between her legs. And fuck the establishment. Fuck them all. And all the while Davy was wondering if he would ever get inside her knickers. But Liz knew that there could never be anything more than a platonic and working relationship between them. They may be distant cousins, but Liz saw him more like a brother, the closeness that she once had with her brother Lenny.

By the end of the four-week stay Liz was saying farewell to her newfound friends inside and outside the working environment. Her sons had enjoyed their time immensely with their new mates and had promised to return the following year and stay in touch on a regular basis until then. Davy accompanied them as far as the ferry in Dublin and later that evening at about seven o'clock they were back home in West Croydon, much to the delight of Robbie and Cissy, who were already in the house via the spare key, which Liz had left behind so that a watchful eye could be kept on the premises while they were away. Benny and Julie weren't far behind in their enthusiastic welcome home. The boys were allowed to stay up late recalling the great adventures they had in Omagh and all the places they had visited with Alec and Davy including the shenanigans they got up to with the local scallywags! Liz didn't say too much about her part as a cash collector, but her sons were singing her praises, about how quickly she orientated herself with the local countryside and beyond. And what a great asset Davy had said she had become. Liz blushed, just a little. A few days later the five boys were back at school and Liz sat down with a mug of tea and pondered over the four-week stay in Omagh with relish.

CHAPTER 14

MUSIC LESSONS AT SCHOOL WERE REBOOTED early in the first week of term. Of course, PJ was once again the main man. Liz had thought about him occasionally in Omagh, but only because the boys mentioned him whenever music was involved. They took part in several low-key concerts and had mesmerised everyone who listened to them, young and old. The McKenna brothers were without doubt everyone's favourite act, and Liz was so proud of them. She was equally proud of herself by the way she had taken the bull by the horns and proved her metal, in no uncertain terms. But she was still missing the company of a man in her life. If PJ could be persuaded that a friend with benefits was the only way that would be acceptable to both of their lifestyles, which would be better than nothing at all. No strings attached. None whatsoever. Maybe they could both live with that concept.

She might broach the subject the next time they went out for a drink, but it must be a well-kept secret, just to see if it would be feasible. It wouldn't be difficult. It needed to be tried and tested in their own good time and there would be no sleepovers at Liz's house, just shag-overs, but not all night. When the boys were tucked up in bed they never stirred, save Michael, who needed to be lifted for a pee. Yes, that could well be the way forward. As it happened, unknown to Liz, the same idea had occurred to PJ. Not as soft as he looked. Eh?

In November that year a meeting took place in a private members' club situated in a small alleyway off Charing Cross Road, London. The main door in the alleyway was small and uninviting, however the interior was magnificently decorated in a high-class Victorian style. The spiral staircase in the entrance hall led to a floor of suites used for very private soirees. Some for business, some for pleasure. James Montague and John Phillips were waiting patiently outside one of the suites when a very well-dressed, clean shaven man with broad shoulders opened the door and ushered them both inside. To greet them were a couple known as Roberto and Jemima Martini, sitting in two large leather armchairs. Each had a flute of champagne in their left hand and an E-cigarette in the other. She always sat on his left as if to recognise that he was the master and she was his lady-in-waiting. They were both slightly chubby and both follically challenged. He didn't care about the lack of hair but she disguised her challenge with an ill-fitting wig, which was reminiscent of a papier-mâché hat gone terribly wrong. Make-up was not one of her strong points.

He lovingly addressed her as Jem and she him as Bobby. No one else, absolutely no one else, would dare to presume that they could adopt such informal salutations. Mr M and Mrs M were to their liking. That, among other points of respect and protocol, were explained to the two visitors on immediate entry by their usher. There were no available chairs so they both stood in the centre space about ten feet from the small table in front of Mr and Mrs M. The door was locked by a well- dressed lady in a trouser suit and a fluffy white blouse. The key was left in the lock, the usher and the lady then took their places, he at the right shoulder of Mr M and she at the left shoulder of Mrs M.

The visitors listened in great detail from the well-spoken Mr M. Not too posh, but not too common. He sounded as if he had worked on his south of England accent to impress his business associates. He intended to sound well-educated, although those that knew him and his wife since the old days were well aware that they were brought up in the East End of London and had both left school at fifteen years of age. They looked as if they were in their early sixties. It had taken some considerable time to set up this meeting. James and John had spoken to a number of go-betweens before being granted an audience by way of the lady in the trouser suit, who they knew as Veronica. They had explained that they didn't mind dealing with Mr M's contact in Dublin (Pascal Murray) but wanted more of the big gear because that was where the really big money was.

The only way to do that was to deal with Mr M or his associates in London, and arrange transportation to Omagh using their own operatives. They would still deal with Dublin for MDMA (ecstasy), cannabis (skunk) the supply of cocaine (coke) but with a stand-alone service from London consisting of a much larger supply of coke. They wanted to expand their operation from the north-west coast of Ireland to the north-east coast, which of course would include the biggest money spinner of all: Belfast. Mr and Mrs M listened intently, although they had already been briefed to the tiniest detail by Veronica. They both liked what they heard. James did most of the talking with John chipping in with the monetary details.

After a brief silence Mr M said, 'Now then, gentlemen. On my right stands Reginald McCabe and on my good lady's left stands his wife Veronica. Reggie and Ronnie! Get it? Reggie and Ronnie! Well, Ronnie makes sure that all our bills are paid on time. If not, well, that's when she will hand over your account to her lovely hubby, Reggie. Now, Reggie leads our enforcement team. A visit from Reggie and his team will not be a happy event. We will get our money one way or the other, with interest, a big fucking interest clause, which will be in the contract that you will both sign immediately after this meeting.'

He looked lovingly at his wife and added, 'Am I making myself perfectly clear, Jem?'

To which she replied, 'Crystal fucking clear, Bobby!'

James and John assured them that every detail was in fact, crystal clear.

Mr M turned to Reggie and asked, 'What say you, Reggie?'

'Yes, Mr M.'

He then turned to Ronnie and asked, 'What say you, Ronnie?'

'Yes, Mr M.'

He then turned to his wife and asked, 'What say you, Jem?'

'Yes, Bobby.'

Mr M looked at the intrepid duo and said, 'Gentlemen. You've got four yeses.'

With that, they were taken out of the suite, along the hallway to another room where they finalised all the nitty-gritty details of the deal with Ronnie. In their absence, Mr M instructed Reggie with the following details: 'Reggie! Send in the waiter and waitress and then go downstairs to the bar and get yourself a well-earned drink.'

Without a word, just a nod, Reggie motioned for the two members of staff that Mr M had summoned, who were hovering along the hallway to enter the room. When they did so, the waiter locked the room, leaving the key in the door. They knew the drill. They were both dressed in identical uniforms. White long sleeve shirts, black bow-ties, black waist-coats, black trousers and black shoes. He stood in front of Jem and she stood in front of Bobby. They were both obviously adolescents. Bobby said: 'Right then, you two! Get naked! You can proceed to give us both our weekly servicing. And don't spare the fucking horses!'

James and John celebrated their newfound business operation in great style that night in the West End of London. No holds barred. Within a week of their return to Omagh, they received the first phone call from Ronnie. Both parties had agreed that all communications by this means would always be by a pay-as-you-go mobile phone, using a different one on each occasion. She gave them strict instructions for their first pick up in London, as per her briefing that night after the meeting with Mr and Mrs M.

It was agreed that there would be three pick-ups per year. Christmas, Easter and August. The plan was that Davy would pick up the gear at Christmas and Easter, as he had been visiting his relatives in West Croydon, on and off over those holiday periods for the last few years. They would involve Liz in Davy's pick-ups and of course give her a nice little sweetener, just to let her get a taste of easy money on her doorstep. A little Christmas and Easter bonus, so to speak. By the time she made her second trip to Omagh the following year for the summer holidays, she would be more than tempted by a much larger bonus to carry out the August pick-up on her own, stash it in the back of her vehicle and what with all the luggage for her and her five sons, it would be easy to conceal it. Using the vehicle and ferry system every time was by far the safest mode of transport.

After the call from Ronnie ended, James and John settled down in front of the blazing fire in the rather over-sized sitting room, which in days gone by was referred to as the drawing room. They both wore a brightly patterned bathrobe. The two matching armchairs had seen better days and James had promised himself that not just the chairs but the whole house would be restored to its former glory in the not too distant future.

'It's all going to plan, James.'

'I never had any doubts, old friend. The operation in London is slicker than slick. Even the way the gear arrives in England from Holland. It's so fucking simple.'

As this stage John stood up and walked the short distance to a small mahogany table and proceeded to pour two large glasses of Bushmills Whiskey from the nearly empty bottle, enhanced with several ice cubes in each, taken from the small ice bucket close to hand. He handed one to James and then returned to his armchair while sipping his own.

'I agree with you there, James. Into the south-east coast of England from Holland by a light aircraft or chopper. I'm not sure which, or maybe they use both on different trips.'

James drank from his glass and nodded in agreement and added, 'They certainly have the resources to have both on standby. The use of all those old, disused RAF air fields along the coast. They have been pretty much dormant for many years, and make it so simple to get in and out in a matter of minutes. And easy to switch if and when they need to for whatever reason. The Martinis are fucking raking the cash in. Hand over fist.'

There was a brief pause and then James spoke again. 'According to the bar man in that club in Charing Cross, those two old fuckers have a big fuck-off apartment in Cheney Walk in Chelsea, a big fuck-off villa in Spain and an even bigger fuck-off house in the Kent countryside. They have what I want. What I was destined for. What I would've had, if my parents, especially my father hadn't been so bloody blinkered in that old-fashioned outlook on life. It won't take long to get myself back on track and I'm taking you with me, old friend.'

They both finished their drinks, made their way up the creaky, steep, oak stairs and into the master bedroom they both shared. They shed their bath robes and crept naked under the crisp white sheets and soft duvet and then lovingly embraced. Never leave your best friend's behind.

The festive activities over the Christmas of 2017 at the McKennas went as well as they always did. Davy of course arrived at Heathrow Airport as per usual but on this occasion, he picked up a hire car and drove to West Croydon. His brief from John was that Davy was intending to visit some old friends in Liverpool on his way home. After a few days on the piss, he would then catch the ferry to Belfast and onwards to Omagh. Plain and simple. The truth of the matter was that he would of course drive straight to the ferry in Liverpool with the gear and get home pretty damn quick. But of course, he had to pick up the gear at a location somewhere in West Croydon. This is when he would tempt Liz into helping him. Although he would have a sat-nav he would encourage Liz to help as she was much more familiar with the local area than he was. No point in taking any unnecessary risks and of course the promise of a tempting cash-in-hand bonus for Liz would make it all plain sailing.

So, on the 27th December after a long and meaningful conversation with Liz they both made their way in Davy's hire car to a petrol station not far from Liz's address. Ann and Wheelie Ferris had been invited to visit that afternoon and agreed to keep an eye on the kids while Liz showed Davy to the local shop so that he could buy some cigarettes. It was almost ten to five and night had fallen when they pulled into the large car park adjacent to the brightly-lit location. Davy drove into a dark corner at the left-hand side of the car park, away from the lights and any closed-circuit cameras that were covering the fuel pumps, as per the detailed instructions he had received that afternoon on the pay-as-you-go mobile phone. A small dark-coloured vehicle parked opposite the entrance had been paying close attention to them, noting the make, colour and registration of the hire car and also the occupants.

Davy's mobile phone rang. Identity verification and code words were exchanged. At precisely five o'clock a dark-coloured smart car pulled up beside them, facing the same way with the driver's side window fully lowered. Liz did likewise with her passenger side window. The driver of the smart car, who was wearing a dark hoodie immediately shone a torch into Liz's face, which blinded her for a few seconds, and then quickly pushed a very large canvas bag through both open windows and into her hands. She had it on her lap in a split second and quick as a flash, the smart car was gone. Without further ado Davy pulled away and returned to Liz's address.

Not a word was spoken throughout the short journey. When they alighted the car Davy was carrying the large canvas bag which was then hidden under the bed in Liz's room but only after Davy completed a quick inspection of the contents. Their actions were carried out so quickly the kids and their minders hardly realised they were back inside the house. Ann and Wheelie were being treated by the five boys to a little impromptu jamming session around the kitchen table, prompted by Liz on her and Davy's departure to the shop.

The following morning, bright and early as promised, Davy arrived in the hire car at Liz's house. She was more than just relieved to see him as she had watched nearly every hour on the clock throughout the night. Her sons were all still fast asleep and because Davy had made a big deal the previous night with his goodbyes, there was no need to wake them as he collected the canvas bag from Liz at the bottom of the stairs. Davy checked inside the bag to make sure nothing had been disturbed, and then gave Liz a sealed brown envelope. A hug and a kiss and he was gone. Liz sat on the sofa in her sitting room and opened the brown envelope. When she counted out the wad of £20 notes it totalled £500!

Davy arrived in Belfast Docks the following morning and after handing over the hire car was picked up by one of his drivers, and they quickly made their way back to Omagh. Davy transferred the canvas bag into the Micra and proceeded to deliver the gear to the cabin in the woods. John was ready and waiting and on Davy's arrival quickly checked inside the bag. He thought that all his Christmases had all come at once. He could hardly believe that the whole operation had gone so well. It was time for him and James to get to work, as it would take considerably longer to break this much coke down ready for delivery. And that, after a long hard week's work for the two friends, was the understatement of the decade.

They still had the other different types of gear that they were still getting from Dublin. They had a long way to go, but were encouraged by the large amount of the top stuff they had already prepared for delivery during that first week. If this was going to be a regular occurrence, as everyone had planned, then they would have to think very seriously about bringing in some help. But, for now, they would keep beavering away and keep reminding themselves about all the lovely lolly that would soon be rolling in. Much more than had been forthcoming before.

The Omagh Cartel was beginning to spread its wings, slowly at first and before long the demand was greater than supply. Easter 2018 came round in no time at all, which saw Davy back in West Croydon for his scheduled pick-up, accompanied of course by his almost, seasoned accomplice, the one and only Liz McKenna. Another hire car, another location, another canvas bag, another series of identity verifications and code words. On this occasion the kids were visiting their grandparents when Davy and Liz went out for a quick drink the night before his return to Omagh via Liverpool. They had plenty of time to stash the gear in the same place as before. Davy even tried to get a leg over, as they had the house and more importantly the bedroom to themselves, but to no avail. He didn't know about the arrangement Liz had with PJ, but she knew. Oh yes, another £500 for good old Liz. It couldn't have been simpler.

When Davy arrived back in Omagh and consequently at the cabin in the woods, once again John was waiting patiently, if not a little anxiously. He shook his head in disbelief, as he once again checked inside the bag. That very day, James and John found themselves in at the deep end for another three hard weeks. Some days they were at it for more than twelve hours with just two flasks of coffee and a box full of sandwiches, courtesy of housekeeper/cook, Mona Lisa McKibben.

The easiest part of the operation was getting rid of the gear and collecting the dosh. Payment to a third-party account in the Bahamas by bank transfer, from their own business account in the Channel Islands, that would eventually find its way into the Martinis' coffers, was equally as simple. But the intrepid accountant soon realised that an individual offshore bank account would be required for himself and James, sooner rather than later. But good old John knew that his contact in the City of London financial square mile, who had already proved to be invaluable, would help them both out, albeit an addition to the princely fee already in operation.

August 2018 was looming on the horizon and Liz knew well that this scheduled pick-up was going to be a solo effort for her. She had been well groomed by Davy. She had been coaxed and re-coaxed, and assured and re-assured, that it would be easy-peasy, and a much greater financial reward would be definitely on the cards! The mobile phone she had to use was sent to her by recorded delivery from Davy. She was contacted the day before the pick-up by those unknown to her, with the normal detailed instructions. Her heart was pounding from the moment contact was made by the suppliers, even through the night and all through the following day. In her almost panic-stricken state, on the morning of the operation, she carried out a dry run through just in case of any traffic problems or unforeseen road works.

Every so often she would get the shakes, just like in her hey-day with Sharon when they both suffered with the hangovers from hell. She cooked for her sons, cleaned the house, the washing machine was going non-stop, but no matter how busy she kept herself her heart pounded more and more. She never heard a word any of her sons said to her and she quite often gave the wrong or a senseless answer. The eldest two of the five siblings, Steven and Connor, thirteen and eleven years old respectively, made several lame excuses to their younger brothers, thinking it was that time of the month for their mum, not realising that that time of the month was no longer an occurrence since the birth of Michael, the youngest and possibly the feistiest of the brood.

The pick-up and stashing the gear went exactly according to plan, as did the car journey the following day to Holyhead. She hadn't noticed on her last holiday journey twelve months previously, just how many staff there were at the port. There were people wearing different types of uniform and all wearing high-vis jackets or vests. Liz and her kids were waved through from the dockside and onto the ferry just like August the previous year. With only a nod from Liz and lots of hand-waving from the five boys, resulting in smiles and returning hand-waves from those in authority, who should know, but did not know, any better. Not even a cursory check! Davy met Liz and her merry crew at Dublin Port and in less than two hours, with Davy at the steering wheel, they arrived safely at Davy's house in Omagh.

While the five sons offloaded their luggage, Davy, unbeknown to them, slipped away with the contraband and made his way to the cabin whereupon he would be awarded a promotion and a substantial pay rise. For all intents and purposes, he would still be the top dog of Omagh Reliable Services. However, his official title on the drugs operation would be junior partner. This would in time validate the creation of another offshore bank account for him. James and John knew full well, that Davy would be the help they badly needed in preparing the gear for distribution and now would be the right time to introduce him to the top man, namely James himself. They both knew that this moment had to arrive but were never sure if they could fully trust him, but who else could they trust? And dear old Davy always had an inkling of who the top man was. He wasn't the sharpest tool in the box but he was far from being completely stupid, so better to take him into their confidence, rather than he find out some other way. When James arrived at the cabin and the formal introductions took place, Davy found it difficult to comprehend how much more responsibility and trust was being placed in him. On his return journey to Omagh he realised that he had suddenly found a new lease in life, a newfound feeling of great confidence. His new official title of junior partner played over and over in his mind and he just loved the sound of it. Junior partner! He was on the way up. Oh yes. He was definitely on the way up. All the way fucking up!

Meanwhile Liz was settling down at the kitchen table to a nice mug of tea and a biscuit. She felt that she had shed a load of weight in sweat and anxiety and, although her under clothes and blouse were still slightly damp, she couldn't have cared less. She was home but not dry, and the boys, well the boys were already out in the back garden kicking a football around. She had done it! Yes, she had fucking done it! On her fucking own!

The following morning, when Liz and Davy were alone in the kitchen, he handed her another brown envelope. It was much bigger than the previous envelopes she had received and very bulky to handle. He watched her count out the £20 notes onto the kitchen table.

'Holy fuck,' she whispered. She thought that she would never get to the end.

'Holy fuck!' This time it was a little louder. All of a sudden, she looked up at Davy. He was simply smiling. She was simply aghast. There, on the table was the total sum of £5,000!

'Holy fuck!' she shouted.

'Keep the noise down,' he whispered.

'But Davy! What am I going to do with it all?'

'Don't worry yourself, love. I'll keep it safe for you. You just say when you want some cash and I will give it to you. Simple.'

'But Davy! For fuck's sake. How will I spend it all?'

'Spend within reason while you're here and when you get back to West Croydon, I'll arrange for a few hundred at a time to be transferred to your bank account. No one will be any the wiser. Trust me, Liz.'

'Are you sure it will work, Davy?'

'Of course it will. That's for sure.'

Over the next four weeks Liz was kept busier than ever. Davy soon re-orientated her to the various routes which meant he could spend more time with his new partners in the cabin. One of his trusted drivers, Jimmy Banks, was promoted to operations manager to help in the company office, and although Liz still helped out as a controller, Jimmy knew that she was a law onto herself. She also kept a detailed account of her clients, which were growing by the week and sometimes by the day. She kept the information in a small hardback notebook. It was a form of abbreviations, a sort of personal code that she could understand perfectly but anyone else would have found extremely difficult to decipher. Even Davy, with all his expertise, would be slightly baffled regarding the relevant names and locations. She was trusted with both the delivery of the gear and the payments made thereafter. Davy was always on call to help out at really busy periods and solve any minor problems over the phone. Liz had become, without doubt, Davy's most valued asset. Each time she returned to West Croydon his workload practically doubled, or on some occasions even trebled, thus more responsibility was passed on to Jimmy Banks. He half-knew what was going on but found it difficult to refuse the extra cash he was earning. He too would welcome Liz with open arms when she hopefully returned the following August.

Davy also knew that she would need more time off to enjoy her newfound wealth and independence, which in turn led to a few late nights with Davy and a few other couples at very upmarket establishments, but she was never tempted to drop her guard, or her knickers.

Babysitters for her sons were not a problem. She also relished the fact that she could well afford her five boys, whatever money they needed, to pay for all the increasing activities they were taking part in, especially with their mates from in and around Omagh. Nothing was out of her reach, including a small collection of new summer outfits, some fancy jewellery and expensive perfume that she would keep well hidden from her parents when she returned home. She would be able to treat PJ to a meal in a nice bistro in West Croydon, or even in the West End of London, even take him to a West End show! She was also looking forward to wearing her ill-gotten gains when she and PJ got together for their lust-filled trysts. They never needed a lot of alcohol to get the juices flowing. They had a genuine passion for each other, but Liz knew in her heart of hearts that if they went public with their relationship, it would most likely go sour, like so many other things in her life.

They were both more than happy with their set-up, and the only other person that knew for sure about their arrangement was PJ's aunt, Kaz Coulter, and she couldn't have been happier for them both. She was beginning to worry about who would look after PJ when she was no longer there. He had always confided in her especially about Liz, even from those early days when he was struck with love at first sight. Kaz was not getting any younger and she dearly loved PJ and Liz and she was also the adopted Aunt Kaz to Liz's five sons. But she was a little concerned about what she felt was an unhealthy relationship with Davy. She was positive that Liz would never cheat on her nephew, but she didn't trust Davy as far as she could spit. She knew that he was the ultimate twat!

CHAPTER 15

SEPTEMBER 2018 SAW LIZ'S SONS back to school. Her parents, Robbie and Cissy, along with Benny and Julie quizzed her about the time she spent with Davy in Omagh, under the same roof, but Liz assured them that they were close but only as close as family. The sisters-in-law had remarked between themselves, that because Liz didn't have to worry about getting pregnant again, if it was either of them at her age, then they would be swinging off the chandeliers. Mind you, if the truth be known, that's what they were doing on a monthly basis anyway, regardless of their age.

Liz loved having the upper hand over her nosey family, not just about her law-breaking activities but by having the independence she had craved all her adult life. She didn't like keeping PJ in the dark, but he would go off his trolley if he knew what she was up to and of course, he would tell Kaz and that would go down like a bag of bollocks. No, for now it was her well-kept secret and hers alone, that side of the Irish Sea.

Christmas, 2018. Davy was back in town. Not one sinner in the McKenna family had the slightest notion what he and Liz were up to, and Liz bloody loved it. Gear picked up and away to Omagh via Liverpool. Another £500 for Liz and another shot at bucking the system and a poke in the eye for the establishment. She had a permanent grin of satisfaction on her face and an exhilarating feeling, down to the very depths of her emotions, which in turn led to an eruption of sexual frenzy when PJ turned up for his ration of hip-grinding and oral love-making. It didn't take long for them to get naked and cover each other in bodily fluids. He only wished that he had inherited the same recent energy that Liz had conjured up. She was like a wild cat at times but could also hold him like a baby when they had both climaxed. He never wanted this experience to end. He wanted her forever.

For the McKenna clan, 2019 was another cracking year.

Work hard and play hard. Liz agreed to work part-time in their head office because even her youngest son, Michael, who was now six years old, was at primary school until two o'clock each day. Sixteen hours per week on the books would not affect her benefits and a few more hours off the books would come in handy. Watching her dad and uncle each day hatching contracts over the phone or rushing out to an important meeting was always exciting to witness. Every so often her attention was diverted to Cissy and Julie, who were the epitome of business women. All four had a lot to offer. They made the daily grind of running the family business look easy and all four were bloody good at it. They were without doubt a formidable team. The two brothers were still as handsome as ever, each having acquired a hint of distinguished grey hair. Cissy and Julie had managed to hold on to their youthful figures and model good looks, enhanced by the labour of love by Jethro, the hairdresser who had once employed Liz and her friend Sharon. It just bothered Liz that her mum and aunt could be so deceptive, so unfaithful and so down-right fucking cows to their husbands, who worshiped the ground they walked on. She knew that they still had their various, all-in fuck buddies, at all-in fuck parties, somewhere near Guildford in Surrey, as well as tearing the beavers off each other whenever they got the chance. So why should she feel guilty about her own wrong doings? Fuck them!

Once again Easter came round fast and Davy was back in town. On this occasion he would return via Holyhead and Dublin. James and John thought it wise to change the route with the view of possibly using the Stranraer-Belfast ferry as another alternative. Although Liz pocketed another £500, she felt a bit short changed compared to the £5,000 she had received in August the previous year. It was great to have that amount of money, but even though she spent it sparingly it had already gone. And she wanted more. More than the occasional £500 back-hander.

August that year saw her venture in her second solo run. She was much more mentally prepared than last time. She was much more brazen than last time. She was much more anti every man and his fucking dog than last time. But much more important than anything else, she wanted it, much more than anyone would ever realise. And no one would deter her in her quest for bucking the system and for the rush of adrenaline that was flowing through her veins and of course, the big bucks, yes... The big pay-off of another £5,000. Yes. This was it. The ultimate mind-blowing experience. And the five boys unknowingly played their part like seasoned professionals. What a fucking turn on!

Once again, the month of August flew by in Omagh. Another £5,000 for Liz plus what she earned as a controller, plus all the extras she was earning in the resident drop-off and pick-up, which was always a Micra. She had surpassed everyone's expectations in the control room. Jimmy Banks would quite often ask for her input regarding the day-to-day running of the business. He and the other two controllers, Suzie and Gertie, couldn't help but admire her dedication and enthusiasm, although no one in the company was aware of the extensive rewards that she received from the powers that be. Davy had to admit that once again, she would be sorely missed when she and her sons returned home. Her nights out were still a real hoot and one of Davy's mates, having failed once again, to get her into a smooching mood, sighed in a frustrated tone, 'Are you sure that Liz is not a fucking lesbian?'

Her sons were going from strength to strength regarding their music capabilities. They were playing on a regular basis at various summer activities indoor and outdoor, afternoons and evenings. All five could sing and play their instruments to extreme proficiency and had acquired a small fanbase of both young and old. They all realised that they had been fully accepted into the local community in Omagh, especially by their mates, quite simply because their full names had all been shortened by mutual consent. If the truth be known the shortened version had been in use with their mates in West Croydon for many a year. So, to all those outside their immediate family they were known as Steve,

Con, Ry, Anto and Mike. This in turn gave the five boys an idea for a name change for their folk group. On previous performances on both sides of the Irish Sea they were known as the McKenna brothers, but that was about to change forthwith. They decided to use the first letter of each of their Christian names to form an unusual but catchy title. They were now billed as 'SCRAM!' The exclamation mark was an absolute must on their billing.

Liz was quite pleased with their endeavours, even the name change sounded almost professional. On one such occasion they won a local talent competition, which was held in the Omagh Folk Park. Not only did they win it by a country mile but were presented with a huge shield and a cheque for £200. The name of their folk group, SCRAM! would, eventually be added to the already large number of previous winners by means of a small plaque, and the icing on the cake was that they would be invited back in the New Year to take part in the annual four-day folk festival in the same location. Their line up when they performed was from right to left: Steve on guitar, Con on banjo, Mike on bodhran, Ry and Anto on button accordions. All of course supplied by PJ at a knock down price and all, of course, paid for, by their dotting grandparents. All the tuition on the various instruments that they had received from PJ was definitely paying dividends. Their singing voices were very impressive but most of all, it was their perfect harmonies that stole the show every time. One elderly member of a particular audience was heard to remark, 'The last time I heard harmonies that good, it was the Everly Brothers!'

When they all arrived home at the end of August, prior to the new school term in September, all five boys had lots of stories to tell both at home and at school. Liz as usual, kept her cards close to her chest. It didn't take long for PJ to arrange a night out but to his surprise Liz had beaten him to it. She organised the next-door neighbour's daughter, Jody, who was twenty years of age and attending the local college of music, so the babysitting fee that Liz paid was most welcome. Plus, the fact she could play a number of string instruments that she would gladly bring with her. Liz knew that they would have a great jamming session but not too late, as she wanted her boys in bed at a reasonable hour so that when she checked on them on her return from her night out with PJ they would be sound asleep. Then he and she could get down and get with it.

They both wished that they could spend a complete night together and that would happen sooner, rather than later. Liz had a devious plan for Jody to stay overnight on a Saturday and she would take the bull by the horns, book a double room in a posh hotel for one night of pure unadulterated passion. She would explain to PJ that she had been saving most of the money she had earned in Omagh for just such an occasion, with no mention of her illegal earnings. And, as he was always footing the bill for their nights out, it was her turn to splash the cash. He would of course initially object, but she knew that she would talk him round.

In early October that year, 2019, PJ's Aunt Kaz asked for him and her legal representative, namely one Bartholomew Barnard Coulter, semi-retired barrister and in fact her brother-in-law, to meet at her home in West Croydon for a formal discussion regarding her estate. PJ always referred to him as Uncle Bart. She decided as she was not getting any younger, (she never gave away her age to anyone except her late husband, Reginald) that it was time to document her wishes in her last will and testament. She had indicated to Bartholomew a few months earlier what she thought would be the right thing to do and he had agreed wholeheartedly with her wishes. He had no design on his late brother's estate. Bartholomew, after all, had been left the large family home in the country and was financially secure in no uncertain terms. The trio met in Kaz's kitchen, sitting at the kitchen table with a pot of tea and some chocolate biscuits, just as she and Reginald had always done on many previous occasions. Reginald used to say, 'There's nothing that can't be sorted out over a nice cup of tea and a biscuit.'

PJ was absolutely gobsmacked when Uncle Bart read out

the entire will across the kitchen table. He couldn't comprehend the legal jargon but as soon as Uncle Bart ended his oration he leaned across the table and said, 'Quite simply, my boy. You will have more money than you know what to do with.'

Kaz added, 'And if you decide to sell this place to move away then that's not a problem. Just take my Reggie, he's in the stone jar on top of my dressing table, and me, of course, and scatter us under a tree in your back garden.'

Poor old PJ didn't know what hit him! He was still shaking as he drove to Liz's house, but there was only one catch. He promised his Aunt Kaz and Uncle Bart that the contents of the will must remain secret until after her death. Kaz was a little anxious that if the news got out then PJ would be up for grabs by many a gold digger, who may be found lurking with intent, and of course there were still cousins and such back home in Dublin, as well as the odd hanger-on in London. That night of all nights was the night of the big event. It was a Saturday and Liz had organised Jody the baby sitter to agree to a sleepover, with a well-earned bonus for the extra responsibility for the overnight stay.

Well, the car journey from West Croydon to the Majestic Country House Hotel near Woking, was like a ride in a dodgem car. Liz kept asking why PJ was driving so erratically but he just answered her in gibberish. The reason they had chosen this particular hotel was because it had a swimming pool and spa facility, and the likely-hood of running into any of their friends was practically zero. They arrived at six o'clock and were soon in the pool for a quick dip before their romantic dinner at half past seven. The whole evening couldn't have gone better. At about ten o'clock they strolled from the restaurant, through the large entrance hall and up the thick carpeted stairs to the first floor, along the corridor to their room and never once did they take their eyes off each other. Liz couldn't believe the change in PJ when they entered the room. In the past she had always taken the initiative in their foreplay, but this time, this bloody time, he was like a man possessed. Gently possessed. He was in complete control and she knew that for whatever reason, she had woken a hidden self in her lover.

But, of course, there was the fact that there were no children who might discover their extra, exuberant, sexual curriculum. Do not disturb! Or did the news of PJ's newfound secret wealth also have a helping hand in promoting his desire to satisfy both their sexual appetites? He was in charge for the very first time in his life. He was definitely on top of the world and on top of Liz. But he didn't mind swapping positions later, as he knew she would like that. He didn't mind at all, top or bottom, any way up and any way down. And God bless all who sail in her!

The following morning they had a cooked breakfast served in their room, brought by a lovely lady of about fifty years of age. She was the ultimate in service style that would have been expected at any top hotel in the land, not that Liz or PJ would have any previous experience of any hotel, much less a top class one, but this was special and as far as they were concerned it was as top class as they were ever going to get for the foreseeable future. Little did Liz know that PJ had plans of his own, regarding further use of top hotels and restaurants, but he mustn't jump the gun!

After eating breakfast, the charming lady that had brought it to their room returned to take away the trays of dirty dishes. When in the ensuing conversation she realised that the young couple had not yet sampled the delights of the spa facility, apart from the swimming pool and hot tub, she encouraged them both to pay a visit as there was a special offer that weekend for residents. A massage and a good rub down would be a heavenly experience for them both. Liz thought that after such a heavy breakfast it would be unwise to succumb to temptation, but the lady advised them that the management would allow them to book by phone from their room, leave their overnight bags in the left luggage when they booked out at midday, and then spa time any time after that. Howzat! Well, they did just that and the spa experience was every bit as good as promised. They reckoned that the lady who recommended the whole episode must have been on commission. She was definitely great value for money. Although she booked the hotel using her debit card, Liz discreetly paid the bill by cash at reception, which caused a slightly raised eyebrow from the young man on duty accepting the cash. He should be so lucky. PJ had suggested once they had showered and dressed in their respective changing rooms, that they meet in the coffee lounge for a quick brew before heading back to West Croydon.

Liz was relaxing on a soft leather armchair, just flipping through a glossy fashion magazine when a lady dressed in what was obviously a designer sports outfit, with very tight-fitting leggings, which left little to the imagination, bumped into the small table beside Liz. When Liz looked up, the lady in question let out a little gasp, as if she had seen a ghost, or maybe she didn't believe her eyes. Liz couldn't tell. The lady who was possibly a little younger than her parents, appeared to have a great figure and spoke in a soft, well-educated accent.

Liz asked, 'Are you all right?'

'Yes, yes, thank you. I'm sorry for being so awkward but I'm trying to locate my husband and you, well, bumping into you… Here… Like this. It's just uncanny.'

Liz was confused and asked, 'Do I know you from somewhere?'

'No. I don't think so, but you look remarkably like a friend of mine and my husband. You are her younger double! Maybe you are a relative?'

Liz was intrigued and inquired, 'Well then, if you tell me her name maybe we can shed some light on the subject.'

'Well now. Her name is Cissy McKenna and she and her sister-in-law help to run the family business with their husbands, who happen to be brothers. They live in West Croydon. I don't know exactly where but we meet up now and again for a social event.'

Liz gave a little smile and added, 'What sort of social

event would that be then?'

'Oh, just a girls' night out, now and again.'

Liz gave another little smile and asked, 'Do their husbands not go along as well?'

'Well no, not really. It probably wouldn't be their cup of tea. All us girls together. You understand? Just a friendly get-together.'

Liz could hardly contain herself but looked up and said, 'Just a friendly get-together, in the all-together... Yes?'

Just then a gentleman of a similar age to the lady, appeared in what appeared to be another expensive designer sports outfit and asked in a similar accent, 'Who is this delectable specimen of sex on legs? Is she all alone? I do hope so.'

They both looked down at Liz's subtle cleavage under her V-neck sweater, tongues practically hanging out. Liz stood up and looked them both up and down with complete distaste and said, 'I may look like my fucking mother but there's no way you two perverts are ever going to get me to one of your any-way-you-like fuck parties. Are we clear?'

To which the lady replied, 'What ever do you mean? We just have harmless fun. Don't we, Simion?

'Yes, of course we do, Daphne.'

'Tell you what, Simion.'

'What's that, Daphne?'

She leaned close enough to whisper into his ear, 'A mother and daughter at the same time would be absolutely scrumptious!'

PJ appeared and wondered why Liz had such a scowl on her face when she said, 'Come on, PJ. The bill's paid. Time to go home.'

Without another word, they left the gobsmacked couple standing in what can only be described as a form of utter amusement. Daphne was definitely wet in her lower region, and Simion was putting his imagination into overdrive!

As Liz and PJ headed for the main door carrying their overnight bags, Daphne and Simion couldn't help but notice the young tight buttocks under the tight-fitting sports bottoms that the young lovers were wearing. Once again Daphne whispered into Simion's ear, 'Mother and daughter and boy-friend and me. Just think of the kicks you would get watching and, of course, taking some nice kinky photographs, my lovely horn-ball of a husband.'

To which he replied, 'Maybe not those two but... Thought for the future, my love. Thought for the future. We must put another ad into our monthly magazine. It's paid premiums in the past.'

PJ tried in vain to quiz Liz about what seemed to be an unusual encounter, but she just brushed it aside and said that it was a simple case of mistaken identity. The remainder of the drive home consisted of the usual banter they had developed over the years. They had been close before but the hotel stay had now cemented their relationship, without a doubt. That's for sure.

On their return to Liz's house they were met by her five sons, who were full of joys of spring. Not just because their mum was home but because they all liked PJ and were pleased that he had taken her away for a great night out. Little did they or PJ know just how expensive it was, but Liz insisted that PJ take the credit otherwise tongues might wag. Between them, Liz and PJ had the good sense to pre-warn Cissy and Robbie of their plans. Ask no questions, get no lies, but if the truth be known, Liz's parents gave the plan the nod of approval.

The Christmas festivities of 2019 went as usual with an almighty McKenna bang. Everyone in the immediate family was there, including Lenny, who was on leave from the Royal Navy. He was being posted back to Gibraltar early in the New Year with promotion to petty officer first class, and everyone was making plans for another holiday there once he got settled. Benny, Julie, their three daughters and husbands were all chomping at the bit. Ann and Wheelie Ferris were in great form. It had taken a while for the unfortunate wounds to heal fully, after the fallout concerning baby Michael's arrival, but that was more than six years before and everything seemed to be on the up and up for now. Of course, Davy was back in town and for the first time PJ was also invited. Davy didn't much care for PJ, especially when he saw how much Liz's five sons reacted when he walked into the party. Davy never knew when to give up on a woman, any woman. He had always worn-them down eventually, but it now dawned on him that he would never get into Liz's knickers, not then, not ever. Bastard!

But he had a plan that he wished to discuss with Liz that would be highly profitable for them both. He was finding it difficult to get her on her own, which hadn't been a problem in the past... Before that bastard PJ showed up. Davy always knew that Liz and PJ were friends, because he was the music tutor, that her sons looked up to him and admired him, but he didn't want that to get in the way of any future ventures that he had in mind. He had also promised his co-partners in Omagh, namely James and John, that he could convince her to take part in an extra pick-up early in the New Year. Mid-term for the schools and the annual four-day music festival in the Omagh Folk Park fell on the same week in February 2020. What a golden opportunity to put a plan of action into operation with a most profitable ad-hoc pick-up.

The London connection had already sanctioned it, but it was up to Davy to put the last piece of the jigsaw into place. He was positive that Liz would be up for it, tempted for sure, by the extra bumper bonus she would receive. He just needed to get her alone, but not just for five or ten minutes. He needed time to explain how it would all work. A much bigger consignment and a much bigger payday for Liz. Then, in the early evening Liz's phone rang and when she answered it, she told everyone that it was Sharon and Gino who were in Southampton until early January and they would like to arrange a visit. She apologised to all present and then withdrew to her parent's sitting room to continue the conversation. PJ jumped at the chance and volunteered to keep an eye on her sons, especially Michael, who at this stage was hanging precariously from a tree in the back garden. He was always causing a bit of a commotion, but in this case also a great deal of laughter.

Davy sneaked from the garden and waited patiently in the front hallway, immediately next to the sitting room door, which was slightly ajar. Liz was obviously enjoying catching up with Sharon and Gino but Davy was becoming impatient by the second. When eventually the call ended Davy pounced onto Liz like a bat out of hell. She was startled to say the least.

'What the fuck,' she began to say, when Davy put his index finger of his right hand against her lips.

'Look, Liz. We need to talk. This is important. I mean very, very important.'

'Well then, Davy. You'd better hurry up and don't try that old, let me into your knickers routine. Change the fucking record. What's up?'

'You're what's up, Liz. You're definitely what's up, Liz.'

'Stop mucking about, Davy, and tell me what's so very, very important.'

Davy went on to explain that the folk festival that her boys were invited to play in was during the same week as mid-term break in February 2020, Thursday through to Saturday. He would arrange their travel arrangements via Holyhead-Dublin as per usual and he would, as per usual meet them at Dublin Port. Because her boys had won the talent competition the previous August, they would be invited to play on two of the afternoons. Night-time performances were for over eighteens only. He would also arrange with his contacts that because of the travel time from West Croydon to Omagh and back again, the preferred afternoons would be Friday and Saturday. So, outward journey on Thursday and homeward journey on Sunday.

Davy would also explain to her family that due to the distance that she and her sons would have to travel, the local council in Omagh would foot the bill for all travel expenses. If they believed that they would believe anything but as far as Liz's sons' musical talents were concerned, anything was possible. He added that Liz could also enthuse what a great opportunity this would be for SCRAM! Surely everyone would be more than supportive, not just the family but PJ especially. He would be able to boast that his tutorship was the basis on which the boys could build their future success. It has to be said that on this occasion Davy was really turning it on... Full blast!

The pick-up for the gear would be the night before, as in previous operations. The time and location to be relayed by the same means, a pay-as-you-go mobile phone which in fact would be delivered once again by recorded delivery. A much larger than usual consignment due to local demand in Omagh and Belfast, and a much larger bonus. If the truth be known, the demand had also grown in Dublin, but most of all in London, which was swiftly becoming the cocaine capital of Europe. Liz took a few moments to try and take it all in when Davy suggested that she sleep on it, but assured her that it was another stroll in the park for them both. 'Come on, Liz, show the lot of them what you've got.' With that said they rejoined the party with Davy hanging back, to give Liz a few minutes' grace before he made his appearance. As she walked along the hallway Davy whispered after her, 'No need to make PJ jealous. Is there?'

The following day, Boxing Day, Davy phoned Liz and asked if he could come round for a quick cuppa and have a bit of craic with the boys. He also reminded her that she was required for the Christmas pick-up that evening at a time and place yet to be determined. He wanted to make sure that PJ would not be there. Liz agreed and as PJ would be visiting his Aunt Kaz, they could talk in private. No sooner said than done. He was outside her front door pronto by means of his hired car. Her sons were pleased to see him, and thanked him once more for the great Christmas presents he had given them at the family party the previous day. Once the dust settled, Liz and Davy made their way into her sitting room. Liz ensured that they sat opposite each other in her well-worn armchairs, just in case he was feeling a little amorous, using the festive spirit as an excuse, which had been the case in the past. She had no problem with that evening's intended operation and the securing of the gear under her bed. Davy insisted that PJ did not spend the night while the gear was in the house. Well, Liz lit on him like a banshee.

'How dare you assume that PJ made a habit of staying here overnight. How dare you assume anything of the sort. You're a cheeky fucker. Yes, we are an unofficial item, but we wouldn't dare throw it in the faces of my boys. Just who the fucking hell do you think you are, Davy? Eh? And for what? Five-hundred bloody quid?'

To say that Davy was on the back foot would have been a vast understatement. He had to make up ground pretty damn quick.

'Not just five-hundred bloody quid, Liz, but a damn sight more. A damn sight more. Believe me.'

'What are you on about, Davy?'

'Well, Liz. Not if, but when, we pull off the pick-up and delivery in February, it will be worth much more than you've earned in the past. Just think about it, Liz. Although you keep your ill-gotten gains under your hat, with my help I might add, you could use an extra big bonus. Yes, or no?'

There was a brief silence, and then she meekly nodded her head.

'Well then, Liz. If you do this for me – no, for us – then your pay day will see you through for quite some time. Trust me, Liz. You will still have plenty left when you come over to Omagh for your usual summer trip in August. Plus, the bonus for the gear you bring with you at that time. How good is that? Eh? How good is that Liz?'

'How much are we talking about, Davy? For the gear you want me to pick up in February?'

Once again there was a brief silence and then Davy answered in a very soft voice, almost a whisper, 'Ten fucking grand.'

Liz sprang upright in her armchair, her eyes nearly popped out of her head and then, once again there was a brief silence, 'How fucking much?'

'Ten fucking grand Liz.'

'You do mean £10,000?'

'You've got it in one, Liz. Ten fucking big ones.'

'Okay, Davy. You arrange everything. It's a fucking deal.'

That night was another sleepless night for Liz. She was already planning what she would do with all that extra money and how she would hide it from her family. She felt a little guilty, especially regarding PJ. But she promised herself that she would find a way. She would bring the ten grand back with her, well hidden in her luggage, when she and the boys returned from Omagh in February. She could make up a simple but believable story about winning it on the lottery. No, winning it on a scratch card she bought on one of her shopping trips. Yes. That sounded good. Her dad was always telling her off for wasting what little spare money she had on scratch cards that were on sale on every shop corner. Yes, that would do for now.

CHAPTER 16

THE FOLLOWING DAY DAVY COLLECTED the bag of gear and was soon on his way back to Omagh. Sharon and Gino had phoned to arrange a visit the same day. When they arrived that afternoon and the initial pleasantries were exchanged, Liz and the two lovebirds settled down around the kitchen table with a nice cup of tea and a biscuit. Then there was an unusual silence. Gino spoke first.

'Go on then, Sharon. Just start at the very beginning, love.'

Liz looked at them both and asked. 'Sharon, please tell me, you're not up the duff, are you?'

'Look at the teapot calling the kettle black, as if butter wouldn't melt.'

'Oh, come on Sharon,' added Liz. 'I didn't mean it like that. If you two were planning a family, then it wouldn't be so bad. But, with your job commitments, your budding careers. It would be an abrupt end to all your dreams.'

'It's not me, Liz. It's my mum. Well, Mum and Dad both. Well, as you know we've hardly spoken more than a few words on the phone for quite a few years... Well... I couldn't understand what the problem was when Gino and I decided to go to sea. It was more Mum than Dad. He's always been on a tight leash. Mum rules the roost and always has done.'

Liz became anxious and asked, 'They're not ill, are they?'

'No, not ill, just a little bit sick in the head.'

Gino held Sharon's hand as she went on to tell Liz the complete story in detail. Because her mum and dad had washed their hands of Sharon, she was determined to find out what was so wrong with going to sea with Gino and creating a good, sound career together. She never had any contact with any other members of her family. Unlike Liz who had a large family circle. Her mum had always made the excuse that although there were a few family members, most of whom had passed away when Sharon was very young, she probably wouldn't remember them. Those still living had simply lost touch with each other. So, Sharon searched the internet and found a site called 'Trace a Relative UK'. Now as it happened it wasn't free, so Sharon and Gino were a little apprehensive to pay the start-up fee. But they were encouraged by the offer of a free trial and they were both suitably impressed with the information they received. They always asked questions that they knew the answers to, just to make sure that the site was on the up and up. Eventually they signed up and what followed was a real eye-opener. Sharon's mum had a living older sister. Sharon had a real live aunt who was living in Ipswich. Sharon had family apart from her mum and dad.

Liz never spoke a word. She just listened like a best friend should.

Sharon continued, 'Well then, would you believe it? We managed to get her contact details, and with a great deal of persistence and bridge-building, we spoke on the phone to each other. We spoke on the phone, Liz! Her name is Barbara Mary Baxter. She is the head teacher of a primary school on the outskirts of Ipswich and she is as convinced as I am that we are truly related. She has never married but has dedicated her life to teaching. She sent us photographs and other family documents that strongly suggest that she is my mum's sister. They showed that mum's full name before she married my dad was Sally Sofia Baxter, which I know is true. My aunt was also able to tell me that my dad is Harold Peter Jackson, known as Harry and that they left Ipswich to marry and set up home somewhere in the London area. There is so much info here, and I refuse to believe that it is all a coincidence. So, with that in mind we are going round to my mum and dad's later this afternoon with the photos and paper work. We don't want to use it as an excuse to confront her, we just want to get to the truth. And guess what? Aunt Barbara is going to meet us there!'

Liz was really taken aback to say the least but she knew her friend of old. She was on a mission and she would not allow herself to be deterred. She was determined to find out why there was so much secrecy in her small family. What was so shockingly disgraceful that would result in downright lies? Lies that would fester for a lifetime. A little while later, the three friends said their goodbyes and Liz wished the intrepid duo good luck. She knew that they were certainly going to need it. Oh, to be a fly on that wall.

The following day Sharon and Gino returned to Liz's house. Sharon looked a little bit flustered but had a smile on her face. Liz wasn't sure if it was a happy smile or a smile of relief. Once more the three of them sat round the kitchen table and once more out came the tea and biscuits and slowly, Sharon revealed all. When she, Gino and Aunt Barbara met at the Eagles Nest as previously agreed, they had planned to give Sally and Harry a pre-warning phone call and then about fifteen minutes later, all three would show up at the front door. They carried out their plan and after yells and exclamations, embraces and tears all round, the gathering was a complete success and the following story was revealed.

Her dad, who was ten years older than her mum, was a long-distance lorry driver living in digs in Ipswich. On one of his few days off, Harry met Sally in a pub in the centre of Ipswich. She was only seventeen but looked much older. Harry was smitten, as was she, especially with the older man who was treating her like a lady. Not like the hopeless male adolescents that were trying hard to impress Sally and her mates with their drunken childish behaviour. It wasn't long before they became a regular item. Three months to be precise. That's how long it took for her to fall pregnant. Well, her mother, who was a widow, threw a complete wobbler at the audacity of the 'slut of a daughter' (quote-unquote) who was not yet eighteen years of age, who had committed the unforgiveable sin. She had a bun in the oven. Her mother was a devout church-goer who was a long-time member of the choir and a very active member of the select vestry in her local church. And before long, Sally was shown the door and told to take herself off, to the lorry driver that she had given herself to. Harry was still in digs but his landlady agreed to let Sally move in on a part-time basis. They would need to find somewhere soon as Harry's room was very basic, with a bathroom that was shared with two other men. In no time at all, Harry managed to get an inter-company transfer to a depot in West Croydon. Initially they had to make do with a very small bed sit, once again with a shared bathroom. Although it was with another young couple who had found themselves in the same predicament.

Harry's boss in the West Croydon depot was a local councillor, and informed them that they would stand a better chance of getting a small council flat if they were married. An imminent babe in arms would be an asset when their case was being assessed. Although Harry and Sally were smitten, it didn't mean that they were in love, but they both agreed for the sake of the new baby, which was due in only a few weeks, that they must pay a visit to the local registry office and marry as soon as possible. Then, Sharon decided to arrive a little early, unfortunately out of wedlock, something her maternal grandmother would never forgive or accept. Harry and Sally both knew that the acceptance of a so-called bastard, in a so-called Christian family in Ipswich, was out of the question. Tongues would definitely wag and fingers would definitely point. Harry had been brought up in foster and care homes until his eighteenth birthday so, as it stood, they had nobody only themselves and of course the newborn baby. Their wedding ceremony was plain and simple with only the bride and groom, baby Sharon and two volunteers from the town hall staff to act as witnesses.

The local council duly allocated the young family of three a small one-bedroom flat on the first floor of a terraced house in a run-down area of West Croydon but, with their own dedicated bathroom and a small kitchen and a short walking distance from Harry's work. Another upside was that a single middle-aged man lived on the ground floor called Joe Skates, who Sharon would come to know as Uncle Joe, who also had his own dedicated bathroom and even smaller kitchen and, as luck would have it, he was also a driver at the same depot as Harry with a similar shift pattern, so there was always a friendly atmosphere in the shared house. But they persisted in their endeavours to find a better home and just before Sharon's fifth birthday they moved into a three-bedroom semi-detached house in a brand-new estate on the outskirts of West Croydon, dutifully supplied once again by the local council. It was an absolute Godsend, and they had lived there to that day and intended to live there for the rest of their lives.

Sally's older sister, Barbara, was told by her mother while she was still at university that her younger sister had run away to London with some lorry driver who was much too old for her. Barbara did try to find further information, but because Sally's flit was so sudden, even her mates at college didn't know anything about where she might have ended up. Her mother refused to have Sally's name mentioned in her company and when she passed away almost five years previously, she did so with what most people would say was a guilty conscience. Maybe not. Who knows? Thus, the reason that Barbara lost any and all contact but she had hoped, prayed even, that someday a minor miracle would happen and that she and Sally would meet again.

And so, when Sharon announced that she and Gino were off to sea together, her mum, more so than her dad, just went into one. Sharon remembered the whole unnecessary scenario, describing it as a complete meltdown, with her dad unable to reconcile the situation and then, he felt duty-bound to side with his aggrieved wife, who had him firmly under her thumb. And soon it got completely out of hand, with things said and done, that should never had been said or done and then, it was too late to do anything but to accept it and lump it, until now. Sally's only reasoning for her reaction to Sharon and Gino going off together was that it brought back all those bad memories and she didn't want the same shaky and uncertain start in life for her daughter. This was not meant as any sort of criticism of her husband, but it was probably more luck than judgement that they had stayed together and remained loyal to each other all those years.

At this stage and completely out of character, Sharon's dad held her mum in his arms and softly said, 'I wouldn't change any of it for the world and from now on, Sally, we must say nice things to each other, more often than we have done before and we must also stop blaming each other. It was a joint decision to get away from prying eyes and all those hypocrites and we're still together.'

Apparently, it was the first time in living memory that Harry had ever been so forthcoming.

So, it was smiles all round, but Sharon and Gino had further good news to share with Liz. They would be on their travels again on Saturday 4th January 2020. Their company, British Maritime Cruises, was flying them both out to Miami USA to join what was known as the Caribbean circuit, for the whole of 2020. They had been engaged for almost two years and they intended to marry at sea at the six-month point. Shortly afterwards the ship would dock in Miami for the usual maintenance to be carried out, and then Sharon and Gino would have a ten-day honeymoon in Florida. They would then reunite with the ship and finish their contract with BMC, who in turn would fly them back to London in December that year.

They had invested in a small one-bedroom maisonette in Southampton and had rented it out on six-month leases for the past three years. They had made a tidy sum from those transactions, which were managed by a local leasing agent. When they returned at the end of 2020, they would sell the maisonette. With the proceeds of the sale and with the substantial amount of savings they had gathered over the many years they had been a couple, they would have ample sums to finance suitable premises for Sharon's dream come true: her own hairdressing salon! Having accommodation directly above the salon was an absolute must! Gino had already been headhunted on many occasions by prominent entrepreneurs, who had guaranteed him a position in any number of bands in the theatre land of London's West End. They had planned a three to six-month buffer zone on their return to the UK, so as to give themselves plenty of time to put everything in place. If it all went pear-shaped, then it would be back to sea and try again another time. Liz was nearly in tears as she listened to her best mate's tales of what was going to be a very exciting year ahead, and she also felt sure that Sharon's dream of having her own hair dressing salon would be a forgone conclusion. She even joked that she could work for Sharon, but would obviously be a little bit on the rusty side. As Sharon and Gino were leaving, they promised Liz that they would meet up for a few drinks, with PJ in tow, in the Eagles Nest before they flew out to Miami.

Later that night, when Liz's sons were all in their rooms she sat at the kitchen table with the obligatory cup of tea and a biscuit, and for the first time in a long time, she almost felt sorry for herself. Five sons that she adored but with none of their fathers around to see how well they were all doing at school, how well they were progressing in their music abilities but, most important of all, how they were all developing their own lovable personalities, and would all grow into responsible young men in their own right. She had no real reason to complain except… Her life could have been every bit as promising and exciting as Sharon's, but as her mother and Julie had often said, especially when they'd had drink: 'You've made your own bed so you'll just have to lie in it.' A cup of tea and a biscuit was never going to change that.

The festive season of 2019 came and went with the usual bravado. Liz decided that on this particular occasion, it would be a nice change to celebrate the arrival of the New Year with her five sons, and of course PJ, around the fire in the cosy atmosphere of her sitting room. The boys just loved the idea of staying up late with PJ telling ghost stories, with a humorous twist, well into the small hours. Liz thought that her kids would end up having nightmares but to her relief they all slept well. So well in fact, that she had to wake them just before noon the next day for a well-deserved hot brunch, which PJ duly cooked. But soon it was back to school for the boys and back to work for Liz and PJ. But although Liz was extremely proficient at her job in the family business, she was occasionally distracted by the adventure planned for February that year. Yes, this trip, she had decided, would set her up for quite some time to come and once again the adrenaline would kick in, only it came at the most inopportune moments thus giving cause for concern for Cissy or Julie who, in all honesty, could not quite work it out.

The half-term break was looming in the middle of February, and although PJ was thrilled for his protégés, he found it difficult to accept that Liz had insisted that he did not make the trip with them. Once again, she found herself reassuring him that she had nothing to hide regarding Davy or anyone else in Omagh. She began to wonder if he was becoming a little possessive. She wasn't sure but they could work it out when the merry band of travelling musicians made their return. Oh yes, SCRAM! They were definitely on the road again. The ferry from Holyhead-Dublin was booked for 2 pm on Thursday 13th February. They would leave early doors just as always and Davy would meet them on the Irish side and take over the steering wheel. After the two planned performances on the afternoons of Friday and Saturday, the return journey would follow a similar format on Sunday 16th February making sure that the loot was well hidden, and boy she was going to enjoy her ill-gotten bonus with just a hint of arrogance when she arrived back in West Croydon.

The morning of their departure was wet and miserable, but all six travellers were in high spirits. Liz made sure to place the larger than normal duffle bag containing the gear well under all the other baggage that was loaded on board the people carrier. The pick-up the evening before went like a dream. No one ever seemed to notice the extra bag in the past so it was highly unlikely that they would on this trip. They arrived at Holyhead in good time as usual. During the journey they made two short stops for toilet and snack breaks but they always looked forward to the fresh hot, homemade sausage rolls and drinks at the ferry terminal at Holyhead. The same lovely elderly lady always seemed to be on duty when they arrived and always had a kind word for them. When they received the signal to move into position to drive onto the ferry everything went just as they had in the past. A short distance from the final boarding area and behind a security fence there was a layby facilitating spot searches. They had never been stopped before but on this occasion, they were. A man wearing the usual high-vis jacket and cap approached the vehicle. Liz lowered her driver's side window and he instructed her to pull over into the layby. As she did so another three men suddenly appeared from out of nowhere dressed in the same garb. One of them had a small dog on a lead and Liz knew instinctively that it was in fact, a sniffer dog. Her heart began to pound like a sledgehammer and her pulse began to race insistently. 'Holy fuck,' she said under her breath.

At this stage Liz was invited to alight her vehicle, as were the five boys. The brothers were shepherded into a small shelter adjacent to their people carrier, but Liz was instructed to accompany the inspecting officers in and around the vehicle. Another two officers appeared, female on this occasion, also dressed in hi-vis jackets and caps, and stood either side of the five brothers who although now wearing their overcoats, were huddled into a tight group inside the small shelter with a full view of the proceedings taking place. The wind and the rain seemed to grow stronger, or was it just Liz's imagination? No one except the officer who seemed to be in charge said a word. His instructions to his subordinates and Liz were short and simple and before long, the large duffle bag containing the gear was discovered. Liz was then instructed to open the bag and no one in authority seemed in the least bit surprised as to its contents. They all remained standing still, just for a few moments, but it felt like a life time for the mother of five. Was it tears or the downpour of rain on her cheeks? Her heart sunk into the depths of despair and she nearly lost control of her bowels, but the sight of the anguish on her sons' faces helped her to man up. After all, she had always thought that she was as good as any man she had come to know in the drugs trade. Or was she? She looked at her five sons being led away to a nearby office block by the two female officers and broke down completely. No sound, but cramps in her stomach that made her almost keel over and her head began to spin. So much so, that two of the officers had to help to support her, otherwise she would have definitely hit the ground.

Once inside the office block, the boys were handed over to two social services representatives. They introduced themselves as Debbie and Gary, who were obviously fully paid-up members of the Anorak Brigade! Hot cups of tea and chocolate biscuits were the order of the day as Debbie explained briefly that their mother was helping the Border Control Officers with their inquiries. Young, as they were, all five whispered among themselves that it was more serious than anyone was letting on, but they were united in keeping calm, led of course by Steven. Michael was the only weak link, but the others took turns to comfort him. At the same time Liz was also assured that her sons were in no trouble and that they were being looked after by qualified personnel. She was left alone in a small, dingy, cold, interview room for about half an hour, with just a table and two chairs for company, one of which she was sitting on. She was worried out of her wits about her beloved boys, who wouldn't have a clue just how much trouble their mother was in. Then, suddenly, a tall man with short sandy-coloured hair, who was suited and booted, entered the room. He was in his late thirties or early forties. He sat on the empty chair on the opposite side of the table to Liz. Immediately behind him was a uniformed constable who took up his post beside the door, which was then closed.

'Well now, Liz. That is, your name, isn't it? You don't mind if I call you Liz. Do you? Elizabeth?'

Liz remained silent but she noticed a distinct Irish accent coming from the twat facing her across the table.

'Cat cut your tongue, Liz? Liz McKenna... Mother of Steven, Connor, Ryan, Anthony and of course we mustn't forget little Michael, must we? Well now, Liz, let's see. Where shall we begin? Oh yes... You are a single mother of five boys, all under the age of sixteen. What must they think of their mum? What will they think once I place her under arrest?'

'Where are my sons? You arrogant bastard!'

'Oh, my, my, Liz. You're the one with a shed-load of cocaine in your nice little people carrier! And you call me arrogant. You hard-faced bitch. Your sons are on the verge of going into foster care and you are looking at not seeing them again any time soon. Oh yes, and a nice long stretch at Her Majesty's pleasure. Fuck me, Liz, you'll be a right old age by the time they let you out! And as for your five precious sons, they'll be all grown up and most likely find it extremely difficult to forgive their stupid excuse for a mother for being totally instrumental in a complete and utter fuck up. How do you feel about fucking up everybody's life, Liz? Ah but, sure, you're used to it. You rely on your parents for just about everything, do you not? You've been doing that for most of your adult life... You fucking loser!'

Once again Liz tried to stop the tears but alas, to no avail. She wiped her face with her sleeve and began to take deep breaths. She stared at her tormentor and shouted at the top of her voice, 'Where are my sons? You can't keep them from me... you... fucking... fucking...'

'Trying to man up, are we, Liz? Trying to tough it out! Are we, Liz? Fucking forget it, Liz... I'm calling the shots. Just me... No one else, Liz... Just me. Like it or not, Liz, I'm your new best friend for fucking ever, Liz. Are you listening to me, Liz?'

She could take no more. She sat, crumpled up in a neat little ball on the chair. He had broken her in record time. He was very, very fucking pleased with himself. He was Detective Chief Inspector Jim Patterson of the Metropolitan Police, originally from Belfast but now firmly based in London. He had been part of an anti-drug task force for the past three years, known as the Anglo-Irish Drug Enforcement Teams (AIDETS). They consisted of The Met in London, AnGarda Siochana in Dublin and the PSNI in Belfast. Little did Liz know that she was a vital part of the investigation regarding the top men in Omagh and their major contacts in Belfast. DCI Patterson signalled to the constable to get Liz a cold drink from the water fountain next to the door. He thought just a plastic cup of water would suffice. No point in spoiling the fact that he had the upper hand. No point in spoiling her, period.

Liz gulped down the small cup of water. It was almost tepid, but she was thankful for it. Her mind was racing in all directions but nothing made any sense. How did this twat know so much about her and her family? How did the officers at the ferry terminal know that she was carrying such a large amount of gear? Why this trip and none of the others. Why? Why? Why?

The DCI gave her a few moments to compose herself, if that was at all possible. He knew that he was known as the maestro of maestros in interrogation techniques, especially with very vulnerable women. Single mothers in particular. And he revelled in it. Everyone in the force knew he got his rocks off – to the extreme – in situations such as this. Rumour had it, that he even carried a spare pair of boxer shorts just in case he was overcome, or just cum, with emotion.

'Now then, Liz. Let's put our cards on the table. Shall we? We haven't been formally introduced, have we? I'm DCI Patterson and you are Liz McKenna. Born 14 February 1985. You have an older brother called Lenny, born 21 March 1983. Bit of a shirt-lifter? No matter, I wonder if any of this will affect his Navy career. Your parents moved to Kings Cross, London, when you and Lenny were very young. Your father Robbie and Uncle Benny became very successful in the building trade, as did your mother and Aunt Julie in the cleaning business. Some of their methods are known to be very much under the table. Know what I mean? You scratch my back and I'll pave your hand with dosh. Apart from Lenny the poof... Oops, shouldn't say poof, should I? Anyway, apart from "Hello Sailor" you all live in West Croydon. You see, Liz, I know everything there is to know about you and your family, warts and all, but I'm not concerned about the warts, just you and your slime-ball of a cousin Davy in Omagh. Oh, and by the way, the least said about your mother and auntie's clandestine love life, the better. Know what I mean, Liz? Know what I mean? Nudge, nudge, wink, wink and double wink-wink. Eh, Liz?'

She didn't answer, not because she was playing hard ball, but because she didn't have a fucking clue what the ball game was all about in the first place.

He continued, 'You tell me everything I need to know and maybe I can arrange for you and your boys to have a hot meal together. Now, how does that sound? Eh, Liz? Oh and by the way, Liz, tomorrow is Valentine's Day. It's your fucking birthday, Liz. Thirty-five years old, five kids and not a husband or a father in fucking sight. Happy fucking birthday, Liz.'

She had a distinct dislike for this smarmy bastard and she needed more time to think, but he wasn't giving her an inch. He kept pushing her, and pointing his irritating bloody finger at her. He was judging her. He was continually reminding her of her pitfalls. In such detail, it's as if he had known her and her family all their lives. But how could that be? As he continued to wear her down, she began to regain some sort of semblance of the nightmare that had surrounded her. If she agreed to something, anything really, then the bastard of a detective might let her talk to her sons. That would give her more time to try and work something out. Oh fuck. Who did she think she was kidding? But she had to try something.

Meanwhile, the five brothers were becoming more and more agitated, and slowly but surely they were proving more and more difficult to pacify. The plan they hatched earlier was beginning to upset the apple cart. They would continue their disruption until they could be reunited with their mum, no matter what. An hour or so later their two minders had to give in and sought further advice from the senior officer present, Detective Chief Superintendent Josh Williams. He had watched DCI Patterson from behind the one-way mirror throughout the dismantling of Liz's family skeletons, piece by piece. He didn't always agree with the DCI's tactics, but the ends had always justified the means. He received the untimely news about the brothers in arms with just a hint of disgruntlement.

He wasn't one for showing his distaste or disappointment at any given moment, but it was time to take a break from proceedings and tally up the pros and cons of the situation. He gave the signal for the DCI to join him by simply opening the door of the interview room and in a soft unassuming voice said, 'DCI Paterson. Can I have a word?' As they discussed their progress, or lack of it so far, they were still able to observe Liz in her panic-ridden state.

The two detectives agreed that time was marching on and if the overall plan of the three police forces each side of the Irish Sea was to be successful, then they needed to get Liz on side sooner rather than later, so it was decided that Josh Williams would step in for the next part of their interrogation strategy. He looked at his watch. It was now almost 4 pm. He needed to get a move on.

He joined Liz in the interview room. As tall as Jim Patterson, mid-forties with short black hair. Suited and booted but with a flair for fashion that would not be out of place in a James Bond movie. Without further ado he began his spiel in a quiet and controlled manner.

'Well, Miss McKenna. I am DCS Josh Williams. I will talk and you will listen. I need you to make a phone call to your cousin Davy. I have it all written down for you, so we can have a little run through to make sure it all sounds kosha. Okay so far?' Liz nodded in complete bemusement.

'Right then, Miss McKenna. You called to let him know that you had arrived at Holyhead as planned. Yes?' She nodded again.

'Now, you're going to call him again and tell him that your vehicle broke down at the dockside, just as you were about to start up in the carpark to drive to the slipway and onto the ferry. You called the AA and they didn't arrive until well after the ferry had gone. The vehicle could not be repaired on the spot so it had to be towed to a local workshop. The mechanic informed you that he would have it ready for the road but it would take a while because the part he needed – a starter motor – would have to be picked up from a supplier forty miles away, so it would be some time later tonight, maybe about ten o'clock before he could get your people carrier back to you. Am I going too fast for you?'

'Yes, you are! He'll ask why I didn't phone him earlier and tell him that I missed the ferry. He'll tell me he's more than half way to fucking Dublin by now!'

'Well then, Miss McKenna, you tell him that you just panicked. You tell him that you were hoping that the vehicle would be repaired in time to get the next ferry until the mechanic told you different. Okay?

'I will also give you the address of the only Premier Inn in Holyhead. You will tell Davy that you and the boys are staying there tonight and you are all booked on the first ferry in the morning, which is due to leave at 8 am. If you do this right now, I promise you that you can join your sons soon after, whereby you can all enjoy a hot meal together. If you do not comply with my instructions, I will have no alternative but to hand you back to DCI Patterson, who plans to arrest you and find temporary foster care for your children. Now, having said all that, Miss McKenna, it's unlikely that all five boys will be accommodated in the same location so, you will have to advise us as to who will go with who. Probably two or maybe even three foster homes. I'm not entirely sure. It's your choice.'

She made her mind up in a split second and agreed to make the call. Several rehearsals later and with the specialised orchestration from the DCS, the call was a major success. Well, you should have heard Davy at the other end. It did help that he was driving in heavy rain and heavy traffic, which hindered him from asking too many awkward questions, but Liz knew that once he returned to Omagh, his bosses would require more detailed information on the situation. So, okay so far.

CHAPTER 17

AS PROMISED, LIZ AND HER SONS were allowed to spend some time together and share a hot meal. The two minders, Debbie and Gary, had arranged for a box-load of McDonald's to be brought to the custody suite where the boys were accommodated, which was on the same floor as Liz's interview room. They all enjoyed the food, but in particular Liz gulped down the ice-cold Diet Coke. After the tepid water she had been given throughout the afternoon it tasted like nectar. She looked at her sons, who were faring better than she had expected. Steven and Connor took her to one side while the other three were still play fighting over the ice cream sundaes.

Steven whispered, 'Mum, what's going on?'

Connor joined in, 'Yes, Mum, what's going on?'

She simply answered, 'Don't worry, boys. I'll get this whole sorry business sorted out and explain everything when we get home.'

'When will that be, Mum?' asked Steven.

'If I have my way we will be heading home sometime tomorrow,' she answered.

Connor then said, 'Fucking tomorrow, Mum. What's going on?'

'Don't you swear at me, young man. I'm doing my bloody best.' She quickly looked over her shoulder to make sure the other three sons were still enjoying their ice cream.

'Look, you two, I need you both to stick by me and your younger brothers for the time being. I promise, to make it up to you all when we get home.'

Steven and Connor nodded, and it had to be said that they were not best pleased, but they both agreed that the best thing to do right now was to stick together. At this stage Debbie suggested that she gave Liz a guided tour of the accommodation. Apart from the small sitting room, which was now very overcrowded, what with Debbie, Gary, Liz, the five brothers, the DCI and the DCS all cramped in.

There were two armchairs and a two-seater sofa, all of which had seen better days, with a small colour TV in the corner. The bedroom contained two double beds with very little room for anything else. A small bathroom and an even smaller galley kitchen finished off the mini tour. Being well-fed and watered helped to satisfy the boys' concerns for the time being, and they settled down to watch the TV. Debbie and Gary were more than pleased to have a little quiet time and finally enjoy their hot meal which by this stage was no longer hot.

The DCS took Liz into the hallway leading to the front door. He then briefed her on the next part of his plan. 'Right, Miss McKenna, when Davy tells his two bosses about the delay they will undoubtedly check our story. When they phone the Premier Inn to confirm that you and the boys are booked in for the night, one of our officers will be there to deal with them. Now, they may well insist on being put through to your room, then our officer will transfer them to this phone, here in this hallway. All you've got to do is carry on with the deception and confirm where you are. The Premier Inn, in Holyhead. Are we clear on that?'

'Absolutely,' she said. 'Absolutely clear. But what if they contact the AA?'

'Listen, Miss McKenna. The AA will not give out any personal details of any call outs they receive. It's one of their golden rules. Any information must be obtained from the customer themselves, unless they were involved in a serious accident, and even then they would need to contact the police for further information. No personal data will ever be released, unless you have a warrant.'

With that, he smiled and added, 'You play ball and we may consider allowing you to stay with your sons tonight. Only after we have all the information that you have in your notebook. Two of my staff have being going through it and although we can decipher most of it, with the intelligence we have already gathered, we need you to put the finishing touches to it. But for now, you can relax with your sons, and if I was you, I'd prepare myself for that imminent phone call.'

When Davy gave the bad news to James Montague and John Phillips they were absolutely fuming, but common sense prevailed. They agreed it was totally unexpected, but Liz's story must be checked out, right away. All three were in the log cabin in the woods of the Montague estate where so many other meetings had taken place, this time the only gear they had to break down was the stuff they got from Dublin the previous afternoon. It was a sizable amount, but not the vast quantity they were expecting from London. Davy was instructed to call Liz's room via the Premier Inn switchboard. Davy's phone would be put on loudspeaker so all three could listen in. James and John would not speak at any time; they would just listen and assess the situation.

The switchboard answered Davy's call but initially they refused to confirm the identity of any of their residents. It was against the house rules. But Davy persisted with a sad story about his favourite cousin and her five sons being stranded in Holyhead because their people carrier had broken down. When the receptionist asked why Davy couldn't contact his cousin on her mobile phone, he explained that he couldn't get a signal. He suggested that she may have inadvertently left it in her vehicle while it was taken away to be repaired. Throughout the conversation, John was whispering prompts to Davy, because he couldn't be trusted to think all this up by himself. Davy smiled with sweet satisfaction when the receptionist finally agreed, against all the rules, to put him through to Liz McKenna and her family.

The DCS stood beside Liz in the hallway as she answered the phone, making sure that he pressed the loud speaker button. Liz pause for a moment and then inquired, 'Hello… Hello… Can I help you?'

'It's me, Liz. It's Davy!'

'Oh, Davy. It's so good to hear a friendly voice. But why did you not contact me on my mobile?'

'Couldn't get a signal, love, but I used my deadly charm on the receptionist and against all the rules she put me through to your room. Who's a clever boy then?'

'Oh, Davy, I'm so sorry about the break down but it wasn't my fault. I did the best I could. And do you know, if we get the ferry first thing in the morning, we will still make the afternoon gig in Omagh.'

'Where's the people carrier now then, love?'

'It should be here in the next hour or so. The mechanic's been on the blower and said everything was going to plan, no probs.'

'Listen, Liz, where's the gear?'

'Where do you think it is? Under my bed covered with my big winter overcoat. I told the boys that it was a load of cheap cigarettes, that one of your mates dropped off for me to bring over to you.'

'Good girl, Liz. Well done. Now how are the boys?'

'Well, to tell you the truth, Davy, they are all dozing on their beds trying to watch the TV. They've had a really long day. We all have. We've been on the go since six o'clock this morning. We're all completely knackered.'

'It must be a big room, love.'

'It's two rooms with an adjoining door. With a TV in each room.'

'But your Steven always make sure that all his little brothers are well tucked up before he gets his head down and then, and then, he likes to read one of his books... Doesn't he, Liz?'

There was a distinct pause when Davy added, 'Oh go on, Liz, let me speak to Steven. He's always the last to go to sleep.'

At that very moment, Steven appeared in the hallway. He had been listening to the whole conversation from behind the sitting room door, which had been left slightly ajar. The DCS nodded to Liz to pass the phone to her son, but she felt as if she was paralysed. Steven decided to take the initiative and called out, 'Who's that on the phone, Mum?' Liz told him it was Davy and he took control of the phone. The conversation that followed went like an absolute dream. Steven was like an old pro and proceeded to convince Davy and the other two listeners that all was as it should be. He even cracked a joke with Davy, which was always part of the banter they shared on many previous occasions. When both parties hung up, Liz hugged the breath out of her son. The DCS patted him on the back and said, 'I couldn't have done better myself, young man. You got us out of what could have been an almighty mess. Thank you very, very much.'

The programme on the TV had kept the remainder of her sons busy throughout the phone call, aided by Connor turning up the volume. Liz hardly had time to draw her breath when the DCS suggested that they return to the interview room for the final chapter of his plan. As they were leaving Steven and Connor, both gave her the thumbs up and a loving smile. That was all she needed to see this horrible experience through to the bitter end.

Once again Liz found herself sitting opposite the DCS at the table in the interview room. She liked his fairly easy-going style, and by this stage felt as if she had known him for a lot longer than just a few hours. She most definitely preferred his company much more than that twat Patterson. Bastard! Without any prelims the DCS said, 'We're nearly there, Liz.'

It was the first time he had called her Liz. She felt almost relieved as he continued, 'All we need now is for you to confirm the information that you have in your notebook. My two associates have got most of it decoded, to coin a phrase, but I need you to confirm and to elaborate on certain points. Okay? I will bring them in now and all four of us can go through it together. Okay with you?' Liz nodded and two more plain clothes policemen entered the room. They were much younger than Jim Patterson, equally suited and booted and possibly mid to late twenties. They didn't introduce themselves, they just stood each side of the DCS and took notes. She couldn't remember seeing so many, well-dressed policemen before. Correction, she couldn't remember seeing so many, any-way dressed policemen before. Everything went like a song, much to the delight of the

DCS. When she thought it was all said and done, the DCS said, 'Now, Liz, all we need to do now is for you to confirm where the drugs are kept on the Montague estate.'

Liz smiled and said, 'Do you know what? I'll tell you, but what are you going to give me in return? And don't even think about threatening me with that bastard Patterson again. It won't work this time, Josh.'

'Why won't it work this time, Liz?'

'Because we've come too far down the line for you to throw it all away on a small-time mule who is a single mother with five kids. That's why, Josh.'

'You're almost right, Liz. But let's say if I can get everything I think you know, or even something that you think you don't know, but I know that you probably do know, I promise you, Liz, that I will reciprocate the favour by looking after you and your five sons. You have my word, Liz.'

The two young policemen still standing either side of the DCS were completely and utterly confused, but guess what? Liz understood every word that Josh said. She smiled once again and then revealed what Josh believed to be the jackpot answer. 'There is a small log cabin hidden in a small but dense wood. It's set well back from the driveway to the right as you go through the front gates of the estate. I don't know exactly where in the cabin but, with the manpower I'm sure you have, you'll find it in no time.'

Josh asked, 'How do you know it's there?'

'Davy took me out for a spin in his car one night. You know, one of those spins when he was trying to get into my knickers. He was trying to impress me. Bumming his load about being a junior partner, and all the shite that goes with it. He couldn't wait to tell me, the fucking eejit.'

Josh was now like a dog with a bone. 'Liz, are you sure about this? Because we know that Davy picked up a load of gear from Dublin yesterday and some of it will still be on the premises, apart from the load they got off to Belfast today.'

'If you know so much, Josh, then why don't you just

arrest them all straight away?'

'Because, Liz, there is a lot more at stake here than you could ever imagine. Now then, Liz, can you help me to shed some light on this last page? There is no trace of these abbreviated items anywhere else in your notebook. This is the only time that they appear and they are on the very last page of entries.'

Liz smiled once again and said, 'No comment, Josh.'

After a short but well-earned break with a mug of strong tea and a chat with her five sons, Josh and Liz resumed their places at the table in the interview room. Once again Josh got straight to the point.

'Now, Liz, these last entries in your notebook? Please, help me out and tell me, what exactly do they mean?'

'Am I not entitled to make a phone call somewhere along the line, Josh?'

'Now, Liz. We are making so much progress, what's this about a phone call? You're not under arrest, you're just helping us with our inquiries. I've given you my word that you and your boys will be well-looked after.'

'The last entries in my notebook are the two coded addresses of the Belfast contacts. They are the big boys, apart from James and John. Although I've never been inside the addresses, Davy has made several trips with me as his driver.'

Josh had to contain himself in no uncertain terms. This was going to be the icing on the cake, and what a big cake it was going to be. The joint operation with three different police forces, in three different countries, was going into action in the early hours of the following morning. He needed those two addresses in Belfast to tie up the final loose ends, well and truly tight. The Met in London, the An Garda Siochana in Dublin, the PSNI in Omagh and Belfast were all waiting for the green light. 'No Stone Left Unturned' was the motto of the AIDETS. This would be the very last nail in the coffin.

'Okay, Liz. What do you want?'

'I want to make a phone call.'

'Who to, Liz?'

'To the one person I feel I can really trust and rely on.'

'Ah for fuck's sake, Liz. Will you wise up!'

That was the first time she had heard him swear.

'Hit a sore point, have I?'

'Now, Liz, listen to me. Just give me those addresses and you'll be on your way home in no time. You and the boys will be well out of this mess. Trust me, Liz. I'm giving you good solid advice!'

'If I give you what you so desperately need, you'll most likely hand me over to that twat Patterson and I won't see the fucking light of day, Josh.'

This was the first time that he felt that she had the upper hand. He left the room briefly to confer with his learned colleagues and returned about ten minutes later.

'Okay, Liz. You can make your phone call but it will be made on one of our phones next door, so as we can make sure you don't try to make contact with any of the numbers we have on file, that would relate to any of the illegal activities that you have been involved in. I promise you, Liz, if you try to screw this up you won't have to worry about DCI Patterson! I will put you behind bars for a very long, fucking time!'

Liz just smiled and was allowed to make her phone call in private, as was her right. The number was checked by the police operator and was registered to Liz's on off boyfriend, PJ McGrath. When she and Josh returned to the interview room she insisted on saying nothing else until she heard back from PJ. Josh left the room absolutely raging and once again sought solitude with his colleagues in the viewing area at the other side of the one-way mirror.

'What do you think she's up to, boss?' asked the DCI.

The DCS hesitated and said, 'I'm not sure, Jim, but we have to start pushing her soon. The whole operation is waiting on us. If we get the green light without those Belfast addresses, then we won't catch all of the slippery bastards at once. Which means some of the big players will go underground until they feel safe enough to start all over again. We're so close to snaring the whole fucking lot of them.'

A few minutes later the operator informed them that a call had come in from West Croydon for Miss McKenna. The two detectives did their best to conceal the grimace on each of their faces but alas, it was impossible, and Liz was allowed to receive the call, which was very brief. As she replaced the receiver, she turned to the DCS and said, 'I'm saying nothing more until my brief arrives.'

Well, you could have knocked the two coppers over with a feather. DCI Patterson grabbed her by the arm and frog-marched her back into the interview room and practically slammed her arse down onto the hard, plastic chair.

'Temper, temper, Jim,' she said, accompanied by a very sarcastic smile. DCS Williams was right behind them and couldn't help but slam the door so vigorously that it made the one-way mirror shake. Liz explained that she had been advised to make no further comments until her brief arrived. The journey from the southeast of England to Holyhead would take the best part of five or six hours. It was now almost nine o'clock. The two detectives once again left the room to confer in private and make several important phone calls, near and far. Liz waited patiently for one or both of them to return when Josh arrived alone. He had regained his composure and once again sat opposite Liz at the table.

'Now listen, Liz. We need to tie down the last two addresses in your notebook. If you do not play ball, we will add obstructing the police in their investigations to your charge sheet.'

'I thought you were going to look after me. You gave me your word, Josh.'

'Look Liz, I'll be honest with you. I have the local police in Belfast standing by with a search warrant that needs to be signed by a judge. We need to give them the addresses before the judge will sign it. He's aware that we are on the verge of getting that information, but we need it sooner rather than later. Look Liz, we have a lot of resources standing by at this moment in time and if we don't get this vital information, we will have to go in without those all-important Belfast locations.'

Liz simply answered, 'No comment.'

Josh left the room, and by this stage the DCI was able to relay some detailed information to him. According to PSNI, raiding the locations in and around Omagh was not a problem, as all the paperwork had been completed, but they desperately needed the Belfast addresses at least two hours before the green light, which was to be 6 am the following morning, involving all units of the AIDETS on both sides of the Irish Sea. For the next five hours or so every copper in the custody suite in Holyhead simply counted the minutes, when, out of the blue, the cavalry arrived. The door of the interview room opened and in walked PJ followed by none other than, Mr Bartholomew Barnard Coulter, semi-retired barrister who was carrying a large black briefcase. They were both dressed in dark sportswear and seemed extremely perky considering it was 2.15 am and they had just completed a long drive. Apparently, PJ did the driving while Uncle Bart prepared some of his paper work.

The detectives once again left the room, and after ten minutes or so of consultation with Liz, Uncle Bart summoned for someone 'with a semblance of authority in the Crown Prosecution Service to make themselves available.' The DCS entered the room and invited Uncle Bart to join him along the corridor whereby he would be introduced to a CPS representative, leaving Liz and PJ to enjoy a lull in the battle. Uncle Bart bellowed, 'To whom shall I be speaking?'

The DCS replied, 'Mr Richard Dunwoody.'

Uncle Bart bellowed once more, 'Ah! Good old tricky Dickie. Take me to him and let the jousting begin!'

Just before 3 am Uncle Bart returned to the room and, making sure the door was shut tight behind him, he spoke in a soft but commanding tone and both PJ and Liz listened intently. He removed a buff folder from his briefcase, opened it and explained its contents.

'Now, this is the deal. The powers that be have agreed to

complete immunity for you, Liz, as long as you give them the addresses in Belfast within the next hour, otherwise they will throw the book at you. I strongly advise you to accept this one-time offer and let's get you and your sons home as soon as possible.' PJ was nodding in agreement, but Liz had a question.

'What about the gear in the duffle bag? Davy and the likes will wonder just how I got away without being prosecuted.'

'That's a very good question but let me put your mind at ease. In the official police report it will state that you pleaded guilty to carrying a large number of cigarettes that were illegally brought into the country by persons unknown. You agreed to transport them at the request of your cousin, one David Beggs, in your vehicle while travelling to Omagh via Holyhead-Dublin. You were prevented from looking inside the bag because when it was delivered to your home in West Croydon by persons unknown, it was secured with a small chain and a combination lock, which made it impossible to check it contents. The official line is, quite simply, the police believed you, which resulted in a caution being recorded and the incident will be kept on file for the foreseeable future.'

At this stage, PJ, who was sitting beside Liz put his arm around her shoulders and said, 'Uncle Bart knows what he's doing, Liz. You've got to say yes!' There was a brief pause, and then she nodded in agreement. Uncle Bart also added, 'This version of events must be conveyed to all and sundry. To your sons, your whole family circle and you must convince everyone that this is the absolute truth, otherwise the bad guys may or may not get suspicious, but if any of them do it won't be for long, Liz. There's an old saying. "Honour amongst thieves." But not for long, especially when their backs are against the wall. They will all eventually turn on each other and jump ship in the hope of a reduced sentence. As far as the CPS is concerned, this is the only official version of your plight that will be recorded.'

'What about that bastard, Patterson?' asked Liz.

'He's all mouth and trousers, Liz. None of the police involved thus far will feature anymore as long as you give them the information they so desperately require. All you have to do, is write down the addresses on the sheet of blank paper in this folder and I will pass it to Dickie Dunwoody of the CPS and you will never have to worry about this unfortunate incident again, and you Liz, you and PJ and your sons will be on the way home, just as soon as I can organise your release.'

'How long will that take?' asked PJ.

Uncle Bart pondered for a moment and then said, 'Just as soon after six am as I can manage. The powers that be will want to make sure that the information given to them by Liz is above board. No last-minute hiccups, if you understand my meaning.'

Liz took the pen and paper proffered by Uncle Bart and proceeded to write down the Belfast addresses. He left the room, and when he returned a few minutes later he had some unexpected good news. He, PJ and Liz were allowed to move to the custody suite and spend the next few hours with the five brothers. When the trio arrived at the small flat, all five boys were sound asleep. Steven and Connor in one of the double beds and Ryan, Anthony and Michael in the other. For the time being Liz could see just a hint of light at the end of the tunnel. About two hours later, 'Operation Stand Off,' got the green light to 'take off', and what an absolute blast it was. Blood, sweat and yes, even tears, every-fucking-where!

After a little nap, Uncle Bart slipped away and, true to his word, he completed the final paperwork and returned to the custody suite just after 7 am, with the news that it was home time for everyone. The boys were already up, washed and eager to begin the journey home, but a stop at the nearest motor way service station for some well-deserved hot breakfast for all, including a very hungry Uncle Bart. After they had eaten, PJ joined Liz and the boys in the people carrier so they could share the driving and good old

Uncle Bart drove PJ's car to his own home in the Suffolk countryside. He would drop off PJ's car sometime over the coming weekend, but for now the worst was over and PJ prayed that this incredible but sometimes naive woman of substance would wise up and begin to take life a lot more seriously, if not for herself then for her five sons. If the truth had been known, she was driving him crazy. Not with desire, but with sheer anxiety! He promised himself there and then that things would have to change, and he was beginning to feel sure that he was the man to bloody well change them!

Over the next few days Liz, supported by PJ, repeated the story ingrained by Uncle Bart so many times she lost count. She never wavered, never added or subtracted any point of detail and soon the natural human inquisitiveness from her family circle began to subside, much to her relief. And would you believe it? It wasn't long before the media at home and abroad got wind of what was taking place on both sides of the Irish Sea. Liz made sure that her sons didn't see too much of it on television, just in case the eldest two would be able to put two and two together. The names of some of the top players became apparent quite quickly and the raids on various premises came to the fore: addresses in London, Kent, in and around Dublin, Belfast and throughout Northern Ireland, including several family residences. After two to three weeks, her nerves began to settle. The amount of arrests that were continually being made pushed her further and further down the food chain. If was as if she didn't exist. Uncle Bart was as good as his word. Not one iota of a mention of Liz, not a jot! Not even a hint of DCI Jim Patterson or DCS Josh Williams. She half expected some sort of a sarcastic phone call or a text message. Nothing. It was well into the school summer holidays before she could convince herself that she was home and dry. Phew! And it was well into the following year, 2021, before anyone was brought to trial in London, then it spread like wildfire to Dublin and Belfast. The clouds of doubt returned as she followed the media reports, until one day PJ gave her a good old-fashioned rocket up the arse, and told her everything was done and dusted. If anything was going to go wrong, it would have happened by then. 'So wise up and get on with your life. Our lives, for fuck's sake, Liz!'

And that's exactly what she did.

EPILOGUE

WORTHING IS A SMALL SEASIDE TOWN on the south coast of England, in the county of West Sussex. About two miles east of Worthing, along the A27, is a little hamlet known as Grey Abbotts. It consists of a pub and five small cottages scattered along a winding road as it makes its way north to the beautiful South Downs. A two-storey, six-bedroom house sits on a small hill and is a ten-minute walk from the pub. The driveway of the house is short, however the front lawn that it divides is more than one hundred yards wide. To the left of the house is a double garage and to the right a small converted barn. The upper floor of the conversion is a studio flat with all the mod cons while the ground floor is equally divided into a music room and recording studio, with a small shower room and kitchen. The English Channel lies two miles to the south. The garden area to the rear of the house is open and flat with two apple trees in the left-hand corner and two pear trees in the other corner. The boundary of the property is marked with a wooden fence, five foot in height so as not to restrict the beautiful panoramic view. August 2022, is exceptionally hot but perfect weather for moving house. The couple and their five sons decided that moving during the school holidays made perfect sense. To all concerned it had been an eventful summer so far, what with the wedding in July, the honeymoon in Disney World in Orlando, to which the newly-married couple brought their five sons, and now to round off the adventure a move into a state of the art house, courtesy of good old Aunt Kaz. PJ's aunt had passed away over the Easter period of 2021. Uncle Bart got the ball rolling as soon as possible regarding her will but it did take almost a year before everything was settled, including the sale of the three-storey town house in West Croydon. The legal procedure was also hampered by the worldwide pandemic of the Coronavirus which was now under control. Only three people apart from PJ knew just how much money he had inherited, Uncle Bart, Liz and the bank manager, but it was rumoured to be in excess of two million quid, possibly more? Who knows? Yes... Who knows indeed. The McKenna brothers would all start at their new schools in the September term, with Michael being the only one still at primary school. He could hardly wait until next year, when he would be at the same secondary school as his brothers, with the exception of his eldest brother Steven. By that time, Steven would follow in his Uncle Lenny's footsteps and join the Royal Navy, and SCRAM! were still going strong. When PJ and Liz decided to get married in July 2022, they both agreed that it would be a small family affair in the West Croydon Registry Office, followed by a slap up meal in a posh restaurant in Mayfair. What was not to like? However, there was one small point that was to be the exception. PJ thought long and hard about it. Liz would become his wife and they would be known as Mr and Mrs McGrath. They would be living in a house with their five sons known as McKenna. It would be too much to ask them to consider being legally adopted by PJ, thereby changing their surnames to McGrath. So, PJ came up with what he saw was the perfect solution. He and Liz nearly fell out about it, but when the boys were all asked for their opinions, it was unanimously decided that there was only one road to take. PJ would change his name to McKenna. Unusual to say the least, but not illegal. And so, it came to pass that the McKennas were as close as ever. That's for sure! Yes... That's definitely for sure.

Lightning Source UK Ltd.
Milton Keynes UK
UKHW010659030621
384853UK00002B/58

9 781800 318694